I0758177

ALSO BY OMARI BAYI

Michael – *A Detroit Saga*

Michael III – *Pimps and Poachers*

Esmeralda – *A Harlem Creole Madam*

Esmeralda II – *Assault on a Mambo*

Short Shorts - *A Collection of Very
Short Tales of Fantasy-Fiction*

VISIT WWW.BIKOBOOKS.COM

MICHAEL II

THE SUNDARBANS PARK

OMARI BAYI

Visite www.bikobooks.com

Prologue

Busta and Michael were throwing heavy blows at one another. Michael would tag Busta with several combinations, driving Busta backward toward the MacArthur Bridge railing, but Busta would recover and land a heavy blow to Michael's chest, knocking him onto his back. Michael had underestimated the power of the old man and was getting his worst whooping ever. Busta tried to stomp Michael as he lay on the pavement, but Michael rolled to his right, and was barely back on his feet when Busta pivoted and struck him again in the face. Michael's knees buckled and he fell backward and went down again. However, Busta could not move forward. He had gotten into great shape, having lost forty pounds, but he was still a big man, over 230 pounds, a lot of weight to lug around in a street fight with the likes of Michael.

Thus ends the final epic battle between the two adversaries in the novel *MICHAEL*, the first book on the McCants family. *Michael II-The Sundarbans Park* is the second novel of the saga of the McCants. The morning that *MICHAEL* ends is the very morning that this novel begins. The shocking ending to *MICHAEL* only intensified as a conspiracy to capture one of the twin sons of Frank and Martha

McCants by a clandestine US agency entangled four generations of innocence.

The family members are:

> Frank McCants – Father of a troupe of eight sons. DOB:1931
>
> Martha McCants – Wife of Frank and mother to his sons, a light-complexion Black woman often mistaken for White. DOB:1931
>
> Mack – Eldest son. DOB:1950
>
> Michael – Twin of Robert. DOB:1951
>
> Robert – Twin of Michael. DOB:1951
>
> Richard – DOB:1953
>
> Louis – DOB:1954
>
> Jack – DOB:1960
>
> Horace- DOB:1961
>
> Ervin – The splitting image of his father. - DOB:1962
>
> Uncle Horace – Eldest of Frank's six brothers. DOB:1929
>
> Esmeralda Dupree – Martha's grandmother. DOB:1883

Other protagonists and antagonists are:

> Dr. Karl Schultz – Robert's military psychiatrist. Head of Psychiatry at Harper Hospital – DOB: 1920
>
> Dr. Joseph McCants – Frank's father – Professor at Eastern Michigan University. DOB: 1906
>
> Commander Peter Cavaletti – Official of the Detroit Police Department. DOB: 1939
>
> Dr. Sekar Patel – Robert's military psychiatrist; an East Indian doctor assigned to the American military while studying with the British – DOB: 1929.
>
> Colonel Austin McGregor – Robert's military commander. DOB: 1942
>
> Antonio Castanza – The Detroit Don of organized crime DOB: 1908

This heart-thumping, action-driven sequel to MICHAEL can only end as the first novel ended: with plenty of shocks and surprises.

Omari Bayi
Author

CHAPTER ONE

Hospital Arrival

Fourth week of August 1978

A stern look masked the forty-seven-year-old father's face as he ran out to hail the EMS unit. Frank McCants, Michael McCants' father, called out to his other sons to move their vehicles further down the block, to make room for the ambulance and authorities. After being told the day before that his son Michael was dead, his family found him alive in his bedroom and called 911 for medical assistance.

Police Commander Peter Cavaletti was pulling into the parking lot of the 10th precinct when he heard over the radio that Michael McCants was found alive at his parent's home. He immediately backed out of the entrance to the lot and headed north on Livernois Avenue for the two-mile journey. Three minutes later he arrived at the McCants home on Santa Rosa Drive, minutes before the EMS ambulance arrived. This was his second visit to this home within twenty-four hours. The day before he had delivered what proved to be incorrect news. That the second-born son of the couple had been killed by police while fighting on the bridge to Belle Isle park. It was extremely rare that he could be contradicted, but this time the feeling was grand.

The EMS technicians carefully but quickly moved up the front porch steps and into the house. They climbed the interior stairs to the second floor and found an unconscious man lying in a twin-size bed. The blood which caked the side of his face was now over twelve hours old. His breathing was shallow but consistent. He had an obvious broken jaw and possibly a broken orbital socket. The bruises on his abdomen implied broken ribs. He also had a possible collapsed lung and a bruised kidney. His left hand was badly swollen as well. He remained unconscious.

One of the EMTs, unsure of any cranial or neck injuries, placed a brace around his neck. Once they were sure he was stable, they moved him to the gurney and down the narrow stairs to the main floor. The technician noticed the police commander and the dozen patrol officers standing about but was too busy with his patient to concern himself with the authorities. However, a police sergeant had already assigned escort duty to a couple of the patrol cars. The neighbors on the south end of the block, believing Michael was killed the day before, could only look on in amazement.

"Man oh man. That Black cat sure has nine lives," was heard more than once in the crowd.

Michael was placed in the back of the ambulance and rushed to Detroit's Receiving Hospital. After he was examined to ensure he was not in any immediate danger, he was assigned a room on the fourth floor in the adjacent Harper Hospital. Michael's mother, Martha McCants, stayed with her son, while her husband, Frank, spoke to the admittance desk.

The attendee asked, "Sir, please fill out this form so we can admit your son."

Frank sat in the chair for only two minutes before he had completed the form. Then he hurried to the room.

Commander Cavaletti approached Frank as he arrived on the fourth floor.

He said, "Mr. McCants, I am so very glad your son is alive. I really hated delivering terminal news. However, I am instructing my staff to detain Michael until we can find out why he was fighting on that bridge yesterday. A man was killed, and there has to be accountability for his death."

Frank said, "You told me yesterday evening that you guys shot him. There's your accountability! I don't know how he survived that fall from the bridge, but all I care about is that he's alive. It's a miracle. Do you know my youngest sons were on that bridge? They saw your cop shoot my son and that monster Busta. I understand that the two were fighting. My youngest son said Busta was about to throw Michael off the bridge when he was shot. He saw both of them fall over the railing. I thank God Michael survived the fall. In fact, when we found him, there was no sign that his clothes were ever wet. How he got from Belle Isle to the Northwest side is still a mystery. He most certainly did not drive himself. Not in the condition he's in. His eyes are so swollen... He must have ridden the bus home and..."

"Slow down, Mr. McCants, please slow down. We're going to get to the bottom of this. I'm just happy for you and your wife. But understand, we have to get all of the facts, and until we do, Michael is being detained. Internal Affairs, of course, will be investigating the shooting. Lieutenant Sumanski said he was trying to stop Mr. Johnson from throwing your son off the bridge, and for now, that's how the report is written. Now, if you'll excuse me."

He extended his hand, which Frank, still somewhat rattled, shook, then walked away.

Frank rushed into Michael's room, blowing by the officer standing at the door. His wife Martha was sitting next to Michael's bed. Michael was handcuffed to the railing of the bed. Frank started to object, then decided not to bother. Besides, Michael was not going anywhere anytime soon.

A doctor entered the room carrying Michael's medical chart with information submitted by the EMTs. He compared the information on the chart with the admittance form, looking somewhat confused. He glanced down at Martha, sitting next to Michael, and looked even more confused. So, he ignored her and turned to Frank.

He said, "Sir, I assume you are the patient's father?"

Frank responded, "Yes, I'm his father. How is he doing?"

Martha was too absorbed in Michael and would not remember the slight until later.

The doctor said, "Well, Mr. McCants, is it? My name is Doctor Willem. I will be attending to your son this evening. We seem to have a slight problem with the forms. The EMTs have his name as Michael McCants. But the admittance form has him registered as Robert McCants."

Martha came out of her fog and glared at her husband.

Frank said, "I'm sorry, Doctor. That was my mistake. Michael has a twin brother. In all the confusion, I wrote the wrong name. What do I need to do to correct the error?"

The doctor said, "I will note the error on this form. But I suggest you go to admittance right away and correct it before the error begins to flow through our systems. Now, if I can ask you to leave the room for a moment so I can examine your son."

Frank and Martha stood up to leave the room, with Martha hesitating, then kissing Michael on his forehead. She immediately realized that this was the first time she had ever kissed this son. In fact, she rarely kissed any of the boys once they started grade school.

When they got into the waiting area, the petite Martha roughly grabbed Frank's arm and said, "Frank, we have to maintain that our son is Michael, just as we've done for the past twenty-six years. Robert's name cannot come up, damnit!"

Frank looked at his exhausted wife and nodded. Moments later a group of doctors and attendees converged on the room to join Doctor Willem.

. . . .

Dr. Willem examined Michael's head wound, wiping the dried blood away. Next to the wound was an old scar.

He said, "This looks like a bullet crease across his scalp. He's been shot before. Perhaps five or more years ago. What do these guys get themselves into? He probably has broken ribs, a possible broken orbital, perhaps a ruptured kidney, slight jaw fracture, broken left hand, and his shoulder appears to be dislocated. Wow, he was in a hell of a war. I wonder what the other guy looks like."

There was a slight chuckle from one of the male interns, then one of them said, "I think the other guy is dead. They had to fish him out of the Detroit River."

Dr. Willem said, "So this is one of the guys who went over the bridge. His clothes don't appear to have been wet at any time. Interesting."

After the doctor completed a thorough examination of Michael, he ordered the necessary X-rays and CT-scan. Then he walked out to discuss Michael's condition with his parents. He walked up to Frank, turning slightly away from Martha.

He said, "Sir, your son has been through quite an ordeal. He has numerous injuries, but at the moment none appear life threatening. He has injuries to his hands, ribcage, head, including his eye-socket and jaw, and possible lung and kidney damage. I don't like the bruising I see on his chest and back. It looks like someone stomped or kicked him multiple times. Or possibly he landed on a hard surface. His musculature is amazing. There is minimal body fat on him. This could have proven to be a problem if he were exposed to the elements too long. Hypothermia is always a concern with guys with minimal body fat. We need to keep him warm to ensure he doesn't develop pneumonia.

"The report is that he fell into the river, yet I see no signs of wet clothing. It's obvious that these are the clothes he was wearing during the assault. I also found an old scar, which looks like a bullet wound to his head and a knife wound on his right shoulder. Did Michael ever get shot or stab before? He's of the age for the military. Was he ever in the army and sent to Vietnam?"

Martha started to speak, then noticed that the doctor was directing all his questions to Frank. So, she held back her comments.

Frank thought, *Robert never mentioned being injured in 'Nam!*

He said, "No, Doctor. Michael has never been in the service. He does walk on the wild side, which is why we're here today. He left home many years ago, so we were unaware of any old injuries."

Martha asked, "Is Michael going to be alright?"

Dr. Willem continued to look at her husband but responded, "Your son will be just fine. I see no reason to believe he will be in any further danger. I just need to rule out any internal organ damage, so I must wait for the results of the X-rays and various scans. It may be totally unnecessary, but I will also send in a neurologist to rule out any brain damage. And the head of psychiatry may also visit. That department

has been pushing to visit all CAT scan patients. I think it's BS, but…
anyway, I will keep you posted."

He extended his hand to Frank and shook it. Then he glanced
down at Martha and walked away.

Martha did not miss this third slight either but was too absorbed
in Michael's condition to address it at the moment. However, she
was getting angrier at Frank, possibly because he allowed the doctor
to treat her that way. She would deal with Frank about the doctor's
behavior later.

. . . .

Doctor Karl Schultz walked through the hospital corridors on his way
to his office. He was now the head of psychiatry at Harper Hospital,
a role he had been striving for, after years of tolling in Oakland
County public services in Pontiac and four years in the Army. He
felt uncomfortable having to work with so many Black doctors and
patients, but the pay and higher status more than made up for it.

His favorite phrase, which he created himself, was, *"There's crazy
and then there's Black crazy."*

Deep down inside he knew he was dealing with a prejudice
instilled in him by his father back in Germany. A prejudice which
served him well as a Nazi during the war. He intellectually knew that
'crazy is crazy', regardless of complexion. It was still humorous to him,
however, to make fun of the implied differences.

He stopped by the X-ray and CT Scan administration desk to
see if any new CT scans had been ordered. He discovered that a
scan had been scheduled for a new patient who had just entered the
hospital recently.

*"Hmm, there appears to be a new patient who will be coming down
for a scan soon. I wonder if this Dr. Willem has attempted to contact my*

office. The patient's name is Michael McCants. This city has a lot of Irish living here. Perhaps I should check on him now, before I finish my rounds."

He caught the elevator to the fourth floor and headed to the patient's room, passing by a family distraught by an injured family member. The parents, who appeared to be a mixed couple, were having a disagreement. The apparent sons of the couple were ignoring their parents and merely meandered around the doorway, completely disregarding the police officer standing nearby. Something about the young men, however, gave Shultz a feeling of déjà vu.

"Those boys look awfully familiar. They remind me of someone I met in Germany back in '73. Yes, indeed, they look a lot like Lieutenant McCants! In fact, the patient I'm going to see is a Michael McCants! Well, I guess he's not Irish."

He walked toward the family, then entered the room, knowing the family would not object, since he was a doctor. He looked at the patient, but the man's facial swelling was too extensive for Schultz to identify him. He then picked up the patient's medical chart to confirm the patient's name.

"Michael McCants. Those fellows outside look just like, what was his first name? Rob, Bob, Robert. So, this could be his brother or at least his cousin. Robert was quite a study. Had him in my ward twice, which was unusual. He was a before-and-after patient. Before he was shipped to the warzone and after his return. In fact, on his return trip he was experiencing nightmares and calling for his brother…Michael? Yes, Michael! He kept calling for Michael!

"If I recall correctly that Indian fellow warned us not to ship him to the warzone. Robert did exactly what the little darkie said he would. He went bonkers and killed an entire unit of Cong soldiers. And he was in total denial!"

Schultz walked out to the corridor and began to approach the parents, then had second thoughts.

"I'd better not get in the middle of that argument. That woman is giving that Black fellow hell. She has to be his wife and the mother of this Michael fellow here in the room. I never considered that Robert was a half-breed! Never liked mixed marriages. Only in America."

He turned to approach one of the sons when Mack, the eldest, suddenly stepped up to him and asked, "Hello, Doctor. My name is Mack McCants. I am the patient's older brother. Do you have questions you need answered?"

The suddenness and demeanor of the man was a little unsettling.

Schultz gathered himself and said, "Yes, young man. My name is Dr. Karl Schultz. I am the head of psychiatry at the hospital, not that your family member needs my services. I like to check on all patients that have had or are scheduled to have a CT scan. I couldn't help noticing, however, your resemblance to a Robert McCants, a soldier I met in Germany some years ago. You wouldn't happen to be related to him, would you?"

Mack was not expecting that response. He had noticed the doctor's name tag and title when he walked by, which is why he was acting so forward toward the doctor. He also could not help but notice the slight German accent of the doctor. He knew he was about to drift into dangerous territory, talking with a psychiatrist about Michael. He decided to respond to the doctor just as he had responded the past twenty-five years when asked about Robert or Michael.

He said, "Yes, Doctor. Since you've checked my brother's chart, you know we are named McCants. That is my father and mother over there discussing my brother's condition. And yes, I do have a brother named Robert. In fact, Michael, the patient you just visited, is Robert's twin brother."

Dr. Schultz was taken aback by that revelation. At no time did he imagine that Lieutenant McCants had a twin.

He paused, perhaps a bit too long, then said, "I am sorry your family is experiencing this trauma. Your brother Michael is in good hands here at Harper. Hopefully your brother will not need my department's services."

He reached into his pocket and pulled out his business card.

"Is your brother Robert here at present? I would love to see him again. If not, please give this to him when you see him again."

Mack's mind began to go into warp drive.

"Why would Robert know a psychiatrist? Could this be part of the information that McGregor was telling me about?"

He said, "Sorry, Doctor, but Robert is not here. He is a professor at the University of Michigan and is out of town on an academic assignment in New York. But I will give him your card when I next see him."

Dr. Schultz's intuition told him that Mack was lying. His response was too controlled for a situation that should be nerve racking.

He said, "I'm not surprised that the lieutenant has succeeded so well. He was only nineteen years old when I first met him, but he already had his undergraduate degree. In history I believe. He returned from 'Nam a year later a first lieutenant, with medals for extreme bravery. He is an extraordinary man, and you and your parents must be very proud of him. I'll leave you to comfort your other brother, Michael. Good day."

Schultz walked out of the ward to the elevators. Jack continued to observe him until he boarded the elevator.

Mack could sense that his lie did not convince the doctor.

"Damn, I have never been good at lying for Michael. Why did I have to mention they were twins?"

Then he turned toward his brothers and noticed his brother Jack staring down the hall at Dr. Schultz.

Dr. Schultz continued to have a feeling of déjà vu as he entered his office. He, however, could not put a finger on it. It was not just the familiarity of the family members. There was more. He packed his briefcase and headed home, arriving later than planned. His wife was not amused, since dinner was already on the table.

He said, "Sorry, dear. I know I said I'd be home by seven. But I got delayed by a new patient."

Gertrud refused to accept this explanation.

She said, "Then you should have called ahead to say you would be another half an hour. I hope you enjoy a cold meal."

Then she walked away, to Schultz's delight.

The remainder of the evening had Schultz thinking about Lieutenant McCants. Robert's ability to focus was a major item of interest to him and his colleagues in Germany, especially that Indian doctor. But there is more. Something in Schultz's distant past. He had a near photographic memory, and it took him back twenty years. Back to his role with Oakland County. Back to an assignment in which he sent an entry-level psychiatrist, a Dr. White, to handle. A request from that small Black city named Royal Oak Township in Oakland County. The request was for a kindergarten student whose mother wanted him consoled. He was now recalling the final report submitted by Dr. White. A report he discarded as nonsense.

Schultz eventually went to his bedroom, which was separate from his wife's room. He, however, could still hear Gertrud snoring down the hallway. Her weight gain ten years ago along with a pack-a-day smoking habit had contributed to her sleep apnea condition. The last of the three children had settled into their own family lifestyles, so the house was now void of bodies during the day. So, she made up for her loneliness by overindulging in the kitchen. Gertrud was always a smoker, but the habit really picked up whenever she had the munchies, which was frequent. Now fifty-eight-years-old, she could not sleep well and was most irritable during the day. Her husband, having moved into his own bedroom, did not help her mood either, since they are no longer sexually involved. Ten years sleeping alone was a long time for a woman with an overactive libido. Nor had he ever escorted her to Harper's gala functions since he moved to his current position as the head of psychiatry.

Schultz thought he would have trouble falling asleep because of his thoughts of the lieutenant, but he was unconscious in ten minutes. For only three hours. Three hours of heavy REM sleep, followed by a sudden awakening with a revelation.

He murmured, "Dr. White's report in 1958 and my report in 1971. Her patient was a Robert McCants who had an imaginary brother named Michael McCants! In fact, she believed that either of the two personas could be the actual person. And Dr. Patel was extremely troubled by Robert's tremendous ability to focus. He said it was 'shaman-like.' Perhaps he was so focused to ensure he maintain control?"

Schultz realized that if his lieutenant was also the patient on the fourth floor, then his brother Mack's controlled response to his question was, indeed, a lie. Could it be? Is that Robert lying in that hospital bed on four?

"The family knows! Of course they know! That is why big brother Mack blitzed me. He wanted to know why a psychiatrist would be examining his 'multiple personality' brother!"

CHAPTER TWO

Dr. Schultz

Frank and Martha arrived home from the hospital after a long day of sitting with their injured son. They refrained from speaking in the car after arguing in the hospital. However, when the front door to their home was shut, Frank resumed the argument.

"Michael did it again. He almost got our son Robert killed. We've got to do something about this."

Martha looked at him in astonishment and shouted, "Don't you dare put this on Michael! He's the one who finally got Busta out of our lives! Not you and your fucken warrior clan! Michael did it alone. I asked you to help me with Robert when he was a baby, and you wouldn't have anything to do with it. I placed him with a psychologist when he was five. I asked for help with an agency when he was thirteen. WHERE WERE YOU? I had to go to the school to see about him time and time again, without giving away our stupid little secret. AND YOU STILL WANT TO KEEP IT FROM YOUR

PRECIOUS FUCKING FAMILY! What would dear old dad say? What would your brothers Horace or Herbert think? I don't give a rat's ass what they think! My baby is lying on a hospital bed because he took to the streets to rid us of that monster Busta. Robert wasn't there either! It was Michael! Hell, now we don't even know which of the two is the real person! How do you know that Michael wasn't the baby with Robert being the imaginary friend?! WE DON'T FUCKING KNOW!"

She began to scream, "Now get the fuck out of my face with that shit about Michael! I don't want to hear any more bullshit about Michael from you ever again! You have got to learn to love him equally to all of your other sons! OR ELSE!!!"

Frank, at 6' and 200 pounds, knew not to go any further with his petite wife. He walked out of the house, jumped in his car, and drove away. Before Martha could close the door, the phone rang. She weakly answered it, "Hello."

The voice at the other end of the line said, "Baby gurl. My boi Michael is in some big trobles. Youse better gits yo man's peoples to kno. Yo little gang of eight caint stop da danger my boi is in. Step to it now, gurl!"

The dial tone told Martha her grandmother had hung up. Now she was terrified. She did not know what the warning implied. Her mind went in every direction imaginable.

"Oh my God! The gangsters are going to come kill my boy! Or maybe the police! Oh lord, please help me!"

· · · · · · · · · · · · ·

Dr. Karl Schultz awoke from a troubled sleep determined to find answers to his perplexing questions about Robert McCants.

He spoke to the walls, "If the lieutenant suffers from dissociative identity disorder, then why didn't it manifest itself during our observations in Germany? We had him under close scrutiny for six weeks when he arrived in the summer of '71. There was no indication of a mental illness. Just an extreme ability to focus on any topic before him. When he returned in the winter of '73, he was catatonic, but still did not reveal any signs of multiple personalities. And as he came out of his catatonic state, no other personality revealed itself. Just the same rigidly focused soldier."

He decided to look further into the lieutenant's background before McCants entered the army. So, on the way to his office, he stopped by the Detroit Public Schools' office on Woodward Ave, just off the Wayne State University campus and a mile north of the hospital. After parking his car, he entered the building, examined the building register, and caught an elevator to the fourth floor. He entered a room for student records and presented his credentials.

He said to the receptionist, his German accent slightly more acute than normal, "Hello. My name is Doctor Karl Schultz. I am the head of psychiatry at Harper Hospital. I need to interview one of my patient's counselors. He was born in '51, so I would be interested in any records pertaining to him from 1956 to 1968. I have no doubt he attended your school system."

The receptionist, an elderly woman, barely looking up at the doctor, handed him a form, then asked him to have a seat while he filled it out.

Minutes later Schultz was back at her desk with the form completed. He was really irritated that the receptionist did not speak to him directly, only took the form and instructed him to have a seat again.

"Americans! I've been here thirty years and I still cannot get used to their lack of culture. She is undoubtedly Irish."

He sat in the chairs against the wall and waited for what seemed like hours.

Finally, after ten minutes, the woman returned with a two-page report on Robert McCants. Schultz took the report and smugly said, "Danke schon, gnadige Frau."

Before he could complete his departure he heard "Gerne geschehen, Arzt Schultz."

He paused for a moment, looked back and smiled, then continued out of the room. The woman merely smirked as he closed the door.

"I wouldn't want to be Robert McCants. Wouldn't want that one in my brain. Bet the fucker was probably a Nazi bastard."

Schultz got back in his car and headed south to Robert's high school. He had read the report as he walked from the building and had created a planned route to visit all of Robert's schools before going to his office. He knew it was possible that some of the staff of the schools might have gone to other positions or retired, but he was too excited to approach this task in a logical manner. He pulled up in front of Cass Technical High School five minutes later.

After spending twenty minutes in the school, Schultz was unable to find any information of interest on Robert. So, he headed north to Robert's secondary school, Post Jr. High. There he met the principal, Dr. Johnson. The interview proved to be a treasure trove of information.

Schultz introduced himself and said, "Mr. Johnson, I am doing research on a former patient of mine, a Robert McCants."

Schultz could not help but see the color drain from Principal Johnson's face.

He stammered, "It's Dr. Johnson, sir. Ah, Robert McCants? Yes, I definitely recall having Robert in my school, even for just a few months. He was quite a fine student, straight 'A' student if I recall, but extremely intense. In fact, due to an administrative error, Robert was moved up a full grade. The advancement did not faze him at all, and he finished at the top of his class. So, I counseled him to consider going to summer school so he could begin high school early. I am not aware of his progress there. I recommended him to Cass Tech. That is our top honors school, one of the best in the nation."

He paused for a brief moment then said, "Well, actually his counselor made the recommendation."

Dr. Schultz noticed the poise the man presented when he arrived in his office was now lost.

He said, "Dr. Johnson, you seemed to become somewhat rattled at the mention of Robert's name. He has obviously been gone from this school for over ten years. And he was only here for a few months. May I ask what is suddenly troubling you? Please feel free to speak candidly to me. What is discussed in here will stay in this office."

Dr. Johnson placed his palms down on his desk and took a deep breath. He then crossed his arms at the wrist, placing his palms on his chest.

His speech accelerated as he said, "I am so sorry. I just lost my composure for a moment. I was not expecting to hear his name mentioned. Sorry, Doctor. My apologies. My issue was not with Robert. It was with his twin."

Schultz spent the next hour with Dr. Johnson before leaving the school.

As he opened his car door, he thought, "*No need to go any further with this research. I believe I've found out what I was looking for. Dr. Johnson focused on the behavior of Robert's twin Michael, the one who today is confined to a hospital bed. What he may not have noticed was that he never ever saw the two of them together, which seems improbable. Unless it was impossible. Just to make sure, since the timeline here at this school was so short, I'll make a final trip to Cleveland Jr. High.*"

Twenty minutes later, Dr. Schultz entered Cleveland Jr. High, a school on the east side of the city. He walked into the office and requested to see the principal. He was escorted into Dr. Washington's office. The principal rose and they exchanged greetings. Dr. Washington offered Schultz a seat, but he declined.

He said, "Sir, I will get straight to the point. You had two students here many years ago. Their names were McCants. A Robert and Michael McCants. They were twins. Identical twins. Do you recall them Sir?"

Dr. Washington replied, "Yes, I remember them both, especially Michael. He was a handful. I recall having his mother up here once."

"Do you ever recall seeing both boys together?"

"I never thought about it, but no. As I said, I did have his mother in my office once, but she did not bring Michael. I told her he had to be present as well, so, she asked my staff to get her son Robert. I still don't know why she didn't request Michael. When he arrived, I recall her chastising the boy severely, then ordered him to find his brother. She said they were responsible for each other, since she had so many other children at home. Robert left, and a few minutes later Michael walked in. They may be identical twins but the difference between the two was night and day. Both boys were gifted students but that Michael…"

As Schultz drove back to midtown he thought, *"One last confirmation. I need to find out if Robert has ever visited his brother at the hospital."*

When Schultz finally arrived at the hospital, he went straight to the fourth floor, bypassing his office. After glancing into Michael's empty room, he walked up to the nurse's desk.

He said, "Hello, I am Dr. Schultz, the head of psychiatry. Have any of you nurses seen a visitor to Michael McCants room named Robert McCants, Michael's twin brother?"

Two of the nurses heard the request and approached the desk.

One of them thought, *"Why is this old White guy asking about Michael's brothers? What does his brothers have to do with his mental psyche? I think I'd better make the eldest brother aware of his inquires."*

She responded, "Sir, you are asking about Michael's brothers? Well, all of them, at various times, have been here to see about him. In fact, two of the brothers have introduced themselves to us. One is the eldest brother, Mack. The other was indeed Michael's twin brother Robert. He had just gotten back from, I believe it was New York, after hearing about his brother. Is there anything else we can help you with, Doctor?"

. . . .

Dr. Schultz sat in his office completely confused by the answer given to him by the nurse.

He spoke aloud, "How is it possible that the patient, Michael, could be visited by his twin brother Robert? Dr. Johnson said that Robert was extremely clever during his dealings with the child. That talking to Robert was like playing a complex game of chess. A game that he never won, which is why he got him out of his school as soon as possible. What clever tricks is this family playing? I know I'm on the right track. I know Robert is Michael!"

Mack was immediately leery after meeting Dr. Schultz. So, he contacted Dr. Willem to see if he had referred Michael to Schultz. Dr. Willem's response was that he had not, and saw no reason to do so, just neurology. That's when Mack decided to have their brother Richard introduce himself to the nursing staff as Dr. Robert McCants, Michael's twin brother. He included all the brothers in on the deception. They did not need to ask why.

. . . .

Dr. Schultz was familiar with clever deception. Born in Berlin in 1920, he was educated in prep schools for the elite. His father joined the Nazi party when Karl was thirteen years old. Karl joined the Hitler Youth when he was fifteen years old but was able to continue his education. He got his PhD in psychiatry at the age of twenty-three. He was assigned to work with a group of scientists that were intrigued with twins. What he did not imagine was the horror the scientists would inflict on their subjects. They experimented on working-class Germans, enslaved Jews, and homosexuals. They were also particularly curious about twins from the Romani culture. Half of their study groups were Romani subjects. They gathered them from all over Europe. Even the French and Italians assisted them in the roundup of Romani twins. Identical twins were of greater value for the study. Schultz was never told what goals the study was attempting to achieve; however, he surmised it had to do with Dissociative Personality Disorder. The study was never finished because the war ended before any definitive conclusions could be made.

Two years after joining the German task force, he was in a makeshift American Army barracks, arrested for war crimes. He was only in confinement for a few weeks when he was informed that he had a visitor. He could not have imagined who it might be, since all of the scientists he worked with were also arrested. He soon found out.

.   .   .   .

An unidentified American in a dark-blue pinstripe suit approached the security guard at the barracks outside of Berlin. He handed the guard his identity papers, then requested an audience with a Dr. Karl Baier. The guard examined the papers, handed them back to the American, then escorted him to a conference room near the entrance. Five minutes later the guard returned with Dr. Baier.

After the guard locked the door to the room, the American said, "Dr. Baier. My name is Agent X. My organization has been reviewing your record here at the Bavarian Institute of Psychiatry and have decided we could use your services. However, a tribunal for war crimes is getting organized and may not agree with your release until they have had a chance to review your case. I suspect you won't want them to see what you've been working on at the B.I.P. So, we need to get you out of here before you are summoned by the tribunal. We will be altering your identity once we get you out of here and into the States. We have experiments that perhaps you can help us with. If you are successful, then you will be able to begin a new life in America. A handler will be in contact with you very soon. I assume you have no objections?"

The agent with the dubious name then rose, knocked on the door for the guard to release him, and was out of the confinement area in minutes. Dr. Baier never saw the man again.

. . . .

Agent X, working behind the scenes, helped spirit Baier into the United States with a new identity, an assistance which completely altered his life. He got married soon after arriving in the States. A handler was assigned to him, but rarely had to interact with him and always by phone. After working for ten years on yet another twin project, Dr. Schultz was given a temporary release from his obligations. Again, no conclusions were derived from the research. He could now settle down in Michigan and not concern himself with twins. Until now.

Schultz decided to contact his handler from the CIA. In over thirty years he had never met the man. He told his receptionist he was not to be disturbed. He then placed a call to Virginia. He had to leave a coded message before placing the phone back on the receiver. Ten minutes later his phone rang.

The caller said, "Yes, Dr. Baier, what can I do for you?"

Schultz had not heard that name in thirty-three years and was not comfortable with it.

He responded, "I have not been in contact with you for quite a while. In fact, it's been over ten years. I believe I may have something that might interest you. And by the way, please don't call me Baier."

The Handler said, "Come now, Baier. You can never escape your past. So, what do you have for me today?"

Schultz discussed the work he had done in Germany for the US Army in the early '70s, an assignment the agency placed him in. He discussed the interactions he had with American Army twins that were stationed in Germany. He also discussed the extraordinary lieutenant he met while there, Lieutenant Robert McCants.

The Handler asked, "I see this Black fellow really impressed you. Have you not encountered intelligent Black people before?"

Schultz replied, "I have to work with Blacks, so I've grown accustomed to them. After a while I stopped noticing Robert's race. It no longer was a factor. It rarely came up during the weeks of discussions with my team. It was his incredible mind that fascinated us. His amazing ability to focus on a subject, any subject. We observed him while he slept or ate as well as during various interviews with the staff. He completely baffled my entire staff. He really frustrated a poor Indian doctor on loan from a British psychiatry division. The doctor completely lost his tolerance for the lieutenant."

"And why is this relevant to our work? Why did you not bring this person up before?"

Schultz could not help but hold the suspense as long as possible. He was deliberately taking his time getting to the point of the discussion.

"Why did I wait five years before telling you about Lieutenant Robert McCants? Because now I suspect that he is a twin. And not just any type of twin, if you get my meaning. So, I need to find Dr. Patel."

That evening Dr. Schultz was on a commercial flight to Madras, India.

CHAPTER THREE

Trip to India

Late evening - the day of Michael's admittance

After thirty minutes of total panic, Martha steeled herself and thought, *"My grandmother did not call me with this warning just for me to fall apart. I need to get off my ass before it's too late."*

She called Frank's brother Horace but was told Horace was not home. She thought perhaps Frank went to one of his other five brothers and she did not want to waste any more time searching for him. So, she called her oldest son.

Mack's wife Linda answered the phone.

"Hello, Mother. Mack is still at the hospital. He's alternating with his brothers Richard and Louis, since the full family should not be in the waiting room."

After thanking her daughter-in-law and hanging up the phone, Martha grabbed her purse, backed her car out of the garage, then drove back to the hospital. After she arrived at the parking lot of the hospital, she was back to being the steadfast and alert Martha her sons knew and loved. She entered the hospital and took the elevator to the fourth floor.

"I'm feeling better already. I should not have panicked that way. I'm so glad I was alone."

When she arrived at Michael's room, however, Michael was already gone.

· · · · · · · · · · · · ·

Michael's brothers Mack, Richard, and Louis took turns staying at the hospital. Richard was present when the orderlies came to take Michael to his screenings. He had been gone for two hours when Mack arrived.

Richard said, "Michael has been gone for quite a while. He's somewhere in this massive complex getting scans and X-rays. I wanted to follow them, but they assured me he was in good hands. Besides, I'm sure I wouldn't be allowed in those areas."

Mack said, "That's fine. How are you doing?"

"I'm okay. Just a little tired. Could use some sleep. So, I'll head home and catch some Z's. I'll call Louis to relieve you in a couple of hours. How are Linda and the kids doing?"

Mack nodded his head but did not reply. His mind was elsewhere.

"I wonder what that Dr. Schultz wants with Robert? He surely did not want to discuss old times. Maybe I should contact Dr. Willem to see why a psychiatrist believes he needs to see Michael. And I didn't like the way Dr. Willem was ignoring my mother, so I may just address that as well."

Richard left the building using the stairs, just missing his mother's arrival, since she used the elevator. Before Mack could stop her, she walked into Michael's room, found his bed empty, assumed the worst, placed her hand over her mouth, and gave out a muffled scream. Mack was right behind her and did not expect her to react this way to an empty bed.

He turned her around and said, "Ma, what's the matter with you? Relax! Michael is fine. They had to take him to get scans and X-rays. He'll be back soon, I'm sure. Damn, Ma, why did you come back again today? Why don't you sit down over here and try to catch your breath?"

Martha now had tears flowing down her face. Yesterday she cried when she was told he died at the MacArthur bridge. This morning she cried with tears of joy when she found out her son was still alive. Now she finds his bed empty after a terrifying warning from her grandmother. All this stress came crashing down on her at once, and she began sobbing uncontrollably. She was angry about the error Frank made this morning with the registration forms. She was also upset by the way Dr. Willem treated her. Frank not saying anything to that doctor for ignoring her was really irritating. Her argument with Frank after they got home hours ago only added to her anguish. She realized what her husband said was no different than her own comments in the recent past. As for her grandmother's call with such a cryptic message about Michael's safety?

"How can she possibly know what's going on here in Detroit anyway? And what did she mean HER boy Michael? Have they been in communication? Has he ever visited her? Of course not! He couldn't possibly know she exists!"

Martha asked Mack to go find Michael and confirm that he was alright. He understood her anxiety and left the room. He was back twenty minutes later with positive news.

"I asked the nurse at the desk what test he had already taken. She told me all of the X-rays he required and that he is now getting a CT scan. The staff is new to the use of the machine, so it may take a little longer than usual. So, I walked to the CT scan department and spoke to that receptionist. She assured me he had just been wheeled in. She said I could wait for his release, but I don't think it's necessary. Ma, your son is going to be fine. He's a McCants!"

"It's nice to see her concerned about Michael. It was always Robert who got her attention. Even I ignored Michael's needs. I now know my error. Michael saved my life, and I've never thanked him. That cop would have killed me that day in '68. The same cop who shot him on the bridge. Yet I yelled at him that day! Then I asked Robert, not Michael, was he alright. Wow. I'll never forget his response. He said, 'I just lost my girlfriend.' There's a riot outside and I almost get killed and he's upset because he lost a girl. That should have told me they were two different people."

. . . .

Dr. Schultz's flight departed Detroit Metropolitan Airport and arrived in Amsterdam seven hours later, a layover before his final flight to Madras. It was early morning in Europe, which was six hours ahead of Detroit. He had not been back to Europe in over thirty years. A fear ran through him that he had not considered when ordering the plane tickets. His layover was a long three hours, so he made sure he got a meal he was once accustomed to. However, he never relaxed in the restaurant, even though he had not left the airport. Every person over fifty who looked at him left him feeling the potential of betrayal. After the boarding of the plane was completed, the plane had to sit on the tarmac for another hour while the airport handled weather-related issues. Schultz's imagination began to go wild, as he felt the true reason for the delay was to give the authorities time to come arrest him.

"Was it that old Jew sitting across from me in the eatery? Or the old lady who flew in with me?"

He did not relax until the plane finally began taxiing. After another eight long hours, Schultz arrived at Madras airport. By the time he got through customs and gathered his luggage it was pass midnight.

Schultz had problems communicating with most of the taxi services because of his German accent. They were more accustomed to British or American English. So, getting a taxi to the hotel was not a simple matter.

"I should have taken my handler's advice and met one of his colleagues here. But I don't want to share all my findings with them until I'm sure I'm on the right track. This could pay off all of my obligations to them. I cannot wait to be totally free."

Once he was in a western style hotel, he began to relax. He was very hungry but was not yet ready to try Indian cuisine.

"A hamburger and fries would be grand."

The following morning Schultz took a taxi to Madras University, one of the oldest universities in India. He recalled Patel telling him that he studied at this university, so he assumed that he may have maintained ties here as well. He had already made an appointment before he left the States to see the head of the psychiatry department. He did not want to ask about Dr. Patel over the phone because he did not want to discuss his true reasons for visiting him. He recalled how the lieutenant really rattled Patel.

"No need to get him flustered too soon."

After meeting with the head of the university's psychiatry department, he was promised that they would make inquiries into Patel's whereabouts and contact him. Schultz returned to his hotel room immediately after the meeting. He had no interest in sightseeing and did not want to miss any calls from the school or his handler.

After Schultz left the university, the head of the psychiatry department, Dr. Karapuswamy, called his assistant into his office.

He spoke in Tamil, "I have asked around the department to see if anyone is acquainted with Dr. Patel. None of them have ever heard of him. Obviously, however, I have. We studied together many years ago. I had to be sure that none of the staffers might assist him by answering his questions about Patel. I just don't want that American doctor poking around here anymore.

"I am also curious as to why an American psychiatrist with a German accent is interested in an Indian psychiatrist. I don't believe his story that he worked with Dr. Patel in Germany. Most Indian doctors go to America or Britain. Unless Patel is fluent in German, why would he go to a country that has a language he cannot speak or comprehend? And why would this American doctor with an obvious German accent go back to Germany to practice psychiatry? This man is approaching sixty years old, so thirty-five years ago he may have been in Germany. Thirty-five years ago the Second World War was still going on, so he must have been working for the German government then. Now why would he migrate to America, then go back to Germany to practice psychiatry? Unless he was working for the American government! It is common knowledge that the Russians and Americans fought over German scientist. A lot of them did not get prosecuted during the Nuremberg trials because they were spirited out of Germany before the trials began. So why would the American government be interested in Dr. Patel?

"Nope, we won't be providing any information to our Dr. Schultz until I find out what's really going on. This sister-fucker could be up to something, and I want to find out what that might be."

His assistant merely looked on in bewilderment.

After two more trips to the university over a seven-day period, Schultz was ready to give up the search. He, however, was not convinced that Dr. Karapuswamy was being truthful with him. So, he contacted The Handler and provided him with more information. The next day he knew exactly where to find Patel. His local contact informed him that he could return to the States. They would interview Patel.

What Schultz did not know was Dr. Karapuswamy was in the hospital after being assaulted the previous day. He was found along a rural road, with no identification on his person.

. . . .

Dr. Sekar Patel had returned to India after spending ten years studying in England and working with the British government. He did not enjoy his time in England and missed being so far away from home. He experienced bouts of homesickness since he first arrived in England and made sure to return to Tamil Nadu annually. He also visited West London, which had a large Indian population, as often as possible. His last assignment, however, had him working in Germany, and there was no sizable "Little India" in Kaiserslautern, the site of the US military base.

His pride in his ethnicity was tremendous, and he did not appreciate the small slights he received from his British, American, and German colleagues. He also did not enjoy dating English or German woman, something that did not seem to bother other Indian men.

What proved to be the final straw was his experience seven years ago in Germany. He had met a very interesting but befuddling young Black American who made him question his talent as a psychiatrist. He could not stop thinking about him.

"Robert McCants. Such a young man with so many gifts. He was just a teenager of nineteen years old when I met him and already was promoted to Lieutenant! I have never met a more baffling person. I could not get into his psyche. There was something troubling about him and my diagnosis proved correct. His extremely focused mind indicated to me that he had the capacity to kill without remorse. Without feelings or conscience. Like he would be able to push the memory aside once the act was done. How the American military managed to explain the carnage he left behind in Vietnam shows the level of corruption in the West."

So, he returned to India and began searching for the shaman who might explain what he had experienced with Lieutenant McCants. After a short search he found the shaman and spent the next four years with him, before returning to civilization. He moved to Madurai in Tamil Nadu and joined the staff at Madurai Kamaraj University. For the past two years he had made annual trips to Madras to visit his family. It was at his home in Madurai that he received the visitor from Madras. A woman approached him as he tended to his garden.

She said, "Dr. Sekar Patel? My name is Chandrashekar. Kannal Chandrashekar. I am from Madras. I am home to visit my parents this weekend. I work at the University of Madras for Dr. Karapuswamy, an old colleague of yours. Dr. Patel, my Dr. Karapuswamy was paid a visit from a German psychiatrist. He left three days ago for the holiday, but I'm sure he attempted to contact you. I don't know why but I believe it had something to do with this German fellow. I was lucky to find you without going to your university. One of the jitneys at the airport has serviced you often. I told him I wanted to go to the university to find you, and he knew where you live."

Dr. Patel became alarmed at the mention of 'German psychiatrist.' He worked with a Dr. Karl Schultz during his last assignment before resigning and returning to India. He was never able to relax around the man. Schultz was very pompous and was one of the staffers who was somewhat belittling of Patel's accent.

Kannal continued, "The German, who described himself as an American, was asking about your whereabouts. Dr. Karapuswamy lied to him and told him he was unaware of your present work location. Since I knew the doctor did know where you were, I assumed he was lying to protect you from some evil. So, as I left for home, I also decided to make you aware as well."

Dr. Patel said, "Young child, I have been away for the past three days visiting family. I just arrived back from Madras hours ago, so I am unaware of any phone calls from anyone. I am acquainted and have worked with many American and German doctors. Did you get his name?"

Kannal responded, "I was not in the room when the gentleman introduced himself. He was about sixty years old, but I find Europeans look a bit older to me than their actual age. What I can tell you is that he travelled a long way to India with the sole purpose of finding you. I hope I did not disturb your morning. Please have a good day. Piriyavitai."

The young woman bowed slightly at the hips as she backed away from Patel. She was already gone before he knew she had departed. His mind was too preoccupied thinking of the inquirer.

"She just described Karl. Dr. Karl Schultz. But why would he be seeking me? We did not have any kind of relationship and I don't recall the two of us working on any outstanding projects. Except, of course, the lieutenant."

He paused for a moment, then said aloud, "Of course! He's as baffled as I was by the soldier. That Black fellow has gotten under his skin as well. I must get in contact with him. I am curious what new information he was able to find. I will call Dr. Karapuswamy tomorrow, after the holiday."

The following day Patel called the university of Madras.

When a receptionist answered the phone, Patel said in Tamil, "Hello. I am trying to locate the head of psychiatry of the university, Dr. Karapuswamy. He is an old colleague of mine. Might he be available?"

The receptionist paused for a moment, then said, "I am very sorry, sir. But they have been searching for Dr. Karapuswamy for three days now. His wife reported him missing after calling the university and being assured that he had already departed for home. The police have gotten involved. We suspect a kidnapping and are waiting for ransom demands, but none have occurred. His staff is at their wits end."

Patel hung up the phone, somewhat bewildered about the news.

"Why would anyone kidnap a psychiatrist? That is most extraordinary. I truly hope my fella is alright."

Just then Patel's phone rang. It was his staff at the university.

"Sir, there are two American men here looking for you. They were told you would be in tomorrow. They insisted on our giving them your home address, but we refused. I suspect, however, they already have it. One of them said something about a big house on the corner. After they left, I informed the Vice-Chancellor of their request. He just shrugged but did not respond. Sir, they were really insistent. I did not like them at all. And they had two Indian ruffians with them. Mean looking fellows, sir."

Patel now knew why someone visited Karapuswamy in Madras. He knew that his friend was in serious trouble, otherwise those fellows who inquired about him in Madras would not have known where to find him. Ten minutes before a car pulled up in front of his house, he was headed back to Sundarbans Park.

. . . .

Dr. Karapuswamy got home from work around sunset. The ocean waves crashing down on the rocks was a relaxing sound to him, so he decided he would sit outside that evening and have his staff serve him dinner outdoors. He never made it, however, all the way to his home. Two men accosted him just outside of his house.

"You were asked for information on Dr. Patel. We know you went to school with him and probably know his whereabouts. So, Dr. K., where do we find Dr. Patel?"

CHAPTER FOUR

Michael's Abduction

First week of September 1978

The doctors at Harper were surprised at Michael's rapid recovery. After the first week in the hospital, he was able to move about without assistance. His handcuffs had been removed on the second day, due to the insistence of the medical staff. They proved to be too cumbersome for the nurses. Cavaletti decided that he was not a flight risk so, after speaking to the DAs office, he removed the police presence at Michael's door. Frank decided it was too early to acquire an attorney, after a discussion with his wife and sons.

Michael was heavily sedated for the first three days because he continued to attempt to get out of the hospital bed and the doctors did not want him to cause any further internal damage. After the initial week of convalescence, however, he required minimal physical therapy, which the hospital staff found utterly amazing.

The physical therapist remarked, "I don't understand. This guy has been bedridden for seven days, yet he is walking like he ran a marathon yesterday. And his muscle-tone is still extremely fit. This must be why these nurses are constantly coming in here to check on his dressings and adjusting his pillows."

On the last day of the week, after the hospital corridors quieted down, Michael got a visitor.

He said, "What the! Damn boy, where have you been? I've been lying on my death bed for a week and you're just now pullin up! What gives? Did they get to you, too? Did Busta's boys mess with you? Damn bro, what's up with this ghost shit?"

Robert gave Michael a weak smile and said, "Nothing like that. I don't know what's up with me, but I seem to have lost a week! I don't recall anything over the past few days. But anyway, how are you? And what's up with Busta? I saw him in Ypsi recently. He thought I was you, but I ignored him, which threw him off."

Michael said, "How did you know I was in here?"

Robert said, "Shit, I don't know. I just got a feeling and poof, I was here. But look, we can discuss me later. You look atrocious."

The two brothers talked for an hour. Michael explained that Busta was dead and how he died. Then Robert heard the nurses in the corridor and decided to leave.

"Hey, it's starting to get busy out there. I'd better leave now. I don't feel up to one of those 'twin brother' comparisons. It's too early in the morning for that kind of attention."

He punched Michael in the shoulder, then walked to the door and said, "I'm going to let you get your rest. I'll come back tomorrow."

Michael said, "Okay, younger brother. See ya later."

Less than a minute later, Jack walked into Michael's room. He looked at his brother and just smiled.

"So you've seen Robert, huh?"

.   .   .   .

The two Americans in the dark suits were driven back to the Madurai university after not finding Dr. Patel at his home. They really stood out, even on the school grounds. Not because of their pale skin tones, either. They had their ties pushed all the way up even though the thermometers indicated it was over forty degrees Celsius.

One of them said, "We'd better send these two local guys away for the time being. I think they're scaring the staff."

He instructed the driver to return in an hour, then gave him some money for lunch. They entered the building and asked for the vice chancellor. After a few minutes they were escorted to the vice chancellor's office.

When they entered his office Dr. Chettiar gave them a warm greeting.

"Vanakkam, hello, I am Dr. Raj Chettiar, the vice chancellor of the university. How can I be of assistance to you?"

The taller American said, "Dr. Chettiar? Am I pronouncing it correctly?"

Chettiar nodded and smiled.

"We are here as donors of a very wealthy American organization. We were here earlier, as I'm sure you are aware, trying to find a Dr. Patel. He seems to have left his residence in quite a hurry. So, we were hoping you could help us find where he might be heading?"

Dr. Chettiar understood the American completely, and he was not averse to proper donations.

"Let me be sure I understand your request. You are seeking Dr. Patel, who was on an assignment with your government a few years ago. You are willing to provide assistance to a worthy cause to get information on his possible whereabouts."

As he spoke, he pushed an empty desk tray toward the edge of his desk.

"Your donations are in American currency, of course."

He paused, waiting for a positive response, which he received.

"Then let me leave you gentlemen for a few minutes while I find out the information you are seeking. Please make yourselves comfortable. Would you like some chai while you wait?"

Dr. Chettiar left his office and walked to the Department of Psychiatry. He spoke to Dr. Patel's staff and colleagues. After ten minutes, he returned to his office, walked around his desk, and sat in his chair.

He said, "Gentlemen, I may have found out some valuable information for you. Valuable enough that the size of the donation just doubled. Please deposit it and we can begin going into detail about the probable whereabouts of Dr. Patel. I think the information I've received is concrete. Very concrete."

· · · · · · · · · · · · ·

Martha realized she would have to prepare dinner for her family for the first time in a week. The kitchen, which was never the tidiest during the best of times, was a total mess after a week of carry-outs. Frank was spending a lot of time with his brothers, and when he was home, he was lying across his bed. Since their argument he rarely watched the television in the living room, preferring to sit in front of the one in the basement. It was obvious to Martha that he was avoiding her, and she felt terrible about it. She did not know how to apologize and had never needed to before.

She spent thirty minutes cleaning the kitchen, then drove to the Farmer Jack supermarket two blocks away on Livernois. After shopping, she drove back home and parked in the driveway, not concerning herself with her neighbor's needs for the shared driveway. The neighbors, sitting out on their porch, did not react to the driveway being blocked. They realized they would have to park on the street for the foreseeable future.

She prepared a Sunday dinner, even though it was Friday Beans and Franks Night. Full-course chicken and meatloaf, mashed potatoes, two vegetables, bread, macaroni and cheese, and a store-bought apple pie. Enough food for a family of ten, even though they were now down to just three children living at home. Then she called the family together. Horace and Ervin came down from the upstairs bedroom and sat at their customary seats at the six-seat table. Horace liked to sit where Mack used to sit, with his back to the dining room window, out of the aisle. Ervin sat next to him. Frank walked up from the basement and sat at the head of the table, facing the kitchen. Martha continued to bring the food from the kitchen and would sit at the other end, opposite Frank.

Before she sat down, however, Jack, who had just arrived home in Frank's '72 country squire station wagon, made a grand entrance into the house. With a big smile he proudly proclaimed, "Robert just visited Michael at Harper."

·　·　·　·　·　·　·　·　·　·　·　·　·

The agents had the driver and his associate take them back to their hotel. After consulting with Dr. Schultz and getting his recommendation, they called their office in Virginia. The shorter agent was still irritated by the brutish method his much larger comrade recently employed.

He said to The Handler, "This dumbass Johanson you stuck me with went too far with his questioning of a university official. He left the poor man on the side of the road to die. He even took the man's identification. I won't work with him again.

"I think we need to begin arranging an interview with Mr. Michael McCants. A quiet interview at our southwest Detroit location. There is no hurry, so please wait until we return. I want to make sure we don't make too much noise. We don't need to get the local police involved."

What the agents found out was that Patel had been working on Dissociative Personality Disorder. They were told that Patel found a shaman who had several students with the disorder, and he was studying them to understand it better. Why he was so apprehensive about talking to them was surprising to the agents. They concluded there must be more to it than just DPD. Which is why they needed to 'interview' McCants. It was obvious to them, based on Dr. Schultz's report, that Michael and Robert were one and the same.

How Michael remained active for two years while Robert was in the military was one of the major reasons Dr. Schultz wanted him interviewed. Was he indeed active or dormant during those years? Michael would be the most recent interview.

A report from the local police in a suburb of London stated that a local Gypsy male had been kidnapped. As of this date ransom demands had not been made. Witnesses said the young man, having been diagnosed with Multiple Personality Disorder, was taken by men in suits. The report was dated January 10, 1975.

A report dated June 1977 from the local police in a suburb of Madrid, Spain stated that a young Gypsy man had been kidnapped by men in dark suits.

The agents that interviewed the vice chancellor of Madurai Kamaraj University discovered Dr. Patel had been working with a shaman in Sundarbans Park. The work involved dissociate personality disorder, as the vice chancellor understood it.

The shorter agent thought, *"Money has a way to get men talking. It's better than kidnapping and murder. This dumbass went too far with that guy in Madras."*

Dr. Schultz, having received a report from the agents, concluded Patel's time in Sundarbans Park must have something to do with the lieutenant.

"Why else would someone who had just spent the past ten years living in Europe want to live in a jungle."

So, he informed The Handler, not knowing the agents had already done so.

The Handler, after talking to Schultz, decided to acquire Michael as soon as he is discharged from the hospital. He would not wait for the other agents to return to the States.

. . . .

Dr. Schultz made sure to keep himself abreast of all news coming out of the India operation. Under no circumstances did he want to be out of the loop. He viewed this operation as his ticket to freedom. He also, however, did not want to go back to India any time soon. He did not enjoy the cuisine nor the cities, which he felt were filthy and smelled of animals. After thirty years of living in America's middle-class, he had forgotten what life was like in Germany during the war. When supplies were short and young men's bodies were being shipped home by the thousands.

After he spoke to The Handler he called the agents for a final update but was unable to reach them. Therefore, he was unaware the agents had already contacted his handler.

"Damn, they must be between cities. And I can never reach them when they go to Madurai. The service there is spotty at best. I need more

information so I can give The Handler a final report. I want to get to the end of my obligation."

In addition to calling the agents in India, he also called for Dr. Robert McCants at U of M. However, he was never able to reach him. He knew the receptionist would not give out personal information about school personnel. So, after the second week of trying via the phone, he drove to the university.

He entered the administration building and approached a receptionist.

"Hello. My name is Dr Karl Schultz. I am an old friend of one of your history professors. I have been trying to contact him for weeks now, but he seems to be away from the university. Every time I call, I am told he is not available."

The receptionist was new to the job and was very impressed that such a distinguished-looking man needed her assistance.

She said, "Oh dear, sir. I hope you didn't drive far to get here. Dr. McCants has been away now for some time. I don't know why they just didn't tell you that on the phone when you last called. It's a shame he is wasting your time."

She leaned in a little and whispered, "They're not happy with him here either. To just disappear like that without notifying anyone. And that mess about his brother on the bridge in Detroit. Well, what can one say?"

She smiled at the distinguished doctor and extended her hand, palm down.

He took her hand, smiled, and said, "Thank you so much for being so helpful. Have a pleasant day."

He walked out of the building, feeling assured that he was on the right path. The receptionist could not stop smiling, impressed with his foreign accent.

"That settles it. Robert and Michael are one and the same. I don't believe he is visiting his brother at the hospital. I never did."

He pulled out onto Washtenaw Avenue and headed east with plans to return to Detroit via I-94. Then he decided to take the long slower drive along Michigan Avenue, through downtown Ypsilanti. As he cruised down the street going 30 mph he passed an older Black couple, walking leisurely down the street.

"Now that's how these Blacks should behave. Just like that old Black lady and her middle-aged son over there. They don't have a care in the world. She probably has just retired from cleaning homes or something."

Dr. Schultz did not arrive in Detroit for over an hour.

The observed couple, Dr. and Mrs. Joseph McCants, did not notice they were being evaluated.

. . . .

Dr. McCants was troubled by the call he had just received from a friend and colleague from the University of Michigan. It seems that Robert's attendance was very sporadic. The history department's staff had heard that Professor McCants' brother was thrown from the MacArthur bridge, so they did not expect him to show up for classes the next day. However, it's been over two weeks, and they have not heard from him. They even sent a staff member to his apartment, but the neighbors said they have not seen him either. What's really strange is that the Ann Arbor police had reported his car parked in a mall parking lot. It was reported to have been there for quite some time.

Dr. McCants discussed the call with his wife, Willamae. He was very concerned with Robert's well-being. However, his wife did not recognize her second-eldest son's children quite like she did her other son's children. In her mind, Michael's behavior proved she was right about their mother. She was unfit to be married to her son. She felt Martha was just poor white trash, with a colored brain.

"Now that half-breed Robert is disrupting his grandfather's reputation. Joseph has worked extremely hard the past thirty years to establish the finest possible rapport with the staff of both Eastern and Michigan Universities. He extended himself when he recommended Robert for the position at Michigan. The boy doesn't even know that his grandfather helped him get that position, and his behavior here in this very living room years ago proves it. All our other grandsons that Joseph recommended performed nicely. Now this grandson is interfering with the reputations of all the Black professors in both universities. We Blacks cannot make a misstep. It's just not tolerated."

· · · · · · · · · · · · ·

Second week of September 1978

Dr. Willem spotted Frank McCants in the hospital cafeteria and decided to give him an update on Michael's recovery.

He said, "Pardon me, Mr. McCants. You seem to be here daily, which is good for your son. I want to tell you that all of the second round of testing is completed. Your son will make a full recovery. Personally, I am amazed at the extreme rate of recovery he's achieving. We usually only see this rapid recovery with professional athletes."

Frank could not pass up an opportunity to take some credit.

With a broad smile he said, "Well, he is a McCants, Doctor. These last fourteen days have been rough on my wife and me, but with your attentiveness and the staff's diligent care for him, I'm not surprised he's almost recovered."

Dr. Willem was not expecting such an uplifting response.

"Okay, now let's not put the cart ahead of the horse, sir. He still needs more rest and therapy. But if everything continues to go as it has so far, he should be ready to go home in seven days. You have a good day, Sir. And by the way. Please extend my apologies to your lovely wife. I may have been inadvertently rude to her the morning of the admission. It was not my intent. Also please tell your son Mack that we've spoken about the matter. Again, have a good day."

Dr. Willem walked away, leaving Frank to ponder about the last comment the doctor made. Then it hit him.

"I doubt if Martha asked Mack to speak to the doctor on her behalf. Therefore, Mack must have noticed what I did not notice that day. It's just like him to step into my role when needed."

He could only continue to smile.

A week later the head nurse on the fourth floor received Michael's discharge form, dated for the following morning. When the nurse went to deliver the forms to Michael for his signature, she found his bed empty.

She whispered, "Dammit! I thought when I left for the weekend I remembered seeing a discharge form with yesterday's date on it. I was sorry I wouldn't be here to see him off. Now I have this new form dated for today, which is cool. I'm glad they put off his discharge for one more day. I was looking forward to getting another look at that fine-ass brother again, since I won't be here when he leaves in the morning. Even his brothers have stopped hanging around. His high-yellow mother sure made some incredibly handsome sons. That dark-ass foxy father of his sure can cook. I guess I'll just have to wait until Mister Michael returns to his room."

She went back to her station in the middle of the floor and waited for him to return. He never did.

. . . .

Mid-September 1978

Michael was coming from a vending machine when he noticed the four men walking toward his room. Two of the men stepped inside his room, then exited. He stepped back around the corner, unable to move quickly.

"Hmmm. There's something about those suits."

His ribs were still sore and his right ankle slightly swollen. He didn't have much lung capacity either, since his pierced lung was not completely healed. He headed for the stairs and down into the sub-basement. A security guard, standing ten feet away, saw him walking in the area and asked him why he was not in his room. Before Michael could respond, two men rushed the security guard, knocking him unconscious. Michael turned to run, but his passage was blocked. For the first time in his life, he felt a sense of helplessness.

"These guys are not connected, or they would have already shot me. They look like feds. I'd better not put up much of a fight or my injuries will only get worse. They told me it would take three months to fully recover. Therefore, I need at least three more weeks before I'm back in action."

So, he backed away from the men in front of him, knowing other men were behind him. Before he could turn toward them, however, a hypodermic needle was jammed into his neck, and he fell into a deep slumber. Fortunately, he did not hit the floor, as two sets of hands kept his slack 170 pounds from hitting the floor.

He would not wake up for hours.

CHAPTER FIVE

Dragnet for Michael

Mid-September 1978

After Dr. Schultz parked his car in the hospital parking garage, he went straight to his office.

He contacted The Handler and said, "It's all over the news. Michael McCants has been abducted?! What in the hell did you do? Why in the hell did you grab him from this hospital!? Why couldn't you wait until he checked out of the building? I'm told he was being discharged this morning. If you had waited no one would know he was missing. But to make such a sloppy grab in front of witnesses? Your boys even injured some of the security at the hospital. Now you've placed me in the center of the abduction! That family isn't stupid. All the questions I've been asking all over the city. Those school principals will definitely be contacting the police. The eldest son will put two and two together,

I'm sure. Now I've got to present myself just right and hope they don't suspect I've got some involvement in this!"

The Handler merely hung up the phone.

Dr. Schultz was correct. By the end of the day, the FBI was calling upon him at his home in Birmingham, Michigan, a northern suburb of Detroit.

The agent said, "Hello Dr. Schultz. My name is Thomas Hamilton, a special agent with the FBI. My partner here is Special Agent Stewart. We are here to discuss the disappearance of a Michael McCants. I'm sure you are somewhat acquainted with him. Mr. McCants was abducted from your hospital last evening. The abductors injured a member of the security staff. Do you know anything about this that might help us locate Mr. McCants?"

Dr. Schultz had been working with agents most of his adult career. As a scientist he respected them and knew to take them seriously. He also knew not to lie to them. The last thing he needed was the FBI looking into his records.

He responded, "No, young man, I mean Agent Hamilton. I have never actually met Michael McCants. I am acquainted with his brother Mack. I met him while I was passing through the hospital. I wanted to see if he might be related to a Robert McCants, a young lieutenant I knew years ago while I was stationed in Germany. Once I realized the injured man was not my Robert, I moved on. Since the encounter I decided to look further into finding Robert McCants. Which is why I went to visit some of the schools he might have attended."

Agent Hamilton said, "Sir, you went to Mr. McCants' room to examine him, correct? Then why did you not complete your medical examination once you realized he was not Robert McCants? Why did you merely 'move on'?"

Dr. Schultz started to speak but was interrupted by Agent Stewart.

"Sir, we received a call from a Dr. Washington, the principal of one of Michael's schools, that you were looking into Michael's academic records. We found out you were also down at the DPS Student Records department. Could you explain what your interest is with Michael? What other schools did you visit concerning Michael? There is no record at the hospital of your ever having treated him."

Schultz thought, *"These guys must know every step I took looking for Robert. I'd better not miss anything related to my search."*

"That is correct Agent. I never had a chance to treat Michael. I have a policy to look into any patient who receives a CT scan. Dr. Willem made me aware of his patient and since it was near the end of my day, I went straight to Mr. McCants room before I went home. The next day I went to the Detroit Public School Students Records department; Cass Tech, which is where Robert graduated from in '68; Post Jr. High; and Cleveland Jr. High. I spoke to a Dr. Johnson and a Dr. Washington. None of my searching gave me any more insight into Robert McCants."

Agent Hamilton said, "Insight? Just what were you looking for, Doctor? You haven't treated Robert in over five years. He is now a fully functioning professor at the University of Michigan. Is there a reason you just didn't call the university?"

"These guys are on a witch hunt. They will go down any path looking for Michael, regardless of the viability of it."

"University of Michigan is next on my list. I've already made numerous phone calls. I'm sorry you don't appreciate my methods, agents. But I do have my own personal way to acquire knowledge on someone."

Agent Hamilton said, "Again, Doctor, why all of a sudden do you have interest in Robert McCants, a man you have not attended to in over five years? And haven't you already been to Ann Arbor?"

The questioning went on for another thirty minutes before the agents walked from Dr. Schultz's Birmingham home. They were not convinced of his statements.

As they climbed into their vehicle Special Agent Stewart said, "I don't believe a word he said. This guy just lied to us. He said he was sent to Michael's room at Dr. Willem's request. In fact, he found out about Michael by seeing the CT scan report. He also did not finish his schedule rounds after visiting Michael's room. I believe there is a connection between his search for the patient's twin brother and Michael's disappearance. And since we can't locate his brother, perhaps he is also in trouble."

They pulled away from Dr. Schultz's home, drove north to Maple Road, then East to Woodward Avenue. As they turned off of his street, they did not notice the old '72 country squire parked down the block.

After the agents left the home, Gertrud walked into the living room and said, "I don't know what your business is, but you aren't handling it well. Otherwise, the FBI wouldn't be knocking on our door."

She heard her stove alarm go off and walked back into the kitchen.

He looked at her and thought, *"What a slug. She could not appreciate how I dazzled those two agents. And she still doesn't understand where my extra funds come from. How we're able to live in this upscale neighborhood, with the private schools for her children and the expensive shopping along Maple Rd. boutiques she can walk back and forth to. How she can drive a new foreign car every two years. How did I ever manage to marry someone with an IQ of 85?"*

That evening the agents reported their interview with Dr. Schultz to their commander. The following morning they were told by their superior to drop any investigation into Dr. Schultz regarding Michael McCants' abduction.

· · · · · · · · · · · ·

Martha knew the police had her son. She had no personal connections within the Detroit police department. She had met Commander Cavaletti only weeks before, so he was the only contact she felt she could trust. She wanted to call North Carolina but had already used up that opportunity. She may continue to get calls, but she knows not to make any.

She found Commander Cavaletti's card in the China cabinet and placed a call to his office. He was not at his desk, but the receptionist assured her he would call her back. An hour later Cavaletti called. Before he could finish announcing his name she began yelling into the phone.

"You guys took my boy! You grabbed my son from Harper! I know it was those goons from the 10th! I know it! I need you to get my baby back, unharmed! He's been through enough!"

Now in total panic, feeling extremely helpless, Martha began to beg the commander.

"Please don't let them hurt my boy. Please stop them before it's too late. He's really a good son, just a little wild. But he's never hurt anybody."

Then she began to shout into the phone.

"You guys shot Busta! My son Michael merely captured him for you guys! That pig Sumanski shot Busta and my boy! You've got to stop him from killing my son!"

She dropped the phone and began sobbing uncontrollably, unable to speak anymore.

Cavaletti waited until she was able to pick up the receiver, then said, "Mrs. McCants. I can assure you that the Detroit Police Department had nothing to do with his abduction. We don't operate that way. However, to put your mind at ease, I will personally eliminate any possibility that it was the police who took him. And we will continue to pursue the men that did.

"Please try to relax. I've met you before and you appear to be a very strong woman. Try to gather yourself. You can't help your family if you fall apart. I know you are one half of the foundation of your family. The other half needs you to remain strong.

"I will call you with an update before the day is over. In fact, I'll even come by. Is that okay, Mrs. McCants?"

Martha whimpered, "Commander, I am so sorry I lost my composure. I know Frank needs me to stay strong right now. I can feel your soul and know you are genuine in your concern for Michael. I will be looking forward to your visit later today. Thank you for being so patient with me. Good-bye."

. . . .

Frank knew the gangsters took Michael. He pulled up to his brother Horace's house in Pontiac, Michigan, approximately thirty-five miles north of his home in Detroit. Horace was expecting him and had his front door opened to receive him. The home was now empty of children since all of Horace's sons were grown and married or off to college. His wife was at her job as a nurse at Pontiac General.

Frank sat at Horace's kitchen table and said, "I guess you know they've taken Michael. Those punkass gangsters of Busta's. I know it. Word in the street is that Busta's boys have gone underground. I've got to find my son before it's too late. That means I'm going to start busting heads. I've already gotten Mack, Richard, and Louis involved. We're meeting at Herbert's, so Martha or the other wives won't be able to interfere. I could use your help."

Horace spoke up.

"Frank, we've got to go about this just right. You have to remember that Michael has a whole lot of enemies throughout the city. Not just Busta. He single-handedly destroyed a lot of territory on the east side before he moved to Busta's turf. So instead of us gathering in one spot, I've already arranged for some of our nephews and cousins to hit various east side areas. Just to ask questions, trying to find out who's actually responsible. You go ahead with your meeting and plan to cover the west side with Herb. I suggest we meet here at seven tonight to compare notes. Try not to make any more enemies. We don't need to turn the entire underworld against us."

Frank almost lost it.

"That's easy for you to say. He ain't your boy. They've got my boy!"

Then he started to tear up.

Horace reached out to his younger brother and said, "Frank, you are wrong. They are all our sons. All fifty of them, each and every one of them belong to the Seven McCants boys. So, buck the fuck up, now! I don't want to see no fuckin tears, or you'll get me going too!"

· · · · · · · · · · · · · · ·

Mack knew the mafia took Michael. He sat at his desk pondering what to do next. He was already at his office when word came on the radio of the abduction. Then his father called him to join them in the search. Mack, however, was not in agreement with his father's assertion that it was the drug dealers that took Michael. He believed the gangsters would have gone in shooting.

"Those punk-asses have a 'Damn the torpedoes! Full speed ahead!' type of mentality. No, it had to be the local Mafia. The way they took Hoffa. As recent as last spring they thought Michael had killed that mobster Sammy the Pincer. They even had Robert trapped in the old Packard plant, believing he was Michael. Twenty-five mobsters against me and my brothers. If it wasn't for Ma, that night would have ended tragically.

"I've got to get in touch with someone connected. But I can't imagine where to start. I know they like to hang out at various restaurants in the city, but those places don't open until lunch time. They can be found wherever businesspeople dine in Italian or Greek restaurants. I can start by going

across the street to Nichols. Then a few blocks over to Greektown. Then up Gratiot to Joe Muer. Maybe even go up to Mario's on Second Avenue."

Mack called his father, but no one was at home. So, he left work and went to meet his father at his job at Chevrolet Gear and Axle in Hamtramck.

He said, "Pops, I understand the direction you want to go in, and I don't disagree. However, I've got a different path I want to take, since I don't believe it was street people that have Michael. I've set out a strategy for myself. Only I'll go alone so I don't appear threatening. I will get back to you tonight at Horace's to discuss my findings."

Frank had no choice but to comply with his son.

"First Horace, now Mack. Heaven knows what Martha is doing. Hell, we may have too many hunters in this hunt."

By 1:00 p.m. Mack had already visited three of the four restaurants on his list. He pulled up to the fourth restaurant, Mario's on Second Ave, just south of Wayne State University. Before he could get out of his car, however, a '78 black Lincoln continental pulled up next to him and three suits got out. One of the suits opened Mack's car door and motioned for him to get into the back seat of the Lincoln. Mack knew he had to comply. The suit held out his hand and Mack handed over his car keys. The suit then closed the back door of the Lincoln and climbed into Mack's car. The driver of the Lincoln pulled away. There was no conversation during the trip east.

After twenty minutes the car pulled into a winding driveway in Grosse Pointe Farms. The suits escorted Mack into the side door of a mansion. He was directed to follow them into the waiting room. Sitting on a long lounge was a tall, slim Black man. Initially Mack was confused, as was the man.

He walked up to Mack and said, "Hello. My name is Bordeaux. Pierre Bordeaux. Do you have business with Mr. Castanza?"

Mack immediately knew who the man was.

"This is that uppity lawyer whose son went to U of D Jesuit High. Some of my friends know his son. In fact, some of them told me later that he didn't want his children hanging out with me or my brothers. He called us ghetto rats."

.   .   .   .

Mack was walking to his last class at Cooley High when he was approached by a friend. They greeted with black power salutes, then the teen said, "Hey, brother. I hear your kid brother was trying to date that guy Pierre's sista. You know, the dude who attends that Jesuit school down on Seven Mile? That elite school with all the White kids? Well, word on the street is that he's wasting his time. Nobody has ever gotten close to that fine-ass heffa. She's too good for most of us. Even her brother's friends have not had any success with her. I'm told her father called your brother a ghetto rat. That ain't cool man. The dude said his sister had to leave Wayne because of your brother. I thought you should know. See ya later."

Just then Castanza walked into the room and introduced himself. His consigliere, Vincino 'Vinnie' Ricci, entered a moment later. Everyone called Vincino 'Vinnie' except the Don and his mother. Castanza called him 'Ricci'. Castanza dismissed his lawyer, to Bordeaux's surprise. He hesitated, but got a look from Castanza, and walked out of the room to wait in the foyer.

Castanza said, "Are you the fellow that broke into my house that fateful night a few months ago? Sat in my kitchen and lectured me about my drug business? You know my boys had to pay a stiff price for letting you in. Well, not that stiff." He then smiled and said, "Ha! I know who you are. You're Michael's big brother Mack. You've been looking all over town for him haven't you? Well, son, you're looking in the wrong places. If I wanted your brother dead, he would have been killed while he slept in that hospital bed. You know, I even visited him there almost three weeks ago, while I was getting a test of my own done. He was out like a light due to the drugs, I'm sure. I actually sat in his room! No son, I didn't order Michael taken. Otherwise, you might as well end your search now, unless you're trying to find his body.

"Your father is also wasting his time. The punks on the street don't have the chops to pull off such a caper that smoothly. They are all knuckle-draggers. Just dumbass eggplants. There are smart niggers and dumb niggers. You're a smart nigger, so stop thinking you're Dick Tracy and go back to your cubicle at the bank. I'll call you when I get some information on what really happened to that little thief brother of yours.

"And yeah, I know he was the one who sat in my chair that night earlier this year. It took me awhile, but this old brain still works when I need it to. That's why I visited him. To see if he was capable of killing my cousin. I concluded he wasn't. Otherwise, he would have dumped that nigger Busta into the river when he had the chance. Yeah, Sumanski told my boys Michael almost did throw Busta over the railing but chickened out at the last moment. Almost cost him his life, too. Shit, anyone too skittish to kill at such a dramatic moment can't ever kill, period. Capiche? So, get back to your family and update them on your findings. So long for now son. Arrivederci."

Mack was dropped off at his job on Woodward. The driver gave him his car keys and a parking slip, which indicated that his car had been relocated back at his company's garage.

· · · · · · · · · · ·

After a day of searching Frank pulled up to Horace's home. It was 7:00 p.m. and he was physically and mentally exhausted. He had to find out the hard way that he could no longer chase young boys through the city. Fortunately, he had his young sons with him. Ervin was especially quick. Their efforts, however, proved to be a waste of time, just as Mack said it would.

Mack pulled up a few minutes later. As he approached the porch, he heard another car door open and saw his mother climb out of her car. So, he waited for her, and they entered the house together.

Frank looked up expecting to see Mack, but also saw his wife.

"Baby, what are you doing here? Mack, why did you bring your mother?"

"Pops, you know darn well I didn't bring her. She just pulled up behind me."

"Nobody needed to bring me. I know you and Horace's M.O. It hasn't changed in all these years. You do shit together then discuss it at seven o'clock sharp. I expect it's going to get crowded in here when the rest of the McCants boys show up. But this is one meeting this high-yellow girl is going to crash. And I ain't going into the kitchen to join the ladies either."

By 7:15 p.m. the house was full. Horace started the discussion.

"Guys, our cousins and I covered the entire east side. There was no knowledge of any abduction of Michael. In fact, most of those dudes didn't even know where Harper Hospital was. We spoke to the top of the food chain. All of them have been staying out of sight since those mafia boys were killed by Busta. In fact, they said some of the guys closest to Busta have simply vanished."

Frank spoke up next. "I'm afraid the boys and I have had the same lack of success that you've had. Busta's men have either been killed or run out of town. The ones whose cars are still here are known to be dead. So, it's very unlikely they had anything to do with Michael's disappearance."

Mack got ready to speak, but Martha interrupted him. She looked sternly at Mack who immediately understood the meaning of the glare. It meant, *'Quiet boy. Grownups are talking.'*

She said, "I've been in touch with Commander Peter Cavaletti, that Sicilian cop that came to the house that morning. He investigated the 10th to see if they had any orders to pick Michael up. Afterwards he came by the house at five. He said that there was no way cops were involved. They would have just marched in and arrested Michael after he checked out of the hospital in the morning. And Sumanski has been tied up with internal affairs all week, so he could not have been involved. The report they got from the hospital was that it appeared men in suits abducted Michael. FBI or other government types."

Frank thought, *"Peter? She knows his first name? And he came by the house today? I know she did not invite him in."*

Jack thought, *"Oh hell. Pops is going to focus on mom knowing that cop's first name. When is she ever going to learn just how possessive he is?"*

Mack's thoughts mirrored Jack's.

Mack waited for his mother to finish then looked at her for a long moment. She ignored his implication. He was sending her a look that said, *'I'm a grownup too, Ma.'* He finally spoke up.

"I spoke to several mobsters at various downtown restaurants then was taken to the Don's mansion in the Pointes. Didn't realize just how big and roomy those Lincolns are. He assured me he had nothing to do with Michael's abduction. He even told me that he visited Michael while he was in the hospital."

The entire room said a collective, "Whaaat!"

When the buzz in the room quieted down, Mack continued.

"I believed him. He told me things about Michael's room. He was getting a health test run that day and just decided to pay Michael a visit. It seems he and Michael have history. He thought Michael killed that guy in Greektown back in '69, but later found out it was

Busta. Michael apparently paid him a visit in the middle of the night earlier this year. Got his security in a lot of trouble. I think he likes Michael, even if Michael is an 'eggplant'. Hell, I'd never heard that insult before. Called me a smart nigger but told me to stop being 'Dick Tracy'. Guess being a smart nigger is a compliment. He also knows you guys are talking to the street punks and says you're wasting your time."

Martha took a deep breath at the mention of the Don.

"That must have been Castanza, the one who called me the night of the Packard incident. No need to mention him here."

Frank was alarmed that Mack was taken into Grosse Pointe.

"This is really getting serious. My boy was forcibly taken into the big man's house. I think I need to reevaluate this entire operation."

Horace thought, *"Damn. Mack is one brave dude. Glad he's on our side."*

Herb thought, *"Shit. I've never ridden in a Lincoln. Damn."*

Finally, Jack spoke up. At eighteen, he was the youngest of the men in the room and was still considered a boy to the rest of them. Frank chose not to bring Jack's younger brothers, but Jack insisted on going, so Frank relented.

Jack said, "It was not the street people. It was not the mafia or the cops. I know who took Michael. It was that psychiatrist from the hospital. Dr. Karl Schultz."

CHAPTER SIX

Investigating Dr. Schultz

The morning of Michael's hospitalization

Jack could not help but notice all the movement in and out of his brother's hospital room the day that he was hospitalized. He saw Dr. Willem enter Michael's room and then approach his parents. He saw him completely ignore his mother, only acknowledging his father. This was a strange occurrence.

"This guy thinks mom is a White woman. He obviously does not approve of mixed marriages so he's taking his frustration out on her. Normally she's the one who gets all of the attention. Mom must be pissed!"

He observed all the interns. The frown on the young women's faces as they observe Michael's damaged face. This too was also a strange event. Normally woman cannot resist looking at his brother.

"That one won't make it through medical school. She's too squeamish about blood and the swelling. It's just the men who are doing all of the

gossip. They know Michael was involved with the bridge incident and they can't wait to rap about it."

He also noticed Mack watching Dr. Schultz.

"Why is Mack so concerned about yet another white coat visiting Michael?"

When Schultz came from Michael's room, Mack stopped him, questioning his presence.

Jack thought, *"Oh, now I see. This guy is a psychiatrist. Why would he be going into a trauma patient's room? I'd better keep an eye on this one. Glad I trained myself well, observing Michael all those years. He couldn't have thought I didn't see him scoping us from those rooftops by the house back in the day."*

So, Jack fixed his attention on Dr. Schultz. He followed him to his office, then to his car. The next day he made sure to park his mother's car, which he was now driving, near the doctor's car.

"I'm going to hang out around here between visits to Michael's room. I want to know why this guy is so interested in Michael. I heard him discussing Robert with Mack. How did he know Michael had a twin? Mack must have slipped up and told him. This must be why Mack had Richard posing as Robert. Mack also knows there's something off about this guy."

Jack followed Dr. Schultz to the school records building on Woodward. He followed him to Cass Tech, then Post Jr. High, then Cleveland Jr. High. Later that day he asked Mack if any of them attended those schools. He knew the answers to the questions but wanted confirmation.

Mack replied, "The only one of us who attended all three of those schools was Robert."

. . . .

Mack was also concerned about Dr. Schultz's interest in Robert.

"Michael is laying in that bed, but this guy is asking about Robert. He claims he met Robert in Germany, which must be true. Otherwise, he would not have known about him. So, he's not interested in Michael's condition, but Robert's whereabouts. I really blew it when I lied so poorly for Michael. And I should not have mentioned that damn word 'twin.' I'd better cover all bases and make sure Robert pays a visit to Michael, which of course, is not possible."

So, he spoke to Richard and had him introduce himself to the fourth-floor staff as Dr. Robert McCants, the twin brother to the patient Michael McCants.

Since Dr. Schultz told Mack that he worked with Robert in Germany, the only way Mack knew to confirm this was to contact Austin McGregor in Chicago. McGregor was Robert's commanding officer during his time in Vietnam. It was McGregor who earlier this year had informed Mack of Robert's exploits during the war. The two met during a sales meeting in Detroit. He showed great concern for Robert's wellbeing and might have some insight into why Dr. Schultz is so interested in him.

That evening Mack called McGregor. The phone was answered on the fourth ring.

"Hello, may I help you?"

Mack replied, "Yes, this is Mack McCants from Detroit. May I speak to Austin McGregor please?"

Austin replied, "Mack! How are you? How is your family? And your brothers?"

Mack knew by brothers he was referring to Robert.

"Everyone's fine. Well, that's not true. Everyone is not fine. My brother Michael, who is Robert's twin, has been injured, but that's not why I called you. We never covered the 'Michael' thing while you were here. I was so confused by all the information you gave me about Robert that I never mentioned why you were hearing about a 'Michael' in Chicago. Michael is Robert's identical twin. I may have been somewhat embarrassed that one of my brothers was a thief, ripping off drug dens, but it's true. It was Michael, not Robert, in Chicago. I just did not know Michael was actually in Chicago.

"You may have heard about the incident on the bridge to Belle Isle. Well, one of the men involved was Michael. But he survived the shooting and fall. Don't ask me how. He is now in the hospital. The reason I called you is because yesterday a Dr. Karl Schultz, a psychiatrist, attempted to speak to my brother. I believe he thought perhaps Michael was Robert. My father made an error in filling out the paperwork, mixing up their names, and this may have led him to believe Robert was the one hospitalized. Anyway. Do you know if Robert ever had any interaction in Germany with this doctor?"

McGregor tried to take all of this in at once.

"Give me a moment to digest everything you just said. The guy in Chicago was not a confused Robert, but his identical twin brother Michael. That would explain why he responded to Smith when Smith reached out to him. And your brother Michael was shot on the Belle Isle bridge two days ago? Now a Dr. Schultz is trying to find your brother Robert. Well, I'm not surprised. If it's the same doctor, and I'm sure it is, then Dr. Schultz was the one from Germany who wrote the final summary on Robert before he arrived in 'Nam. Robert spent six weeks under psychiatric observation before he was sent to 'Nam. I don't know if I mentioned that before. No one really understood why the Army felt the need for a fully trained officer to be under observation before he was sent into combat. Especially for so long. Unfortunately, their conclusions proved correct. Robert should not have been sent to a warzone."

The phone remained silent for a short while, then Mack said, "Do you think this doctor saw Robert when he left 'Nam? He gave me the impression that he did."

McGregor said, "It is very likely, since Robert was returned to the same base in Kaiserslautern, Germany. If Schultz was still assigned there, then he would have administered to Robert a second time. But you said Robert returned acting perfectly normal."

"As normal as he was when he left Detroit. He was always somewhat reclusive. I didn't even know he attended Cass Tech or had his degree from Wayne until you told me. Anyway, can you think of any reason I should be alarmed?"

"Mack. I am a West Point graduate. I love my country more than I love myself. But after spending a career in the army, I know not to take anything for granted. I'll tell you what. I'll look into this doctor myself and get back to you. I may still have some contacts that can help us sort this out. Give me your home phone number, since I only have your work number. Have a good day and I hope your brother Michael has a speedy recovery. Good-bye."

Mack held the phone to his ear for a while after hearing the dial tone. He was trying to take in all that occurred over the past two days. He went to bed still thinking about Schultz and McGregor. He could not have known that getting McGregor involved in Robert and Michael's affairs would ultimately lead to McGregor's death.

· · · · · · · · · · · · · ·

Three weeks later, the day after the abduction

Every few days Jack drove past Dr. Schultz's home.

"I'd better not come by here again. I'm not the only observant one and this old station wagon really sticks out in this neighborhood. So does mom's used car."

He was right. Gertrud Schultz had indeed noticed his car after the third trip by. She also noticed the black sedan that was parked around the corner, watching the house. She assumed they were a team.

· · · · · · · · · · · ·

The discussion with the family about Michael's abduction left Frank exhausted and bewildered. His physicality had always provided him with enough energy to resolve any issue to the very end. Yet today it provided him with nothing. He could not bring himself to strike any of the young men he accosted that day, nor could he catch those that ran away. He was now forty-seven years old, too old to be fighting in the streets. Not that he had been fighting the past thirty years. Only once did he have a need to.

The muscular 6' 200-pound dark-skinned man walked into the barber shop on the corner of 12th and Elmhurst.

He said, "I live around the corner. Which one of you dudes spoke to my woman!"

The entire shop, which was full of street people, stopped moving. Then a huge pimp in a bright red hat came from the back of the shop, looked down on the man, and said, "What da fuck do you want? What does it matter? I didn't kiss her, did I?"

The shop erupted in laughter. This emboldened the pimp, so he stepped closer and continued.

"The next time I'm around the corner I'll just kiss her on the pu…"

He never finished the sentence.

Another pimp stepped over his body, as it lay prone in floor dust and trimmed conked hair, and charged into the 6'2" 225-pound man. He, however, was off balance, with one foot still in the air. He soon joined the big fella in the dust. Then the 6'4" 250-pound dark-skinned man grabbed the nearest man to him, who had laughed the loudest, jerked him out of the barber's chair, and bitch-slapped him across the face. White shaving crème flew against the mirror.

One of the women in the back of the shop yelled, "Ohhh! He just pimped-slapped my man!"

The 6'7" 280-pound hulk held the man up and slapped him again. Then he let him go and the man wilted to the ground, his head now spinning. The four remaining men backed away as the 6'9" 310-pound behemoth approached the barber.

"I'll be back in here with my crew if this happens again. My McCants crew! Ask around Eight Mile if you're still curious. You tell these pimps that Elmhurst is off limits. Ya feel me?"

He turned his 7'2" 350-pound body toward the crowd, then Frank McCants walked out of the shop. Only he did not need to duck his head as he exited the doorway, turned left, and walk his 6' 200-pound frame home.

He never noticed his six-year-old son Michael peeking through the window.

What Frank now realized was that he needed to do what Martha had done two years ago when she called her family for help. So, he called his estranged father.

When the phone was answered, he said, "Dad, I need your help. I need your extended family to help me find my boy. Horace and I have reached our limits. Please reach out to your family and ask them to help me find my son."

.   .   .   .

After a long day Dr. Joseph McCants arrived home from his office at Eastern Michigan University. Earlier that day he had followed his usual daily routine and ventured home for lunch with his wife, Willamae. However, before he walked back to the campus, he received a call from his eldest son, Horace. It was Horace who had advised him not to try and visit Michael when he was hospitalized. Horace now made him aware of Michael's kidnapping but advised him to stay out of the matter until he was needed. His wife also asked him to stay away from the city.

"You don't need to lower yourself to that gutter level. You've got a reputation to uphold."

Dr. McCants did not regard his wife's advice as anything but pompous hot air. Her disdain for her daughter-in-law, Martha, made her disown all of Frank's children. So, he was relieved when his son Frank called him for help that evening. After he hung up the phone he glared at his wife, then picked up the phone and called his father. The glare was a signal for his wife to leave the room.

Dr. McCants, now over seventy years old, repeated the same message to his father that his son Frank gave him. "Baba, I need your help. One of my grandsons is missing."

.   .   .   .

Ervin was sitting in the living room when the phone rang.

Before he could speak into the receiver the caller said, "Ervin, this is Dotty at Farmer Jack. Your brothers are in big trouble. There is a gang of thugs standing outside waiting for them. The store manager tried to get them to stay inside, but your brother Horace refused. They are about to walk out of the store. You'd better hurry!"

Ervin dropped the phone and sprinted out the door. He had to run the two short blocks plus the length of the large parking lot to reach the store. By the time he got there, the fighting had already begun.

Three guys were lying on the ground, one of them lay at Jack's feet. Three other men had Jack pinned against a car, pounding him. Horace was still on his feet but was taking as many punches as he threw. Some of the guys were huge, so Ervin went for them first. At sixteen, 6' tall and weighing 170 pounds, he was fearless. He still had the adrenalin after witnessing Michael's fight with Busta on the MacArthur bridge just three weeks ago. He hurled himself into the rumble, knocking one of Horace's adversaries out immediately. The man would not get back up for some time. The odds immediately shifted from 7 men against 2 to 6 men against 3. This excluded the three men already laying on the pavement when Ervin arrived.

Ervin spun around and grabbed one of the teens attacking Jack, lifted him up, turned him sideways, then drop-kicked him. The teen's body struck Ervin's raised knee, breaking several ribs. He then punched the second teen facing Jack in the back of the head, then turned back toward Horace.

Each blow Horace threw knocked out one of the thugs. He was a head-hunter, with one punch knockout ability. Now Horace only had one guy facing him, since the other two were unconscious on the ground. However, he still had a knife sticking out of his side, with blood pouring out of the wound. The man was a huge 6'4" and over 230 pounds fighting a seventeen-year-old teenager. He knocked Horace backward, causing him to grab at his side.

Ervin saw the blood pouring out of his big brother and yelled as he charged the guy. The giant turned just as Ervin stepped up to him with his guard down. Martha would have been most disappointed. The man slammed his fist into the teenager's face. Ervin knew immediately his jaw was broken as he dropped to the ground. He was now out of the fight, barely able to remain conscious.

Jack was now fighting with only his left hand, having broken his right wrist. Horace was still holding his side, blood pouring out of his ribs. He saw Ervin go down and furiously launched himself at the man, ripping his fist into the man's kidneys with three rapid hooks. It worked. The man stooped down in agony. The teenager screamed out as he jumped sideways to get a better footing then punched the former golden gloves champion against his jawline. The man's eyes rolled back in his head as he collapsed to the ground.

The last man looked around for help, which proved to be a big mistake. Jack grabbed him by the throat with his left hand, pulled him forward, kneed him in the stomach, then lifted the man upside down over his head with one quick motion, then released him in mid-air. Gravity pulled the man back to the parking lot pavement. He landed on his head and did not move again.

Horace tried to get to the prince of the family but was unable to move and eventually fell to his knees. Blood continued to run down his side. Jack reached down for Ervin, hooking his left hand under Ervin's armpit. Ervin struggled to regain his footing. His ebony face was now protruding near his left ear.

Several police cars entered the parking lot, sirens blaring. Minutes later multiple ambulances arrived. The police recognized the McCants boys but displayed total indifference.

The police sergeant said, "Okay, who started this shit? Dombrowski, get over here and arrest those three. They obviously jumped these guys."

Dombrowski thought, *"So these are those McCants boys I've been hearing so much about. Wonder if they're related to that guy Michael that's got Sumanski in such hot water. And my big brother lost his job to a Black fella named McCants. That was way back in '65. I wonder?"*

The crowd immediately began to behave unruly toward the police.

An old Irish lady charged Dombrowski and yelled, "Are you crazy! I saw the whole thing. That gang jumped those two boys. They might have killed them if the younger boy over there had not arrived."

The store manager, Abdul, stepped up and yelled, "What are you doing? You are not going to arrest these boys. These are my customers. Those punks were waiting out here to jump Jack and Horace. I tried to keep them inside the store, but they were too proud to hide from them. So, they defended themselves. Bravely I might add. I wanted to help them but I'm too old. In fact, Jack told me to stay inside. None of these other men here wanted to get involved either. Fortunately, their younger brother Ervin showed up when he did."

He pointed at the youngest of the three McCants.

"That redhead freckle-faced punk with the short afro lying over there stabbed Horace. There's the knife. I hope Horace broke the fucker's face! Ibn al Kalb!"

The man he was referring to had not moved in quite a while.

Dotty charged forward, tears streaming down her face, and said, "Yeah, I called Ervin. Those guys intended to kill Horace and Jack. It was so obvious. This was not an ordinary fight. They were here to murder them! You guys must have known about this! We called you ten minutes ago before the fight even started. You're just down the street less than two miles away! It's funny you all show up AFTER the fight. You knew about this, didn't you? Punk-ass cops!"

Dombrowski was now surrounded by the three protesting citizens. More of the store customers converged on him, separating him from the McCants. The murmur in the crowd was getting louder. People walking along Livernois began to merge into the parking lot. Ambulances were trying to get near the fallen fighters.

Jack said, "Guys, come-on. We've got to get Horace to the hospital. You too, Ervin. I believe your jaw is broken and my wrist is as well. I can't use that hand anymore. Those ambulances are going to take these punks-asses to Mount Carmel, west of here. So, we'd better go down to Receiving or Harper."

The police sergeant was too busy dealing with the crowd to notice the McCants leaving the area. Dombrowski did notice but decided not to attempt to stop them.

"This is bullshit. No way those three kids were responsible for this fight. Besides, I hated my big brother. He was a fucking bully to me and my sister. And he only got meaner after he lost his job."

Jack drove out of the parking lot then north on Livernois, heading for the southbound Lodge Freeway. In ten minutes they were pulling into the emergency entrance at Receiving Hospital, which is adjoined to Harper Hospital. Horace was now covered with blood and Ervin was only semi-conscious, so they were attended to immediately. Unfortunately, Jack was wrong about the destination of the attackers. Minutes later several ambulances arrived, bringing ten young men into the receiving room with the three McCants. Fortunately, they were in no condition to cause any further trouble.

Frank and Martha heard about the fight as they drove past the grocery store on their way home. Frank pulled over to ask a passerby what was happening.

The man said, "All I know is this gang tried to kill those McCants boys. You know, the family at war with Busta."

Frank drove into the parking lot but was not able to get past the ambulances and police cars. He ordered Martha to stay in the car, a waste of his breath, then ran into the crowd.

When the store manager saw Frank, he rushed over to him and told him the boys were okay and were heading down to Receiving or Harper Hospital. Frank ran back to the car, but Martha was not in it. So, he had to go back through the crowd to find her.

When he did find her, he shouted, "Get back to the car! I told you to stay in the car! The boys are fine. They're at Harper."

Martha meekly climbed back in the car, and Frank pulled away, running all red lights on northbound Livernois for the next half-mile, and jumped on the southbound Lodge in less than a minute.

Frank knew the boys would probably be at Receiving, not Harper, so he parked at their emergency entrance and he and Martha ran inside. The receptionist knew immediately who they were.

She said, "Your boys are fine. Please relax. But security is not going to let you leave your car there. Please move it into the parking lot. I will escort your wife to your sons, and you can join them once the car is moved."

Frank hesitated, but the look on the nurse's face told him that it would be a losing battle to challenge her. Besides, the security guards were already headed toward his car.

Martha placed her hand on his chest, a move he had become accustomed to, and said, "Honey, go park the car while I check on your sons. They'll still be here when you return."

Frank walked outside while Martha followed the nurse. Ten minutes later he was standing in front of Horace.

He thought, *"How did I fail these boys? Did my recent actions bring this horror on them?"*

Martha thought, *"My fighting Sullivans! I taught them well!"*

CHAPTER SEVEN

Michael's Interrogation

The first week of captivity: Mid-September 1978

The parents of Robert McCants, Martha and Frank McCants, had always assumed their son suffered a mental disorder, often referred to as Split Personality or Multiple Personality Disorder. In fact Robert does not suffer from multiple personality disorder. He and Michael are actually two distinct individuals. They are 'Dual Persons' as a result of their Romani DNA. They have the Romani 'glow' through Esmeralda, their great-grandmother. It manifests itself only in twins with the 'glow' who have lost their other sibling at birth. To the two men their twin is a separate physical entity. They do not know they share the same body. Michael's mind sees Robert's physical presence and Robert's mind sees Michael's physical presence.

The same physical restrictions exist for them as would exist for Michael or Robert and their other brothers. If Mack can appear, then Robert can 'appear'. Mack could not appear in Vietnam because he did not travel to Vietnam. Therefore, Robert's mind would not 'see' Michael while he was in Vietnam. He knows that Michael did not travel with him during the two years he was away in the military.

Michael was able to 'appear' to Robert whenever he was on the University of Michigan campus because Michael 'knew' where to find Robert on the campus, just as Mack would have been able to find Robert on the campus. They are able to appear in front of others merely by one of them leaving the room then returning dressed and behaving as the other. Which is why all their schoolmates and friends believed they were two different individuals. However, if one of them is restricted in movement, the other cannot possibly appear to others. If the restrictions are removed, however, Michael can merely leave someone's presence long enough to change and re-appear as Robert.

Michael knows where Robert is because Robert is willing to share his location with Michael AND Michael can read his twin's mind. Robert cannot, however, read Michael's mind. Therefore, Michael was always walking into Robert's environment, but Robert never walked into Michael's, if Michael did not tell him where to find him.

The twins have learned not to present themselves at the same time whenever others are present. This is due to the mental anguish they experienced as toddlers when Martha and Frank admonished Robert for talking or switching to 'Michael' in their presence, which freaked his parents out.

They are two unique individuals, with separate brains, sharing the same body.

· · · · · · · · · · · · · ·

When Michael regained consciousness from the sedative he received, he was still unable to move. The room was totally dark, and he was strapped to a hospital bed. It would take thirty minutes before he realized he was not paralyzed, but merely tied down. The sounds from outside of the room were vague, but he could make out the horns of freighters sailing by. He could also hear birds, which he identified as sea gulls. There was no automotive traffic or voices, which implied he must be near the river but along West Jefferson Avenue, a dead zone at night. The air had a dank odor to it.

Michael listened for any movement in the room but found none. His injured hand was throbbing, and his ribcage was more painful than it had been in days. He remembered that he did not put up a struggle, so the pain must have been from his transport to this obvious warehouse along the city's southwest side. He could probably scream for hours with no one hearing him. He felt the urge to fall back to sleep, so he did not resist. There was no need to remain awake, since he knew he was not going anywhere any time soon.

He began to dream. He dreamed about Sammy the Pincer. He dreamed about Busta shooting Sammy. He dreamed about Sammy shooting Busta. He dreamed about shooting Sammy and Busta. He dreamed about Busta throwing him off the MacArthur Bridge and two lawyers dressed as hobos drinking up his wine. Then beckoning him to buy more. He dreamed about an elderly couple living in a castle on the east side of the city. A castle with tiny houses surrounding it. And a big house over the castle garage. The garage which stored boats. He dreamed about long bus rides to nowhere. Dropping him off in a distant land, forcing him to walk forever to return home. Finally, he dreamed about a continuous request to turn into Robert. A request that was being made over and over again.

"Okay, Michael. Now it's time to become your twin brother. Bring me Robert. Turn into Robert."

He finally awoke to the request. A light was now on, and a young man was asking him to become Robert. A strange little man was asking Michael to turn off and allow Robert to surface.

"Michael, I have you hypnotized. You are under my control. I need you to become dormant and allow Robert to surface."

Michael thought, *"What is wrong with this fool? How am I supposed to turn into Robert?"*

The 'little' man, named Dr. Alphonse Little, had been working on Michael for three days now, primarily during the day. The lighting in the warehouse was weak, so Little preferred daytime hours. Besides, this place was very creepy to him. The security in the warehouse was minimal since Michael was lightly sedated. However, the sedation was wearing off, at the request of Dr. Little. He had hoped Michael would respond better to his hypnosis if he were fully conscious.

After another hour of failed attempts to get Michael to bring out Robert's persona, Dr. Little left the room. He walked into an office in the back of the warehouse and made a call. Schultz answered.

"Hello, Dr. Schultz. This is Dr. Little again. I have not had the success I was hoping for. He is not responding to my suggestions. I was hoping to have better success once he was alert."

Dr. Schultz wanted to scream at what he considered idiotic expectations, but he had already made his position painfully clear.

"I can't believe these idiots kidnapped him from the hospital. I was lucky I was not connected. The FBI definitely did not buy into my lie. I still don't know why they never called back."

He said to Dr. Little, "Young man. I have asked you not to call me here. I am not familiar with your practices. We always allowed our split personality patients to change personas on their own. We never tried to command or force the transformation. If Michael is indeed Robert, then he will change when he's ready. Remember, I told you he never transformed the entire time he was with me in Germany. Trying to force the transformation may be a lost cause."

> *The scientists in Germany had been searching for Dual Persons within the Romani culture since the late 1930s. On the rare occasion they found one, however, they always assumed the person was suffering from Split Personality Disorder. So, when they had a Dual Person, they were always unsuccessful in their attempts to 'bring out' the other persona.*

Dr. Schultz wanted to go to the interrogation site but realized he could not.

"*If Michael sees me, he may recognize me. Robert knows my face very well and Michael may have seen me walking through the hospital. I also need to stay inconspicuous.*"

Schultz had another reason why he was afraid to go to the site. He could not get over the feeling that he was being followed.

· · · · · · · · · · · · ·

Castanza decided to join his men for dinner at Carl's Chop House on Grand River Avenue, north of the Lodge Freeway. It was a popular upscale place that specialized in steaks and potatoes. His personal corner table was ready when he arrived. As he entered the room his men stood up from the table.

"Chao Capo," came some of the greetings.

"E bello vederti. Good to see you."

He smiled and replied, "Grazie. Grazie," and sat at the head of the table. Various civilians waved his way, and he returned their greetings. The waiter was at his side immediately, even though his consigliere, Ricci, tried to wave the waiter off. Vinni wanted to have a private moment with the boss but soon realized this was not the right time.

He knew the boss did not like to talk about business at the dinner table, but this was important.

The group of men were served wine and dinner and celebrated a good 3rd quarter. They maintain their composure however, since the boss does not like to disturb the other guests in the restaurant. The men knew some of the boss's neighbors from the Pointes were possibly present, and he hated to be embarrassed in their presence. In general, Castanza had always preferred to keep a low profile, unlike certain New York Dons.

After an hour, when it appeared that most of the men have consumed their initial plate of food, Ricci motioned for the men sitting closest to Castanza to move away from the table for a few minutes. Castanza knew why, so both men leaned in toward each other.

Ricci said, "I may have some info on that nigger Michael for you. Word is the feds have him. Not the FBI, but, you know…those 'fed's."

Castanza said, "Okay. Keep me posted. And don't call him a nigger again. His family is somehow connected to New York, and I don't need shit coming from them, capiche? Besides, I kind of like the boy. He's growing on me. To survive falling into that fucken river after being shot by that prick cop Sumanski. If he wasn't a nigger, I'd have him on our team. His big brother Mack is impressive too. Keep an eye on those boys."

Ricci said, "It has to be their mother who's got the connection. She's originally from New York. Don't know the full connection. Not just yet."

· · · · · · · · · · · · ·

Frank's older brother Horace felt the need to visit his parents and discuss the latest situation concerning Frank's sons. He had been trying to console Frank for several days about Michael, and now the younger boys had been attacked. He believed the attempted murder on his nephews at the grocery store was probably caused by the assault they had made on the drug gangs in their attempt to find Michael. Personally, he felt extremely proud of Frank's youngest three.

He said to his wife, "Those boys are true McCants. Frank was always the badass in the family, always the first into battle, and now he's produced eight badass sons. He definitely taught them well. There are ten punk-asses laying up in the hospital because they tried to fuck with my nephews. Ten against two! Luckily our Prince showed up when he did. That young punk is my main man! Dark just like the rest of us! Like our boys. And the word on the street is that my namesake nephew Horace knocked that big mother out cold! Even with a knife in his ribs! And that guy was a heavyweight golden gloves champion of Michigan!

"From what I understand, Jack tried to warn Horace that the gang was too large for them to take on, but hot-headed Horace did not listen to him. Luckily the staff in the store know the McCants well. That phone call that little cutie made to their house sent the 'Black Panther' to the rescue. Man, I love those boys!"

Horace had already called his father about the ordeal the boys endured. This was the third call he had made over the past month. First Michael's bridge accident, then Michael's kidnapping, and now the assault on his three nephews. His father, who had usually been nonchalant when he received news about Frank's family, was now very anxious. His treatment of his second son was now truly troubling him.

.   .   .   .

Dr. Joseph McCants was disowned by his family after refusing to accept the marriage they had arranged for him and instead married Willamae, his college sweetheart. He was forced to live and raise his new family in Ypsilanti, east of Ann Arbor, far away from the family estate in central Michigan. After receiving his doctorate in history in 1932 from Eastern Michigan, during the depression, he had trouble finding work. The doctorate made him over-qualified for most jobs and the surrounding universities were not interested in hiring a Black professor during such hard times. His family's abhorrence to his marriage to Willamae proved extremely debilitating. He subsequently moved his wife and two sons to Pontiac Michigan to teach in a private school.

In 1946, after the war had ended, Joseph was finally partially forgiven by his parents and received a teaching position at Eastern Michigan. When Dr. McCants decided to move the family to Ypsilanti, to be closer to the university, his oldest two sons, Horace, almost 18-years-old, and Frank, now 15-years-old, moved to Royal Oak Township, closer to Horace's job on Eight Mile Road. Horace had shown no interest in higher education, preferring to focus on a music career. Frank enrolled in the nearby high school in Ferndale, Michigan, just east of the township. A year later Frank met Martha. Two years later, in 1949, against his parents' wishes, Frank married Martha.

Ironically, Dr. McCants treated his son Frank almost the same way his father was still treating him. Neither man approved of their sons' marriage, and showed their disdain by shunning their son's wives. Now, almost thirty years after Frank's marriage to Martha, one of Dr. McCants favorite grandsons was missing, weeks after being shot and thrown off a bridge, and the grandfather truly felt completely helpless.

Just as Frank had called upon him for help, he had called his father, a man over ninety years old. Now all he could do was wait for more news from Detroit.

The following morning his doorbell rang. It was his son Horace with his wife, Lucille.

. . . .

Frank was indeed troubled by the decisions he had made recently. He should be out looking for Michael. Instead, he was sitting on the fourth floor in Harper Hospital again, after Horace was moved there from Receiving Hospital. His condition was not serious. The knife nicked a rib but did not hit any organs.

Martha was also troubled, but her mood was due to her desire to call her grandmother. However, she had already used that 'once in a lifetime' opportunity. Now she just had to solve her own problems. She thought about calling her sister for advice, but she knew her grandmother would see right through that attempt. It might make her grandmother angry and cause her to shut her out completely.

Martha thought, *"What a selfish old witch,"* then regretted the thought immediately.

"Suppose she can read me! I'm sorry, Grandma, for that thought. I am just so frustrated. I didn't mean no harm!"

She did not realize it, but she feared her grandmother as much as she loved her. Anyone who dealt with Esmeralda had a healthy level of fear of her.

Mack entered Horace's fourth floor room but was followed by a young nurse.

She said, "Sir, I know you are concerned about your brother. But the floor is getting kind of crowded right now. So, if you would please, with your parents already here and all, could I ask you to wait in the waiting room?"

Mack turned to her and said, "You do know there are people in that room who are waiting to visit their relatives as well. People whose relatives are responsible for my brother being here. I don't think you want me in that room. If fact, I think you should make your security aware of the dynamics here, since the police don't seem to be concerned. No, I think I'll just stay put in here with my parents."

The nurse frowned, then left the room.

Minutes later security was approaching the room. However, they recognized Mack as Michael's brother, since Michael had been there recently.

"Hello, Mr. McCants. We received a call about overcrowding. But we understand your position, so you may stay as long as you please."

Frank and Martha remained quiet, and Mack said, "Thanks, officer. And by the way, how is your colleague? I really appreciate him trying to save my brother. I hope he's recovered from his injuries."

The guard said, "Joe is doing fine. He should be back to work next week. Thanks for asking. Have a good visit."

The guard walked down the hall to the waiting room to assess the potential volatile situation. Then he called his supervisor for more coverage on the fourth floor. Minutes later two additional security guards were working on the floor.

Not long after the new guards appeared, Jack entered Horace's room. He found his parents there, along with Mack. It was obvious to all that Jack was in a very bad mood. He could barely look at Horace, which was puzzling to Mack. He immediately knew trouble was brewing, but he did not know why.

Frank asked Jack, "Son, what's wrong? Is Ervin okay?"

Jack looked at his father but did not respond.

Mack stepped between him and Horace and said, "Jack, Dad asked you a question."

Martha became alarmed.

"What's going on? Jack? Are you alright?"

"Do I look alright? Does this look alright?"

He held up his right arm. It was in a cast past his elbow.

"Do you know Ervin has a broken jaw? And do you know why?"

Horace pushed the button on his bed to lift the back of the bed. He could sense what was going to happen next.

Jack turned directly toward Horace and glared at his younger brother, his two eyebrows becoming one. Frank did not know why he was angry but stepped in front of him as well, since Mack was unable to hold him back without assistance.

Mack thought, "*I used to be the big brother, but now those days are gone. All three of the 'little kids' are noticeably bigger than me.*"

Martha could only stare, totally confused.

"*What's going on? They usually joke around after a rumble. Why is Jack, of all people, so angry?*"

"Frank, what's happening? Jack, why are you so angry?", and tried to touch his shoulder.

Jack jerked his shoulder away, not wanting anyone to touch him. Frank saw that and pulled his hands back before he could touch his son's chest. Jack was now Frank's height, and near his weight. And he was eighteen and angry. A bull in a China shop. He moved his arm in front of Mack, motioning him to back away, and Mack complied. He knew he could not handle Jack alone anyway if Jack were to erupt.

Frank said, "Son, tell me what's troubling you."

Jack's lips were compressed so tight he could not speak. Horace, however, did speak.

"Pops, he's just mad because I didn't listen to him. I don't run from nobody, especially those punks. And we handled them, didn't we?"

Jack finally erupted. "AT WHAT COST?! I told you we did not need to go outside. We could have waited for them to leave! We could have called Mack and them. It was ten against two and you wanted to confront them? That was asinine! And you forced my hand because I couldn't let you go out there alone. None of the punk-asses in the store were going to join us. Hell, you didn't even give them a chance to. You just bulled your way outside the store and started swinging. Now look at you. If that blade had entered you where that red nigger intended it to, you'd be dead now! My baby brother Ervin is why you and I are not dead! He flew in like he was wearing a red cape. Now he has a broken face! Because you can't control your machismo!"

Frank was now forced back all the way to the edge of the bed.

Mack had his hand lightly on Jack's arm, and Martha had backed up against the wall, not knowing what Jack might do next.

She said, "Is Ervin alright? Is my baby alright?"

Jack looked at his mother and said, "His face is broken, Ma! So no, he is not alright. You need to go check on him, not sit here with this fool."

Jack turned to leave the room and bumped into a security guard as he exited the door. He brushed past the man and left the floor.

The guard momentarily looked back at him, then said, "Folks, we can't have trouble in here. Please take any arguing off the floor. We have our hands full with the other families down the hall. We've made an exception with you folks. Do I make myself clear?"

·   ·   ·   ·   ·   ·   ·   ·   ·   ·   ·   ·   ·

First week of October 1978

Three weeks after the abduction Dr. Little was still unable to produce Robert from Michael. He had tried numerous methods, to no avail. He was not sure what he expected, but at least he thought he could get Michael to speak in Robert's voice. He had dismissed his two assistants after the second week, since they were of no use to him. One of them had actually brought in a so-called brain monitor, a knockoff EEG scanner, to observe Michael's brain wave patterns. The data revealed nothing unusual. He viewed the contraption as nonsense.

Michael was getting weak due to poor nutrition and the lack of movement. Dr. Little was too focused on his science to notice. Michael, however, definitely noticed. He knew his body was completely healed. But he also noticed his lack of energy.

"I've got to get the fuck out of here. I'm wasting away. I need to make a move soon or I won't be able to. I don't have to worry about my hand and ribs anymore. I suspect my eye socket is also completely healed. I just don't need to get hit on it anytime soon. I'd better make plans to break out of here in the next few days. There are only four guards in the building. That could be three too many if I don't move soon."

Dr. Little placed a call to The Handler.

He said, "Three weeks and we've gotten nowhere. Whoever told you this guy had SPD doesn't know what they're talking about. That person should be tarred and feathered. I've just wasted three weeks of my life."

The Handler said, "I've been consulting with Dr. Schultz, the guy you want to tar and feather. He has a suggestion. We need to allow Michael to escape. He believes that if Michael escapes, then his brother Robert, who has been absent the past six weeks, will reappear. He suspects that we are dealing with something more than SPD. He just doesn't know what. The staff I have in Europe have an opinion but I don't wish to share that with you just yet. I want you and Schultz to draw your own conclusions.

"Don't inform the guards. We don't want him to suspect anything. Just leave one of his straps loose, just enough for him to free himself. Do you understand?"

Little shouted, "Of course I understand. I'm not an idiot like the person who came up with this dumb plan. Suppose one of the guards hurts him during their attempt to restrain him? Then what? He's obviously too weak to fight them off. Besides, it's four of them. And since you don't want me to warn them, I can't expect them to leave an escape route for him. This is stupid. You people are stupid!"

The Handler spoke into the phone, and Little's face turned ashen. He then said, "Yes, I do understand. I will proceed as you requested."

· · · · · · · · · · · ·

Around 5:00 a.m. Thursday morning, near the end of the third week of his capture, Michael awoke from a sharp pain in his left shoulder. The room was pitch black, as it usually was after the sun went down. He could sense someone's presence. The odor of the person told Michael it was Dr. Little.

"What did he shoot me with? And why did he inject shit into me?"

Dr. Little backed away from Michael and left the room. He had already secretly packed up his office, so he grabbed the one bag and walked to the parking lot. Minutes later he was driving down West Jefferson. He could have driven his car in reverse down the road and not hit a single oncoming car. He turned onto Dragoon, near Fort Wayne, then north to the southbound I-75 freeway entrance. Forty minutes later he was in Ohio.

Michael was more alert than he had been in quite a while. He noticed that he had more movement in his right hand. The strap was looser than normal.

"If I can just move my thumb, perhaps I can flip this buckle over."

It took him thirty minutes to finally maneuver the strap. Five minutes later he was standing for the first time in three weeks. Surprisingly, his legs felt just fine. A shot of epinephrine will work wonders on a super body like Michael's.

He turned to walk away from the bed but knocked over a tray sitting on a cart. That alerted the security that something was moving in his area. The four men on duty were actually Army MPs, assigned to maintain the security of the building from intruders. They were not heavily armed. The last thing they expected was 'the Dummy on the Gurney' to move.

Michael walked gingerly forward until he touched a wall. He used his feet to search out his forward movement, barely dragging his feet along the floor. When his foot touched an object, he would reach out with his hands to examine it. This allowed him to move around the furnishings in the cavernous room. He walked along the wall until he reached a corner, then along that wall until he found a door. He pulled the door slightly open, and light began to fill the room. He was in an interior room and would not need further investigating to find an escape route. The light coming into the room allowed him to see the full layout of this larger room. His exit door was just to his right.

He could now hear the security moving about on the balcony above. So, he jumped back onto the gurney and closed his eyes. One of the soldiers was scanning the room with a flashlight.

He spoke into his radio, "I thought the noise came from below. It must have been a bird on the roof. 'The Dummy' is still asleep."

He walked back to his post, placing the flashlight back in the container. Michael waited twenty minutes to ensure the alert soldier was relaxed again. Then he got up and walked directly to the exit door, moving past any furnishings along the way.

He opened the door, which led to Dr. Little's office. What he did not know was a silent alarm was triggered when he entered Little's room, something Dr. Little had forgotten about. The soldier on the second floor understood that the sound he heard was indeed the prisoner and alerted the other soldiers. They were waiting for 'The Dummy' when he opened the door to the parking lot.

The first soldier pointed his 9mm at Michael and ordered him to back up into the office. Michael complied. However, when the soldier stepped into the office Michael quickly stepped forward, grabbed his wrist, and jerked the gun from the man. He then tossed it away and punched the soldier in the nose.

"What am I doing? This is not a street fight. This is a fight for my life, so act like it. These guys are going to hurt me unless I hurt them first. I know they won't shoot me so..."

He followed the first punch with a roundhouse left and the man went down. He did not recover anytime soon.

The three other soldiers rushed into the room, but Michael caught the first one with an uppercut, causing his eyes to roll back into his head. He joined the first guy on the floor. The next soldier was more fortunate. He caught Michael with a right to his jaw, sending him to the floor. Then the other soldier jumped on him, pummeling him about the shoulders and attempting to hit him in the face. Michael dodged the headshots, then pivoted with his hips, sending the soldier forward over his body. He quickly rolled over and sprang to his feet, blocking a punch from the last soldier. The man was somewhat hampered because he was still holding his gun which proved to be a detriment in a street fight. Michael stooped down and sprang forward, wrapping his arms around the man's legs, lifted him up and flipped him to the ground. Then he kicked him in the head before he could regain his footing.

He now had one adversary left but he proved to be a handful. The two middleweights fought like boxers in a ring for two full minutes. Eventually, Michael won the round by a knockout. He then reached into the man's pockets and took out his pocket change. He noticed that some of the other men were beginning to arouse so he did not wait around for any of them to arise. He walked out of the door and breathed fresh air for the first time in three weeks. His heart rate was 60 bpm. A few minutes later, after a short jog, he was boarding the Livernois Avenue bus at Fort Street. It would be a slow ride back to Santa Rosa. This would also be the second time in six weeks that he arrived to his parents' home via Detroit's bus lines, after a street fight.

Michael, however, did not see The Handler watching his escape from across the street. Moments later The Handler was gone.

CHAPTER EIGHT

The Return of Michael

Thursday morning, 1st week of October 1978

Commander Cavaletti was just sitting down for his morning coffee before leaving for police headquarters. The drive south on Gratiot Avenue would be a smoother drive if he waited another fifteen minutes for the last of the rush hour traffic to subside. However, he would not get a chance to taste his coffee or wait for smoother traffic.

"Commander Cavaletti," he said, responding to his ringing telephone.

He mimicked the caller.

"There is news about Michael McCants. So, what is the news?"

A moment later he hung up the phone, looked at his wife, who seemed to understand, grabbed his car keys, and headed out the door. Twenty minutes later he was entering the front entrance of police headquarters at 1300 Beaubien Avenue in downtown Detroit.

The headquarters' morning shift desk sergeant stopped him and said, "Commander, the original report was that Michael McCants was seen riding a bus up Livernois, passing right by the 10th precinct for Christ's sake! He had to know there's a warrant out for him! Anyway, now a report just came in that McCants was seen entering his parents' home on Santa Rosa. Since there is still an outstanding warrant for him, a couple of cars were dispatched to pick him up."

The commander, normally a very calm man, became furious.

"What in the hell? That warrant was dismissed before he disappeared. You didn't send a car over there before I arrived, did you? Do you know how volatile this situation is? The man was kidnapped from the hospital. No way did you send a couple of squad cars over there! Hell, did you send SWAT and the Big Four too!? That family has gone through hell these past few weeks and now you send over just ANY police representatives there! Get on the fucking squawky and tell those men NOT to approach the house until I get there. DO I MAKE MYSELF CLEAR?! I don't want anyone from the 10th precinct to touch their front porch!"

. . . .

Trigger had been in hiding since that fateful day Busta killed Shapatilo and his four stooges. All five men were made men and the local mafia would not be satisfied until an equal number of heads are delivered to the Grosse Pointe boss, Don Castanza. Trigger and the boys had noticed black Lincoln Continentals patrolling the neighborhood in search of Busta for the entire summer, with no success. By late summer, however, everything exploded when the boss was caught on the MacArthur bridge and killed by Officer Sumanski. That did not stop the Lincolns, however. Day and night they continued to drive through the area. Joker suddenly disappeared without a trace, as had Ray Ray, and no one had seen or heard from East-side Snake in a month.

"Dhose Dagos ain't gonna leaves be what's left. Busta is dead but dai stills looken for em? Nope, da lookin foe jest me now. I cain't keep hidin in dis har garage, sleepin in my ride or dis har partment. And I cain't trust my bitch any moes ether. I's gots ta git outta Dodge. I could call my boy in New York but…What da fuck?! He owe me for da last trip I's paid fo em. Fucker gits har and only stay an hour. Caint help he crashed up his ride."

Trigger, sleeping the last two nights at his lady's younger brother's apartment, looked for his little black book, finding it in the last suit he searched. He dialed a number and after five rings someone answered.

"What's up? Who is this?"

"Hay Dillon. It's yo boy Trigger from Detroit. What's kickin?"

Dillon responded, "Damn boy! What in the hell is going on in Detroit?! The Man killed your boss? Didn't Busta know to keep the cops on payroll? Oh yeah. Now I remember. He went stupid and killed that dago. Not just any made man either. But the top dago in Detroit! Shiittt, I'm surprised he survived as long as he did. He must have been squirreled away fo-sho these last few months. But you can't hide forever. And that hoe's boy was there too, huh? The way I heard it, both them niggas went off that bridge."

Trigger was hurt that Dillon spoke about Busta in such a disrespectful manner. However, he needed his help, so he had to ignore the insults.

"Listen, Dillon, I needs yo help. I needs a place to hang til thangs har cool down a piece. Can I comes to de Apple fo a short stay? Stay wit yo folks?"

The phone line was quiet for a while as Dillon considered his response.

"Alright cousin, Listen up. I have known you since we were teens. But you done stepped in it. I warned you that hoe was connected. Shit, man. That wasn't just any hoe. That was Esmeralda! I don't know how she turned herself young again, but I would swear that was her! Or at least one of those fine-ass granddaughters of hers. I was ten years old the last time I saw her, but I've got her face bronzed in my brain. That woman I saw in Detroit looked exactly like Esmeralda.

"My car crash on the turnpike was no accident! I realized it when I saw that hoe in the doorway. That was Esmeralda! Do you get me! That was the witch Esmeralda, voodoo or whatever her powers are. Anyway, I would like to help yo ass, but I think anyone who fucks with that family in Detroit is in for a rough time. Check out your success kicking their ass and ask yourself if you've had any luck. Shit, word here is that even her boys were kicking yo ass. And that the little one on the bridge gave Busta hell!

"What you need to do is go west and never look back. The trail of bodies Esmeralda left here in Harlem in the '30s and '40s is long. And don't think that cop killed Busta either. Shit, it was that witch-queen Esmeralda, I'm telling you. And she's connected to the mafia here, too. Word is that you motherfuckers had one of her boys trapped in a factory and then just walked away. WHAT DO YOU THINK THAT WAS ALL ABOUT!

"I talked to the older guys here. The real old guys, mother fuckers in their nineties, since most of them fuckers from back then are all dead. They told me even mafia boys who messed with her disappeared. They said that old witch would have to be around 100 years old today. They said she was in her mid-sixties when she left Harlem. Well, I saw her the week before she left Harlem. Back in '47. I remember because I was just ten years old, so I can remember the year. I saw her shoot a nigger dead just for smiling at one of her granddaughters! I was there, you hear me! I was just a kid, running errands for the pimps, but I would never forget it. And the bitch could not have been anywhere near sixty! Still fine as hell, long black hair and all! Well, I'm telling you that bitch standing on that porch in Detroit that day was her, got-damn-it! I know it! A Black diva who looks White.

"Listen, Trigger. We was teens together. I remember when you brought your po-ass Mississippi-talking self up here in the '50s. Well, I'm going to quote a western I once saw recently. 'Go West Young Man.' Take your ass to Kansas or Missouri. Shit, that's where I'd go. Look, cousin, I've got to go. Let me know where you settle down at."

. . . .

Commander Cavaletti was very proud of his Sicilian heritage. His parents had immigrated to the United States just months before his birth. They moved to Detroit the week of his delivery. His father experienced a lot of discrimination from the recent southern White migrants to the city. He had a rough time in school as well, until his parents moved the family into a heavily Italian neighborhood on the east side of the city. Cavaletti witnessed the harsh treatment the Black citizens of the city had to endure and could somewhat relate to it. He did not consider himself a bleeding-heart liberal, yet he still volunteered to join community committees for better police interaction with the city residents. His wife applauded his initiative.

"Honey, I am so proud of your efforts to aid the downtrodden in the city. Someone from your department needs to step up. The city has now had a Black mayor for almost five years, but the relationship between the police and the citizens is not getting any better."

Indeed, Coleman Young, the city's first African-American mayor, was elected in '73. Since his election the 'White flight', which started after the Second World War ended, had only accelerated. The predominately White police force viewed Mayor Young as their enemy, after having had Roman Gribbs, the Wayne County Sheriff, as the previous mayor. Police brutality was the major issue during the '69 and '73 elections, with a Black candidate, Richard Austin, losing a very tight race against Gribbs in '69. Young's win in '73 was against the former police commissioner, John Nichols.

Cavaletti knew that protocol required him to go to the 10th precinct before going to an active operation. He decided, however, to bypass protocol and go straight to the McCants' home, believing time was of an essence. He would deal with any fallout from his actions later. He was somewhat surprised when he arrived. There were three squad cars parked in front of the house, with some officers walking around their vehicles in the light rain, but none having approached the house. There were also squad cars circling the block in an attempt to cut off possible escape routes, if necessary. The commander was relieved that the officers had not entered the property and thought their patrols around the neighborhood were unnecessary.

"What a waste of manpower. Michael is not a fugitive. The charges against him were dismissed during his final week in the hospital. Strange it was the final night of his stay that he was abducted."

Cavaletti drove a few houses up the block, then parked his vehicle. He approached the officers in front of the house, spoke to them for a moment, then walked up the porch steps and knocked on the screen door. Frank unlocked and opened the door for him.

Cavaletti said, "Hello, Mr. McCants. I hope all is well. I understand Michael has returned. I hope he has not been harmed. Would you mind if I spoke to him?"

Frank invited Cavaletti into their home and asked the commander to have a seat, which he declined, then summoned Michael from upstairs. When Michael appeared, Cavaletti saw new bruises on his face and felt a sense of compassion for the young man. He stepped forward and extended his hand. Michael hesitated, looked at his mother, then shook Cavaletti's hand. Cavaletti could not help but notice the bruised knuckles as well.

"Michael, are you alright? Do you need any medical treatment? Do you know who kidnapped you?"

Cavaletti knew he was not handling the situation properly. His nerves were on edge because of the manner the morning started. He was still nervous about the large police presence outside. He also was worried about the actual kidnapping and curious how Michael had managed to escape. The young man had obviously been beaten and was very weary. His father was very anxious, both because of the kidnapping and the police outside. Martha had to restrain him from calling his brothers. Martha and the three younger brothers were now crowding the room as well. When Cavaletti looked at the younger three sons he was shocked at their obvious injuries, which were all new. He had given instructions that he wanted to be kept up to date on any issues this family experienced. Yet no reports came across his desk of the boys getting assaulted.

"Some heads will roll!"

Martha noticed his observation of her other sons and spoke up.

"My sons are having a rough time in the neighborhood due to Busta's killing. You guys killed him, but my young sons are made to suffer. But don't worry. We'll handle it. You should see the other punk-asses. Yes indeed, my boys gave as good as they got. Ten against three ain't too bad odds for these three, huh boys?"

Frank gritted his teeth.

"She asked me to be cool, then she makes such a declaration in front of a cop. Suppose one of those other fellas has a serious injury?"

Cavaletti said, "Ma'am, I am sorry your family is having a rough go of it after the Belle Isle incident. I have instructed my staff to keep me abreast of new developments involving your family. No one informed me, but I will get to the bottom of this. However, it would help me tremendously if I could interview Michael about the kidnapping. I am glad he is okay, and I want to know where my department went wrong."

He then turned back to Michael, but before he could speak, Michael said, "I've already put a call out to Robert. He may be their next target."

Cavaletti was very surprised by this remark, for he could not understand why Michael would be concerned for his twin. Martha and Frank looked at each other nervously and the boys began to stir.

Cavaletti said, "Fine, if you think that was necessary, however, I don't see the connection."

The commander spoke to Michael for approximately thirty minutes.

Then he said, "I can understand if you don't want to go back to the hospital, but I would advise you to, just to be sure none of your old injuries have worsened. Also, the only way I'll be able to get to the bottom of what happened to you is if you come to the police headquarters. I can arrange for you to be interviewed at the downtown headquarters by our best detectives. Besides, I am certain once the FBI find out you're free they will insist on speaking to you as well. Hell, they probably have already been informed and are on their way here now."

Before Cavaletti could finish his sentence, two men in suits began approaching the porch.

Frank said, "I guess you are a prophet, Commander."

The Special Agents of the FBI introduced themselves to Michael and his parents. Frank asked his sons to leave the room so the agents could discuss matters with Michael. Frank and Martha, however, remained in the room.

After Cavaletti excused himself, the Special Agents interviewed Michael for approximately an hour, twice as long as Cavaletti. They wanted to escort him downtown to their headquarters, but Frank objected.

"Guys, Michael only got home a couple of hours ago. He has had no sleep and is in no condition to travel with you downtown for additional questioning. The police commander has already taken up a lot of his time. We promise Michael will be available to you tomorrow morning."

Both agents pondered the request and consented, since they understood the young man needed rest, after such an ordeal.

Ten minutes later Michael was sound asleep in Robert's old twin bed.

. . . .

Cavaletti returned to his office at police headquarters, bypassing the 10th precinct. He was determined to find out why no one informed him of the younger McCants' assault. The desk sergeant explained to him that the responsibility for informing him belonged to the captain of the 10th precinct, Ralph Baker. Cavaletti did not need to proceed any further. Baker was already in his doghouse, which is why he felt comfortable bypassing the 10th. He walked into the Police Commanders office and closed the door. An hour later he had explained the complete complexity of the McCants' ordeals to his boss. The commander promised him that he had the full support of his office.

After working the previous twelve hours Cavaletti pulled into his driveway. He was extremely tired due to the tense day. He parked his car in the garage and entered the house. His wife greeted him in the kitchen.

"Looks like you've had a busy day. I suppose those McCants are a handful. I suspect they do appreciate your personal concern for them."

He smiled at her and lightly kissed her on the lips but did not wish to rehash the day.

He said, "How's James?", their fifteen-year-old son.

His wife frowned and said, "The boys at his high school are still giving him a hard time, especially your fellow cop's kids. They're mad because word is out that you don't support Sumanski's Belle Isle bridge shooting."

Cavaletti was not happy to hear that his son was suffering due to his work on the force. The neighborhood was packed with Detroit police officers, so a lot of the boys in his son's school, Notre Dame High in Harper Woods, were officer's sons. He looked down the street from his living room window. Sumanski was looking up the block at his home.

All Cavaletti was concerned about was that Martha's sons were safe. He hated disappointing her. Unfortunately, he would continue to disappoint.

. . . .

Cavaletti discussed the shooting on the MacAurthur Bridge with Sumanski the moment he arrived on the scene, before Internal Affairs had spoken to him.

He said, "Why did you wait until Mr. Johnson had the young man over the railing before you fired."

Sumanski said, "I was trying to shoot the big guy before he dropped the little guy."

. . . .

Cavaletti saw Sumanski the day after he was brought in for questioning about the cash found in his backyard.

He said, "I heard O'Brian talking to some of the officers this morning. He was saying that Michael looks like the kid you had cornered in the alley on Fenkell back in '68. You remember that day. You were knocked out by a rioter. Could it be that you know Michael was responsible for assaulting you? The crowd said you smiled after shooting the two men. One man said you were dancing an Irish jig."

Sumanski replied, "Sir, I have no idea what you're talking about. As I've said to you before, I saw the big guy about to throw the little guy off the bridge, so I fired. And by the way, I'm not Irish. I'm Polish. We don't do Irish very well."

· · · · · · · · · · · ·

At 11:45 p.m. a Black '78 Cadillac Eldorado pulled into a fueling station on Michigan Avenue in Southwest Detroit. After filling up his tank the driver drove the car over to a vacuum machine and thoroughly cleaned out the front and back seat of any trash and papers. He emptied his ashtray and glove box of trash and paraphernalia. He performed the same exercise in his trunk, leaving only his spare tire and a small toolbox. Then he thoroughly vacuumed the entire car. When he was sure the car was clean of any drugs or alcohol, he drove onto the westbound entrance of the I-94 freeway.

On the front seat was a road map of the Northern United States. A red circle was made around the city of St. Louis, Missouri. The driver accelerated to 69 mph, then locked in the cruise control. The car would not stop again until it arrived at a gas station in Benton Harbor, Michigan, approximately three hours later. The driver got out of the car, paid for a full tank of fuel and a carton of cigarettes, then filled the tank to capacity. Then he got back in his car and re-entered the west bound entrance of I-94. He would not stop again until the sun came up behind him on his left, some three and a half hours later.

CHAPTER NINE

Robert's Ordeal

A middle-aged woman, living in North Carolina, approached her elder and said, "Grandmother, I'm experiencing a lot of trepidation, but I cannot identify it." The grandmother said, "I knos baby. But ain't nuttin we can do bouts it. It jest gots to playitselves out."

. . . .

Friday morning 10:00 a.m.

End of first week of October 1978

As arranged the previous day, Michael met the agents in their office. Since he did not know how long he would be with the agents he drove his own car. Once the FBI went through the regular procedures concerning a kidnapped victim, they asked the obvious question.

"Michael, do you know where they kept you imprisoned for the past three weeks?"

Michael, having been told by his father to cooperate fully with the agents, responded.

"I was kept in a warehouse in the southwest section of the city. I know after running a short while I crossed Dragoon. There was minimal auto traffic in the area, especially after dark. The guy who questioned me the most was a scientist. He was accompanied by two other scientists, but he was definitely in charge. They actually wore white coats as if I was a lab specimen. The enforcers there were military, all armed to the teeth. Big guys. The scientist kept probing me daily. At one point they had a contraption attached to my head. They would sedate me for what must have been hours at a time. They kept asking me to bring out my brother Robert, to switch to my brother Robert, like I had him hiding in my back pocket. By the way, I made a call to him yesterday. He was not at home, so I need to try again soon. I know they are going after him next."

Michael could tell the agents did not believe his story.

Finally, they asked him what the scientist looked like.

He sarcastically said, "White."

When asked how the soldiers were dressed, he said, "Green fatigues."

When asked if he thought he could identify any of the soldiers he said, "No, they were all White."

At one point one of the older agents angrily said, "What's with all this 'White' shit boy; your mother is 'White!'"

The other agent, looking embarrassed, leaned over to the agent, and whispered into his ear, "No, dummy. She is not White. She just looks White."

After four hours of questioning, the two agents arranged for Michael to be taken home. He reminded the agent that he had driven his own car. Both agents were completely confused by his story and assumed Michael was just lying. They did not understand why he would make up such a silly story. They assumed Michael had been kidnapped by the gangsters from Detroit. Or maybe the mafia, since it was rumored that he had killed Sammy the Pincer. In fact, the agents were truly surprised when they got the call yesterday morning that Michael was still alive. The Bureau had written him off as dead the day after the kidnapping.

The younger agent, however, was truly concerned. He was aware of Michael's reputation of going to war against the dope dealers in the city and worried he was merely waiting for the right moment to get payback.

When McCants got off the elevator at the FBI Headquarters on Michigan Avenue, he was met by a small contingent of reporters and two Detroit police detectives.

The Detective said, "Mr. Michael McCants, you are under arrest."

He was placed in handcuffs and walked the remaining distance of the lobby and out the front door of the building. The detectives, backed by two Tactical Mobil Units, placed him in the backseat of their car and drove away. Instead of driving McCants immediately to Police Headquarters, a few blocks from the FBI headquarters, they traveled to the 10th precinct. They placed him in a holding cell until 4:30 p.m., then loaded him into a paddy wagon and transported him to police headquarters. He was marched up the stairs and into the lobby. The detectives stopped at the front desk to speak to the desk sergeant.

He said, "We've got Michael McCants here. Where is Cavaletti?"

The afternoon shift sergeant, not on duty when Cavaletti arrived in the morning, did not want to get in the middle of the drama.

He said, "He's with the Chief."

The detective said, "He doesn't need to be disturbed about this, you got it?" then walked McCants into the holding area.

The outstanding warrant for assaulting a police officer during the 1968 riots was now being enforced. Since the day was Friday, after 5:00 p.m., McCants was placed in the Wayne County jail. He would not be arraigned until Monday morning.

One of the prisoners in the jailhouse was exiting the holding area and saw McCants being marched into the cell block.

He said, "Shit, That's McCants' kid. The one who kilt Busta. They are going to kill him before Monday. This is truly a setup."

Five minutes later Horace McCants got a phone call.

The caller said, "Hey, bro. This is Hammer. We played together on the circuit. I got your number by calling Baker's Keyboard Lounge on Livernois. Listen, my brother. Your nephew has been arrested. The one that kilt Busta. They've got him at the Wayne County lockup. He won't last the weekend unless you get him out now. Or build a wall around him. I owed you one and now we're square."

Horace said, "Solid," and hung up. Horace understood immediately what was happening and what to do about it. He made some calls. Then he called his brother Frank.

. . . .

McCants was relieved to have the cuffs off his wrist. He, however, was not feeling relaxed in this crowded cell. There were eight other inmates in the holding area waiting to be relocated elsewhere in the jail. All were eyeing him, some with fear and anxiety. McCants' reputation was city-wide and any move toward him could prove fatal.

One of the older men thought, *"There must be a hit out for this young man. He may not last the night. I've heard of him. He killed that dago in Greektown back in '69. He also killed Busta last month. I heard he was kidnapped by the mob, yet here he is, walking in here like nobody's business. None of these fools will want to be the first to approach him."*

McCants thought, *"So now what? Do I have to kill again to survive the night?"*

An hour later McCants was still alive. The security came to move him to the gymnasium, an unusual move for a newly placed prisoner. He had to step over a couple of unconscious bodies lying on their backs to reach the entrance of the cell. The guard looked down at the bodies and understood why they were not moving.

McCants was moving through the crowd when he saw his adversaries. They began moving in on him from three sides.

"Wow. They aren't wasting any time. Well, there isn't any running around in here. Too crowded. I'll just have to hit the first guy in and take his weapon. Then perhaps ..."

Before he could finish his thought a second group of men stepped in front of the first group, turned to face them, then backed them down. All the men in the gymnasium knew what was occurring. McCants was getting a wall of protection.

"What's happening? I don't know any of these guys."

Then a little guy walked cautiously up to McCants and said, "When you see your uncle Horace, tell him Junebug said 'hi'."

McCants slept well the rest of the weekend.

Early Monday morning, McCants was taken from his cell into a small room. A man in a suit was sitting at a table. McCants understood he was to face the man on the other side of the table. The prison guard left the room.

The man said, "Hello, Mr. Michael McCants. My name is Juan Rodriguez. I work in the public defender's office. I'm sure your family will provide you with your own attorney, but until he arrives, I have to prepare you for the morning arraignments. All the men here that were brought in after 5:00 p.m. get a P.D. until they can arrange for a personal lawyer. Now what I understand is they have arrested you for assaulting a police officer. An Officer Sumanski. This assault occurred ten years ago in 1968. The statute of limitations does not apply here because, according to witnesses, you left the state for some years, living in Indiana and Illinois. Besides, there is no limitation when you assault a cop. Do you wish to discuss this alleged assault with me before we enter the courtroom? Is there anything you wish to share with me?"

McCants shook his head.

The lawyer, somewhat baffled, said, "Okay. They will be coming for you in a few minutes. Normally they transport you over to cells above the courthouse to help the arraignments run smoother. But your case has been placed at the top of the docket. So, they will escort you directly to the courtroom from here."

Twenty minutes later McCants was facing Judge Anthony White.

Judge White said, "Mr. Michael McCants, you have been charged with assaulting a police officer. This offense occurred on April 4th, 1968, during a civil disturbance. How do you plead?"

McCants stood as erect as he could and said, "Your honor, I was walking out of the federal building when the police grabbed me and placed me under arrest. I have not been told what the charges are. No one had even addressed me by name. They just handcuffed me in the federal building and drove me to the 10th precinct. After a few hours, they transported me down to police headquarters, then threw me into a cell and locked the door. I wasn't even fingerprinted. No mug shots or anything."

The judge paused and looked at the prosecutor.

He said, "Three questions. Why was this gentleman taken to the 10th precinct first. And tell me you have his mugs and prints with you? If he was at the 10th, then they had plenty of time to fingerprint him and take his mug shots. So where are they? And tell me he got his phone call!?"

The prosecutor said, "Sir, I believe he was fingerprinted, but I don't have them with me at the moment. I rarely find it necessary to bring them into court. I don't know why they took him to the 10th first. Perhaps it was because the assault occurred in that precinct. And I'm sure he got his phone call."

The judge looked back at McCants and said, "I am sorry you were treated so poorly, Mr. McCants, but I still need you to plea. I have explained the charges to you. Mr. Michael McCants, how do you plea?"

McCants said, "I don't understand why everyone today keeps calling me Michael. My name is not Michael. My name is Dr. Robert McCants. I am Michael McCants' twin brother."

. . . .

Robert and Michael always traveled with a change of clothing, which is how they were able to appear to be in the same place at once. When the FBI agents entered his parents' house, Michael had already packed his bag and placed it near the front door. The following morning he grabbed the bag then jumped in his car, drove to Harper Hospital to pick up Robert, then proceeded downtown. The two men walked into the federal building, then Robert excused himself and went into the men's room. When the interview with the federal agents ended, Michael walked out of the office and into the public restroom. Robert exited the restroom, then spent the next three days in the county lockup.

. . . .

Second week of October 1978

Cavaletti was having another tantrum in police headquarters. He was furious why a decision to arrest Michael McCants was made without his knowledge.

He entered the police chief's office and said, "I made it clear that any interaction with the McCants family was to go through me. Unless you approved it, then someone is deliberately trying to harm this family. That fight at the supermarket was no normal street rumble! Those teenaged boys could have been killed! Do you know how ridiculous we look? We arrest a man who was shot by Sumanski in front of dozens of witnesses. Then we accuse him of assaulting Sumanski when he was just a teenager. Sumanski and O'Brian were knocked out by a 150-pound teenage kid? Sumanski weighs over 220! O'Brian is even bigger! They deliberately detained him at the 10th before transporting him down here. They placed him in a cellblock full of Busta's gang. Fortunately, his people were able to protect him. We sure couldn't. How were we going to explain how he was killed while in our custody? Or that no one had him fingerprinted or had his mugshot taken? He didn't even get a chance to make a phone call!

"THEN, during his arraignment, we find out we've arrested the wrong man?! We arrested a college professor from the University of Michigan! Do the words 'Keystone Cops' sound familiar! The media is going to have a field-day with this one. They will start to put two and two together. I can see Bill Bonds smirking on the evening news.

"The supermarket fight, the hospital kidnapping, now this dumbass arrest. From a federal building no less. We were supposed to be looking for a kidnapped victim. Instead, we attempt to arrest him, but arrest his brother instead. This shit would make a Kojak episode seem dull in comparison!"

· · · · · · · · · · · ·

After leaving the county lockup, Robert walked back to the FBI headquarters and entered the men's room. He had hidden his car keys in the last stall and needed to retrieve them. Michael entered the restroom as Robert exited the stall and said, "Let's go. I need you to drop me off on Santa Rosa. You can get your own car there."

There was no need for Robert to discuss the weekend with Michael. He understood that Michael probably already knew what had occurred, since he could read his mind.

After a quiet drive and brief stop on Santa Rosa, Robert drove to his apartment for a shower and change of clothing, then drove to the university. He was confused about the past month, recalling very few events during that time. He was also confused why he had pain in his rib area and minor bruising on his face.

"I must be feeling transference pain from Michael. He did not say so, but I know he must have been brutally beaten. Sometimes it sucks to be an identical."

That thought frightened him, reminding him of the last time he had misgivings about being a twin, so he looked skyward and apologized to no one in particular.

Before he went to his first lecture, he stopped by the Dean of History's office. The dean's secretary, Mary Ann Glide, gave Robert a very disappointing look as she escorted him into the dean's office. One look at the dean explained the secretary's mood. The dean, Dr. Alford Burke, was extremely upset. He did not waste a moment.

"Robert, I don't understand these long periods of absence. We had to cover your classes for the past two months, and you never called to explain your absence. How can you expect me to tolerate this? Young man, you are an excellent instructor. Your rating among your students is exemplary. Your colleagues also speak highly of you. But those same colleagues had to cover for you for six weeks! I know your brother was hospitalized, but you still have to report to work! And you don't even call to warn us you won't be returning anytime soon. Please explain what happened."

Robert was not surprised by Dr. Burke's tirade, even though no one had ever spoken to him in this manner before. He did not have an explanation and definitely did not want to tell him he had no knowledge of his own whereabouts. He only remembered visiting Michael once in the hospital and again… *picking me up at Harper Hospital and driving me to the federal building. I walked with him to the men's room, then he asked me to exit the building out the Michigan Avenue door. When I asked him why, Michael said, "Because I think they are going to attempt to arrest me. They were at the house earlier today, but that cop Cavaletti stopped them. I don't know why but he seems to like Pops and Mom. Especially Mom. But now that I'm here I don't think he can stop them again. I think they are going to go through with an arrest. So, let's pull a fast one on them and…."*

Dr. Burke yelled, "Robert? Dr. McCants!"

Robert's mind drifted back to the meeting at hand. His lost time was interfering with his ability to focus, which only confused him more.

"I'm very sorry, sir. I am still somewhat distraught about my brother's kidnapping. Then the police arrested me on Friday, mistaking me for my brother. I had to spend the weekend in the county lockup. I was even denied a phone call. They finally released me this morning after they realized their mistake."

Dr. Burke was flabbergasted. He did not know if he should believe such an extraordinary tale.

"Dr. McCants. I am so very sorry about your problems. But they cannot impact this university. Your family drama should not interfere with your position as a professor of history. I see it's almost time for your first lecture. Please return here once all of your classes are over."

Robert meekly rose, took a step back, nodded his head at Dr. Burke, then left the office. He was still bothered by the lost time, but his McCants attitude was slowly returning. He was willing to let that 'family drama' comment slide. At least for now.

"We'll discuss my 'family drama' situation more when I return."

Four hours later Robert returned to Dr. Burke's office. The dean's secretary was now extremely pleasant as she again escorted him into the dean's office. Dr. Burke motioned him to sit.

"Robert, aww, Dr. McCants, I have to apologize for my emotional outburst earlier today. I did not have time to fully appreciate your state of mind these past few weeks. If one of my brothers were in trouble, I'm sure I might respond similarly to the way you responded. Please forgive me for my rude behavior."

Robert, now perplexed, decided to push his McCants attitude aside.

"Sir, there is no need for you to apologize to me. You were right. I should have communicated better about my family drama situation, as you stated this morning. I will make every effort to prevent this from occurring again."

Dr. Burke stood up, acting somewhat nervous, and extended his hand to Robert. They shook hands and Robert left the office. As he walked past the secretary she also stood up and smiled. Somewhat confused, he merely nodded his head at her, said "Good-bye," and headed for the stairs.

Robert pulled up to his apartment ten minutes after leaving the campus. He sat for a moment trying to understand what changed Dr. Burke's attitude toward him. He believed Dr. Burke was correct in his assessment of his work during the past few weeks, just did not need to be so insensitive about his issues. He, however, was still bothered by his mental confusion. He had always had short periods of lost time, which he viewed as normal. He had experienced them all his life and assumed everyone did. Now, for whatever reason, the periods of time have become much more extensive.

He turned on the evening news, made himself a cup of tea, then sat down to relax for the evening, turning down the ringer on his phone.

"I don't need any interruptions the rest of the evening," and slowly drifted off to sleep.

He dreamed of his return to Germany from Vietnam. His reintroduction to Dr. Schultz. The initial confinement to his hospital bed. A confinement that continued until they realized it was a waste of time. He always managed to escape any method of strapping they attempted to use. He dreamed of the questioning he endured about the final combat battle. The attempt to convince him that he had killed during the firefight, something he knew to be untrue. He dreamed about the sleeping agents that they were using on him, which he had developed such a tolerance for, that they were no longer effective.

Robert eventually awoke feeling extremely rested after eight hours of sleep. Sleeping on his couch was so relaxing. However, he did not have a true sense of time or space and began to realize he was no longer in his living room. In fact, he knew he was not even in his apartment. One thing he did know, however. He was no longer dreaming. He also knew that he was in trouble.

He could sense that the room was large, with a high ceiling, even though the room was pitch black. The air was very cool, almost chilled.

He pulled his arms away from the loosened straps, reset his thumb, swung his legs off the hospital bed, and stood up. He was now standing barefoot on a very cold floor. He checked his clothing and realized he only had on a gown.

"Shit, I bet it's white too. I think I've been kidnapped. I'd blame this on Michael, except whoever grabbed me did so from my apartment. They must have been there earlier and drugged my cup or contents of my tea."

He felt his face and body but did not detect any new bruising or pain. Even his ribs no longer hurt, as they had earlier the previous day.

He heard footsteps coming down a corridor, so he climbed back onto the bed, inserted his arms back into the straps, and lay prone, as if he were still asleep. A minute later the door opened, and a light came on. Dr. Little entered the room, followed by four heavily armed military soldiers. Before the last soldier entered the room, the lead soldier gave instructions to the four men standing outside the door.

"Under no circumstances are you to open this door. The report on the lieutenant is that he is an expert in hand-to-hand combat. The Vietnamese sergeants reported that the villagers found eight Cong soldiers dead from knife wounds or head and neck trauma, all piled in one small circular area. So, forget that 'college-professor' bullshit. And this guy is no good to us dead so keep your safeties on."

Dr. Little turned toward the soldier and said, "I don't want, nor do I need, your protection in here. This man won't be waking up for at least four more hours. Besides, even if he does wake up, those straps will keep him confined. Therefore, please send at least two of your men back outside. They make me nervous."

The lead soldier said, "We have been given strict orders to maintain heavy security around this guy. His brother has already escaped from here before because of the light security you had here. We won't be making that same mistake. That's why I made sure those straps are properly secured."

The soldier walked past Dr. Little to examine Robert's straps.

Then he exclaimed, "What the fu…" as Robert struck him in the throat and grabbed his rifle.

The moment he had the weapon in his hand, his mind switched to extreme focus, combat mode. The three soldiers lifted their weapons toward him, but Robert reacted first.

"I have been trained to aim for the kill shot. Aim for the head and heart." He took aim and all he saw was the eyes of his adversary. He

started to pull the trigger, then at the last possible moment, lowered the rifle and fired, *"Pow Pow Pow Pow Pow Pow."*

Suddenly the only sound in the room was the screaming of the three soldiers. Then he turned the rifle toward the doctor.

Dr. Little backed away and said, "Robert, please don't kill me! I'm begging you! Please don't kill me!"

Robert reached down to the downed soldier thrashing on the floor at his feet, his hands wrapped around his throat. He grabbed a clip from the soldier's belt, then turned as the door swung open. Four soldiers came barreling in and opened fire. Robert shoved an equipment table toward them then dove behind Dr. Little's desk. When he slid out of the other side of the desk, he opened fire.

"Pow Pow Pow Pow Pow Pow Pow Pow."

He switched to the second clip, but it was not necessary. The four soldiers joined their comrades in a choir of screams and moans. The first soldier had passed out and remained unconscious on the floor.

Robert walked over to Dr. Little and jerked him to his feet.

"How many others are out there?"

Dr. Little stammered, "Oh my God! You've got them all! You've killed them all! You are just what we've been looking for. You are Michael and Robert, aren't you? A killing machine, just like the report stated. Just as Dr. Schultz said. You are a magnificent specimen.

"Please, lay back down on the bed so I can examine your brain. I must examine your brain! Please put the gun down so we can continue our study."

Robert resisted the urge to shoot the insane man between the eyes, then walked away from him.

"Robert. Robert. Where are you going? Robert. Please come lay back down so we can continue our study. Don't worry about those soldiers. We can always get more of them."

Dr. Little sat down on the floor and continued to stammer, "Robert. Robert. Robert…"

The soldiers continued to cry out in agony. All of their weapons lay busted beside them.

Robert peeked out of the doorway and listened for more footsteps, but the remainder of the building was very still. He could only hear the raving lunatic sitting on the floor behind him and the anguish of the soldiers. He walked out of the cavernous room, into the smaller office, where he found his clothing. He laid the rifle down, dressed quickly, found Dr. Little's car keys on the desk, then lifted the rifle and walked toward the exit.

Three minutes later he was entering northbound Interstate-75. It was 2:00 a.m. Tuesday morning.

He drove back to his parents' home and found his twin standing outside on the sidewalk.

He picked Michael up then said, "They just kidnapped me tonight. I suspect they took me to the same place where they were holding you. Therefore, we need to stay together until we find out what's going on. I think a Dr. Karl Schultz wants to study us because we're twins."

"Is that why you shot those eight men? Hell, you should have shot that freaken Dr. Little! He kept making the stupidest request. He wanted me to change into you!"

Robert looked confused then said, "Well, I never gave him the chance to ask me anything. He was a very peculiar guy."

Robert arrived home, showered and shaved, and was back in front of his students at 9:00 a.m. He had been arrested and spent the weekend in jail, released, reprimanded by his boss, kidnapped, and escaped his kidnappers over a three-and-a-half-day period. Most of the time during this period he slept.

He left Dr. Little's car with Michael.

. . . .

Mary Ann, Dr. Burke's secretary, had lunch with a group of secretaries from the area universities. The group of women took pride in the power their bosses wield, so Mary Ann was especially proud to tell the group what had occurred earlier that day with a young history professor. It did not take long for word of the reprimand to get back to Eastern Michigan University.

. . . .

The President of the University of Michigan received a call from the dean of history at Eastern Michigan University. Dr. Joseph McCants made him aware that he did not appreciate his grandson being treated so poorly by the dean of Michigan's history department. He explained the trauma the young man had recently experienced. The University president, aware of Dr. McCants' family's long history with the area universities, assured him that he would handle the matter. An hour later Dr. Burke was sitting in the office of the President of the University of Michigan.

CHAPTER TEN

Cavaletti

Final week of August 1978

The day of the Bridge Shooting

Lieutenant Sumanski was elated after killing Busta. He thought that Michael was dead as well and only found out otherwise the following morning. Unfortunately, he could not hide his joy from the crowd. Numerous witnesses, who were on the bridge during the fight and shooting, called into police headquarters about the shooting, keeping the police brutality hotline busy most of the evening. A hotline that Commander Cavaletti helped to initiate.

Sumanski spent most of the evening filling out paperwork and answering questions at the 10th precinct, normally a safe haven for him. That sense of security was now gone. The following morning commanders from police headquarters arrived at the 10th to interview him. A White police officer shooting two Black men involved in a fist fight was troublesome for the force. Especially after the murder of the three teens during the '67 riot. Both men falling over the railing was sensational news for news media, both local and national. The mayor even commented on the shooting, being careful not to place judgement too soon. Then word began to spread that Michael had survived, and the media went wild.

"Shocking news from the east side of Detroit. We reported last evening that two men were killed by police on the MacArthur Bridge at Belle Isle. Now reports are coming in that one of the men shot on the bridge has survived. News at noon."

Sumanski was celebrated as a hero by his immediate colleagues on the force. He also received congratulatory calls from some of his underworld connections. He was floating on the euphoria but his elation would end very soon. Internal Affairs was waiting in the wings.

His interviews with I.A. would last for hours. When he got home that evening, he was exhausted. After parking in his garage, he walked to the front of his property, not proceeding through his customary side door. He stood on the sidewalk and looked down the block at neighbor's homes. There were at least four homes on his block that belonged to police officers. The entire northeast community, just south of 8-Mile and west of the city of Harper Woods, was often referred to as 'Copper Canyon' or the 'Blue Corridor.' It was heavily populated with Detroit police officers, primarily because of a residency requirement by city charter.

As he walked to his front door, he could not resist looking down the block at a particular house four doors west and across the street. The female resident in the home was returning his gaze.

·　·　·　·　·　·　·　·　·　·　·　·　·

The four men were barbequing in Sumanski's backyard during the late fall of '68. The city had already had its issues with civil disturbances that year due to the Martin Luther King assassination. Now the celebration for the Detroit Tigers Major League Baseball World Series victory over the St. Louis Cardinals had gotten somewhat out of hand, and arrest had to be made. Fortunately, only minor property damage occurred as the celebratory crowd convened in the downtown streets. This was of special interest to the four men, since they represented Detroit's finest.

As they relaxed the following day one of the men, an Officer Stokes, watching the rebroadcasting of the celebration on a television screen, said, "Now that's how you celebrate. Not like that April shit last spring. King gets killed and they burn their own neighborhoods down. I still don't understand it."

Officer Thomason said, "What do you expect from jungle bunnies? Fortunately, there were more of us White folks in the crowd then there were bunnies, so the celebration did not get too far out of hand."

Stokes, noticing Sumanski daydreaming, said, "Sumanski, what's going on? Why are you staring across the street?"

"Because Lieutenant Cavaletti just moved down the block."

Thomason said, "You don't like Cavaletti much do you? We've known for some time that he was moving here. Just because he's a nigger lover doesn't mean he shouldn't move into our neighborhood. I know, you don't like him because he's Sicilian," and laughed.

"Shit, those dagoes are going to make me rich someday. I couldn't care less about them."

He paused, then said, "You obviously don't know do you? Cavaletti's wife is a nigger. Why do you think I call him a nigger lover?"

. . . .

Cavaletti's wife Judith had made it a habit of keeping a watchful eye out for her property since moving to Carlisle Street near Kelly Road. Too many strange things have occurred to their property over the years. She especially kept up with Lieutenant Sumanski's work schedule. One late afternoon she noticed a pretty white lady in a pink dress walking from door to door selling cosmetics and hoped she would not stop at her home. She had her own stock of products that she purchased while visiting her mother on Dexter Avenue and did not need any more Fuller Brush stuff.

Judith was especially curious when the lady arrived at Sumanski's house. She knew he was not at home and the lady would be wasting her time. Sumanski's wife had left him a year ago and taken the kids with her.

After knocking on the door and ringing the bell, the lady did a surprising thing. She looked around, then walked into Sumanski's backyard, carrying a small box. When she returned, she had to brush off some dirt from her pink dress. Then she walked back to her car and drove away, no longer interested in finishing her sales. She did not have the box with her when she returned.

The following evening Cavaletti told his wife that a search of Sumanski's finances proved he was on the take from organized crime. They had found a lot of money buried under a rose bush in his backyard, which led to the financial search. Judith, of course, witnessed the search, as did most of the neighborhood. Judith's facial expression did not change as she listened to her husband, but her mind began to race back to the pretty White woman in the pink dress.

· · · · · · · · · · · · · · ·

Morning after Robert's release from jail

Second week of October 1978

The courtrooms were unusually quiet that Monday morning. The staff of a judge was still abuzz about the arrest of a college professor who had been mistaken for his twin. Some of the staff members found it somewhat humorous. Others felt the system had been hoodwinked by the man. That he knew his brother was going to be arrested and traded places with him to upset the system. It did not help matters that the man who the defendant was accused of attacking was now being accused of bribery.

"Do you really think they're going to charge that cop with a crime?" asked one of the men.

His colleague replied, "Hell no. The last thing any police department wants is an investigation into bribery. Most of the upper echelon of the force are solid citizens. They believe in that slogan, 'To Protect and Serve.' But you can't believe that pig did not share his ill-gotten gains with some of his 'boys'. How else do you think he got that promotion to lieutenant? All those complaints of police harassment on him? And do you know how hard that promotion test to lieutenant is? I've seen that cop in here numerous times. There is no way he could pass a sergeant's test, let alone a lieutenant's test."

The last of the trio frowned and said, "What are you trying to say? Are you implying there is a fix in? No way the prosecutor will let this one slide. Shit, the feds are onto this one. His goose is cooked, and if he has to take some of his 'boys' down with him, he will. In any case, he's suspended."

. . . .

Castanza was feeling old. He knew he was feeling that way because his world was getting confusing. One day he received good news. The next day bad news. He had been speaking to Lastanza, the Don in New York, for over an hour.

He said, "Topsy-turvy. That's right, I used that WASP word. Mischiato! Traduzione! I have good times and bad times all at once. I have lost one of the best collectors I've ever had. That nigger Busta was the best. He was smart too, but he sure destroyed the English language. And a mean bastard, which is how I like my niggers. Then he kills my entire staff from the northwest quad! I had to have that dumb Polack kill his ass. Now the dummy Polack is under investigation for bribery! Who could have known? Ha! Shit, what am I laughing at? I'm the one that was bribing him. Well, indirectly. Hell, I didn't even know he was on my payroll. It was Busta who was paying him and not sharing the info or influence.

"Busta killed my cousin Sammy, then he kills my other cousin Little Sammy, then he kills Shapatilo. He actually chopped off my giant cousin's head! That's some mean shit. I knew that practice with the bowling ball bags by Shapatilo would come back to haunt him. And you know who is irreplaceable? The nigger! Not that schmuck Shapatilo. I moved a paisano into that office the next fucken day. With minimum losses. Hell, the only smart thing Shapatilo did was delay the hit. Otherwise, we would have lost half a mil. But now I have no one to run that area because my boys killed Busta's entire team! No collections. I'm betting money is flying away like the geese heading south for the winter!

"My mother is still grieving the loss of Little Sammy. But from what I've been hearing he was starting to talk like the nigger! Saying words like "dat" and "Caint" and shit. We send him in to kill his brother's murderer and the murderer kills him and his entire crew!

What a super nigger Busta was. Fuck, that nigger could have run with Spartacus! And he was a big motherfucker too! Freaken linebacker!

"Worse yet, I'm starting to really like that colored family of yours! Those boys are something special. The one twin, the one who invaded my home that night, fell off the fucken Belle Isle bridge and survived. Sumanski even claimed to have shot his ass before he fell, and he still survived. Busta didn't survive, but the kid did. Then the youngster, if I can believe the word on the street…the word is that the feds kidnapped him from the freaken hospital, but he escaped! Then his twin brother was abducted by the same feds, so you know what that eggplant did? The word on the street is that the soldier-boy killed them all! The feds had to remove eight bodies from that warehouse they think is a secret. The dumbasses don't know I have an afterhours poker game across from their warehouse! And the older brother had the balls to come looking for me! He thought I had his brother! Hilarious! Where did you find these guys? I still don't know why you ordered me to release the kid earlier this year from the Packard plant, but I'm so glad you did. The entertainment is just grand!

"Listen, I've had too much to drink. I hope I didn't say anything offensive or out of place. My apologies if I did. You have a good day. Arrivederci!"

Six hundred miles east of the city, Don Lastanza looked over at his son and said, "Rudolfo, that fucken Detroit is a zoo. And the family running it belongs in a circus. But they'd better not mess up and hurt any of those spooks that's related to that old lady, or they will have hell to pay. And not from me either. I saw what happens to guys who mess with her and it ain't pretty. God, she's got to be at least 100 years old!"

· · · · · · · · · · · ·

Cavaletti entered the Detroit Chief of Police's office, sat in a chair, and waited for him to return. Ten minutes later the chief entered his office, finding an uninvited guest sitting there.

He said, "Now what are you doing here? Do you know the hell-storm brewing out there? The mayor is going nuts about all the fuckups happening around here. The bogus arrest. The alleged bribery within the department. The kidnapping from right under our noses. You know he secretly hates Sumanski and now this shit? Are you sure that dumb Polack is not being set up? I even got a fuckin call from the president of the University of Michigan. He did not like hearing that we arrested one of his professors!"

Cavaletti could never understand the use of derogatory descriptions of ethnic groups. Especially ones directed toward their own group.

He sat in front of his superior and thought, "*I hear Blacks calling each other the N-word. I'm Sicilian, and I would never call a fellow Sicilian or Italian a dago. Yet we do! Some of the Irish cops call other Irishmen 'Micks'! I just don't understand it. I guess it's a level of self-hatred that we're unaware of. We turn these words into a badge of honor.*"

He said to his Polish Chief, "Chief Tomaski, I need to excuse myself from Sumanski's investigation. It's well known within the department that I don't care for the man. Hell, everyone in the 10th precinct thinks I have it out for him. On top of that, we're freaken neighbors. My kid is catching hell in school partly because of my involvement with this case. He was just starting to fit in, then this happens."

Tomaski said, "I asked you...do you think he's being set up? I mean, think about it. Who buries that amount of money in their fucken backyard? Someone planted those notes in the 12th precinct. Right on the freaken front desk! Then calls to report the presence of the notes. Then directs us to the money. His lawyer is going to have a field day with this evidence. The fact that we discovered those bank accounts of his will be lost if the other evidence is tossed. What do they call it, 'fruit of some freaken tree' or something?"

"John, it's 'fruit from the poisonous tree'."

"Whatever. Listen, I don't like the dumb Polack either. He's a throwback from another era. The pre-civil rights era. But we're going to have a 'blue-wall' of hell if we don't handle this right. So no, you're not getting off the hot seat that you helped create. Now, why are you in my fuckin office, because if it was for that, you can leave right now."

Cavaletti sighed then stood and walked out of the office, feeling exuberant. He smiled all the way back to his desk.

"No way was I getting off this case. I'm going to make sure that racist bastard pays for his crimes. I'm going to make him suffer for insulting my wife and son. He doesn't know that word got back to me about his attitude toward my family. My wife warned me when we moved onto the block that he would prove to be trouble, but I didn't listen. Now my boy is paying the price.

"He killed Busta when he could have stopped that fight without the use of deadly force. Those cops just stood there and didn't intervene at the orders of Lieutenant Sumanski! Then he marches in like 'Dirty Harry' and just starts shooting, without any provocation. According to the witness's statements, which collaborates the police reports, the fight continued for minutes after he arrived. And he had the audacity to smile afterwards. In front of a crowd of people no less. What gall! Hell, those young McCants boys were on that bridge!

"I did the proper thing asking to be dismissed from this case. I'm just glad the chief saw through my request and denied it. Now no one can accuse me of targeting that prick. Sumanski, you're going down!"

He got to his desk only to find messages that his wife had been calling him.

He called home, and before the phone could ring, he heard, "Peter, you need to come home. Sumanski and his friends are sitting out in his driveway with their chairs positioned toward us. I don't like this. They've got six-packs of beer and he's even pulled his barbeque pit out front. It's freaking October for Christ-sake! Nobody barbecues in October. How is Tommy going to get home and not see them? You've got to do something about this before it gets out of hand."

She did not hesitate blurting into the phone because she knew it was her husband calling. Now the helpless feeling was easing somewhat. She knew this would be handled as only her husband could.

"My man is going to nail that sucker to a cross. Yes indeed. I am so glad that lady in pink did whatever she did. I don't know what that could have been or who she was, but 'hallelujah' to pretty white ladies in pretty pink dresses."

Her husband was home fifteen minutes later.

. . . .

Cavaletti drove his command car down Gratiot, running light after light, with no sirens blaring. When he got to his street, he slowed down just enough to avoid any complaints from his neighbors. However, he did not slow down when he got to Sumanski's driveway, pulling into it fast enough to make the six men scatter, chairs and all. He stopped just short of striking the barbeque pit. No beer was spilled. No glass was broken. Then he jumped out of the car and marched up to Sumanski, who did not back away. They stood nose to nose without a word spoken. One cop in uniform, one cop in dungarees, flannels, and gym shoes. However, one by one, the other officers, some still in uniform, walked back to their cars and drove away. After two minutes Cavaletti stopped smelling Sumanski's breath, got back in his car, and drove back to work, not bothering to stop at his home. There was no need to. Her wish was his command.

Within the hour word spread throughout all precincts of the incident on Carlisle Street, on the northeast side. The message was clear. Don't mess with Cavaletti's family. Sumanski had broken a code. Families are off limits, and he lost support when he harassed Cavaletti's wife. The other cops in attendance were also getting labeled. Cavaletti knew each of them since they were frequent visitors to Sumanski's home. One of the men actually lived down the block. He chose, however, not to contact their individual captains. He knew the grapevine would handle any communicating needed. He was right. His phone began to ring, and before the day was over, almost all of the captains called his office to apologize and ensure him that those men would be dealt with. It would never happen again. However, one of the captains left an ominous warning.

"Cav, you've got my support, but you need to watch your back. Word is Sumanski is gunning for you. I mean that literally."

Meanwhile, back on Carlise Street, Mrs. Judith Cavaletti decided to reward her husband with a steak dinner. She pulled her Weber barbeque pit from the garage, placed it in the driveway near the sidewalk, and started grilling a 16 oz steak for her man.

· · · · · · · · · · · · ·

Martha McCants was feeling a little low that morning. She had been doing laundry, a job she hated more than any laborious task in the house. There was a time when she would just want to cry at the volume of work involved. By 1962 she had to do laundry for ten bodies! This included diapers, soiled and all. The worst was the diaper pot. For two years she had two babies in diapers. In fact, when she came home with Ervin, Jack was just getting out of diapers!

Now she was down to just washing for five. In fact, the boys usually handled their own. That still left her with her husband's work outfits and his need to change after work. That doubled his output of required washing. She once tried to get him to help but that proved to be a huge mistake. The man put one of her white dresses in the wash with a red dress, creating a new pink dress!

Now, many years later, she was lamenting the loss of yet another dress. One she had just purchased. Ironically this one was pink as well. She had carelessly gotten a stain on the dress two months ago that just would not come out. The soil she stooped down on while wearing the dress must have had fertilizer in it, because it left a lightened smudge near the lower front area.

"Never will I do gardening in pink again."

. . . .

A forty-three-year-old woman approached her ninety-five-year-old grandmother and asked her a question that had been bothering her since early September.

"Grandmother, that call you had me make to the Detroit police headquarters back in September. The call about the notes at their 12th precinct. I didn't get some innocent person in trouble, did I?"

The old woman smiled, a rare expression for her, and said, "No babe. Jest de opposites sweethard. Jest de opposites."

CHAPTER ELEVEN

McGregor

Second week of October 1978

Day after Robert's Escape

Austin McGregor was a colonel in the US Army during the Vietnam War. He was a West Point graduate in the class of 1964, and was assigned stateside, until 1967. He was then sent to the warzone of Vietnam and would remain there for the next seven years. He served as Lieutenant McCants' commander for Robert's thirteen months in Vietnam. His fondness for Robert grew with every mission he assigned him, and Robert proved to be worthy of the colonel's admiration. After McGregor left the army he worked as a software project manager for a firm located in Chicago.

Earlier in the year McGregor was contacted by a man who had reported to him in Vietnam. Jake Smith, who had experienced hard times since his addiction to drugs during his time in the war, sought

McGregor out to inform him about Lieutenant McCants. He believed he had witnessed the lieutenant robbing a drug den in Chicago and felt it was his duty to report this incident to the Colonel. McGregor saw an opportunity to aid McCants, so he contacted his brother Mack in Detroit. After informing Mack of what he believed was a problem situation for Robert, he flew back to Chicago.

McGregor had not spoken to Mack since they met in downtown Detroit last summer. He never found out if his information to Mack was of any use to him. Then, during the final week of August, Mack called him and asked about a Dr. Schultz. Mack informed him that the incident on the MacArthur bridge that made national news involved his brother Michael. Dr. Schultz was making inquiries about Robert while visiting Michael. Mack wanted to know why this psychiatrist would be looking for Robert. McGregor informed Mack that he was indeed familiar with a Dr. Schultz and would look into the matter for him. They exchanged phone numbers and McGregor assured Mack he would get back to him as soon as possible.

The following day McGregor called Mack and told him not to be overly concerned about Dr. Schultz. He had made some inquiries and there was no report on Dr. Schultz that would raise any alarms. Probably just a head shrink showing an interest in an old patient. Since Schultz had worked with Robert in Germany it was probably normal for him to seek Robert out, after finding out that his brother was under his hospitals care. He saw no reason for Mack to be alarmed by the visit.

Now, eight weeks later, he would change his mind. The call he received from the CIA that night made him realize his response to Mack was premature.

"Hello," said the ominous voice over the phone. "I would like to speak to Colonel McGregor."

McGregor knew immediately this was the US government calling him.

"This is Colonel McGregor; however, I am no longer a commissioned officer in the Army. What can I do for you?"

The voice said, "I would like to meet with you to discuss your Lieutenant Robert McCants. I will be in town tomorrow. Meet me at…"

After meeting with the man the following afternoon at a coffee shop near his home, McGregor was more concerned than ever for Robert.

"First Dr. Schultz is inquiring about him, now the CIA. I wonder if Schultz was working for the CIA while he was stationed in Germany."

Austin had never worked with the CIA and knew this could not be a legally sanctioned request for his assistance. The CIA was not allowed to work on domestic issues, and this request was definitely domestic. The man's interest was more than just Robert. He was also interested in Michael, Robert's brother. Which is why McGregor refused to co-operate with the strange man. The agent did not take his refusal well.

The following morning McGregor woke with a revelation he had not considered before.

"If Robert is a twin, and was drafted in '71, then Michael should have been drafted as well. I need to look into Michael's draft status to see where he was stationed. Maybe that will shed some light on the doctor's interest in both of them."

He called an old friend who was an instructor at the West Point Academy.

"James Hooks, how are you? This is Austin McGregor. Hope all is well. We haven't spoken since I left the service in '74."

The two men chatted for ten minutes about their time at the academy, then McGregor got to the point.

"James, I have a favor to ask of you. I am trying to find the records for a Michael McCants from Detroit Michigan. He was born in

December 1951 and would have been drafted in March 1971. He had a twin brother who was stationed with me, and I'm just curious about Michael. Can you help me find out his military status?"

The following day Austin received a call from Colonel Hooks. After a brief discussion he hung up the phone, satisfied with the search. The records indicated that Michael had failed his medical and was excused with a 4-F deferment due to poor vision.

. . . .

A late night in March 1971 found an intruder breaking into the offices of the induction center at Fort Wayne, on West Jefferson Avenue, in southwest Detroit. The intruder searched for the medical records of the young men who were examined earlier that day. He found the report on a Robert McCants and replicated it, making only three changes. The given name of the candidate, social security number, and the medical results. Then he replaced the records back in the file cabinet, making sure to put the duplicate form at the back of the pile, since the forms were in numerical order. Then he departed as quietly as he entered.

The following day the receptionist noticed a pad of forms was misaligned on her desk. She did not, however, notice the top form missing.

. . . .

Now that the question about Michael's military status was resolved, McGregor needed to know what to do about Robert. He knew his refusal to the CIA was not going to be received well. It was common knowledge within the military that the CIA performed illegal operations during the war, and at times the upper echelon of the army contributed to their request for assistance. He, however, wanted to know why the CIA was interested in Robert, so he planned another trip back to Detroit. He called Mack to alert him of his desire to meet with him again but was unable to reach him.

Before he left Chicago, McGregor contacted Ralph Brooks, a sergeant who reported to him and was often assigned to Lieutenant McCants platoons. He and Brooks had left the service on the same day and had managed to keep in touch, even though they had little in common.

After a few attempts by phone Brooks finally answered.

"Hello. What's up?"

"Ralph. It's Austin. Austin McGregor. How are you?"

"Colonel Austin McGregor! I haven't heard from you in a while! Man, it's so nice to hear from you! I'm doing fine. How have you been, sir?"

After some pleasantries McGregor got to the point.

"Ralph, the reason I'm calling you is about Lieutenant Robert McCants."

Ralph cut him off and said, "McCants! Boy, I haven't heard that name in quite a while. Now there was a Brotha! Boy, could he shoot that rifle of his. And anybody else's too! Ha!"

McGregor had to cut back in.

"Ralph, yes, McCants was a hell of a soldier. Tell me Ralph, you soldiered with him. Patrolled with him. Fought alongside him. How did he do it? What did McCants do that the rest of us soldiers could not do? Can you explain him to me?"

The phone got quiet for a short while, then Brooks said, "Colonel, there is no way to explain the lieutenant's methods, except for one important thing. He was fearless. Almost as if he felt invincible. Seriously. No showboating or anything like that. Just cold-hearted fearlessness. Like he had been in lots of mini wars back in Detroit and was always victorious. He was always fixated and attentive, whether he was walking down a trail or eating his food. Always on alert. We used to talk about him at the barracks. He never actually relaxed the same way the rest of us did. Half of his mind seemed to be checking out his environment, you know what I mean? His eyes would be looking at you but at the same time, looking through you. I would bet he checked out everything he saw as he entered a room. Every pencil on a desk. Every bird in a tree. I may be exaggerating but he was always 'on,' you get me? He never fully relaxed, but I bet he thought he was relaxed. He would appear natural to the untrained eye, but all of us noticed his alertness, considering where we were. This may have been why he was short on small talk. His mind was too busy checking out anything and everything all of the time. Almost robotic, but in the most natural way?"

McGregor understood Ralph, for he had the same reaction whenever he was talking with McCants.

"He never seemed to fully relax, but was always calm and steady, always measured in everything he did. He also had the perfect answer to any question you asked him, almost as if he knew what the question was going to be before you asked it."

McGregor had one more question about the lieutenant before he got off the phone.

"Ralph, did McCants ever mention to you that he had a twin? Did he ever mention his brother Michael?"

Brooks waited for a moment before answering.

"You know, Colonel, he did mention that he had a lot of brothers. But he was never specific about any one of them. I know he was a second born. But that's about it. And no mention about a twin."

After a few more minutes of small talk about each other, they both said their good-byes and hung up.

.   .   .   .

Friday, Second week of October 1978

Dr. Schultz sat in his office at Harper Hospital, a sanctuary for him since the day he first ventured into Micheal McCants' room. Now he dreaded going home. His wife was becoming unbearable, always asking him about his whereabouts ever since that FBI visit. He was now feeling very uncomfortable about the twin experiments. A lot of men had been seriously injured, a fact he was not supposed to know about. His handler let it slip during their last phone call. He had never known his handler to get hysterical, but apparently the last abduction went horribly wrong.

"At least that puny twerp Dr. Little is where he belongs. In confinement!"

Just as he was leaving for home, his phone rang again. His face revealed just how much he dreaded answering it.

"Don't pick it up. It's either Gertrud or my fucking handler. Why don't I know his real name? Like that Agent X fuck many years ago after the war. Why don't they use real names! Why does everyone call him 'The Handler'!"

He knew he could not let the phone continue to ring, so he answered it. It was not who he expected.

"Hello," said the man on the other end. "My name is Austin McGregor. I was a colonel in the US army, stationed in Vietnam while you were working in Germany."

Schultz was alarmed that someone from the US Army would be calling him after all of these years.

"First the FBI. Now the Army?"

"Colonel, what can I do for you?"

"Yes, Doctor. A Lieutenant Robert McCants spent some time with you before he was deplored to Vietnam. I'd read your '71 summary report on the lieutenant numerous times, so I know he must have been a special case for you. I see you are working in Detroit, Michigan, which is where the lieutenant lives as well. Have you had the fortune of meeting him since his second stay with you in '73?"

. . . .

Schultz was feeling bewildered. How did things get so far out of control? His trip to India proved fruitless since he never found Dr. Patel. Then his fool handler kidnapped Michael. Then the FBI inquiries. So, he suggested that they let Michael escape, only to have them kidnap his brother Robert! They were supposed to only locate him, not abduct him. What a fiasco that proved to be! Robert went on another shooting spree and almost killed all of those soldiers! They should have known Robert was immensely dangerous! Now he gets a call from Robert's commanding officer.

"And I can't get rid of this strange feeling that I'm being watched! Freaking FBI!"

After a ten-minute phone conversation, Schultz arranged to meet McGregor the following day at the hospital.

When he got home, he walked through the kitchen to see if there was a plate of food in the oven for him. He retrieved the plate, turned off the oven, then walked straight to his room. At no time did he notice the piercing eyes of Gertrud, staring at him from her darkened room. Nor could he sense her thoughts.

"He's supposed to be a doctor, but he brings danger to our home. What a moron."

. . . .

That evening the McCants were trying to settle in for a quiet dinner, which was unusual considering the recent occurrences. Ervin and Horace were away visiting friends. Jack, however, felt the need to stay closer to home. Closer to his parents. His instincts told him the drama all of them were experiencing was not over. Also, he and Horace had not gotten over the argument they had in Horace's hospital room.

Martha began setting the table. She placed five plates on the table, out of habit, even though she knew the younger two were away.

"Those boys should be here. They still have not healed from their injuries."

Every few minutes Jack would walk over to the living room window and peer out.

Finally, Frank asked him, "Son, you need to relax. You're home now. Everything is going to be fine. What are you glancing at anyway?"

Martha said, "He's probably looking at those two White dudes parked in that Tool and Dye shop driveway on Lyndon."

Jack looked at his mother in amazement. Frank jumped up, alarmed, and rushed toward the window, but Jack stopped him.

Martha said, "Frank, we don't need them to know we're aware of them. Please just sit back down and enjoy your dinner."

Frank asked her, "How long have you known they were there?"

"Hell, Love, we're always under some kind of surveillance. Busta had two of his men renting an apartment down the street on Chalfonte back in late '69. They were also probably paying some of our neighbors to spy on us. They were always hawking on us. They drove by multiple times a day. No big deal as long as they stay on that side of the door. Ain't that right, Klaw?" The shepherd just wagged his tail.

Just past midnight a shadowy figure approached the sedan parked in the driveway of a tool and die shop on Lyndon, facing the residential block of Santa Rosa. The occupants inside the car had fallen asleep after a long night of talking and drinking cup after cup of coffee. The dark figure opened the passenger door and pulled the first man out of the car and struck him hard on the jaw, knocking him unconscious. The man's partner awoke and reached for a holstered gun but was dragged over the passenger seat and put to sleep before he could withdraw it from the holster. Then the assailant put their car in drive, turned the wheel eastward toward Livernois Avenue, and let it coast down the street. The two men recovered in time only to witness their car crash into a telephone pole just before it entered the Livernois traffic. When they looked around, the dark figure that accosted them was nowhere to be found.

Jack heard a muffled crash, and a few minutes later someone entered their back door. He knew it was his father by the behavior of the two shepherds. They usually get more excited when Horace or Ervin entered the house.

After Frank got in bed, Martha wrapped her short arms around him and said, "Do you feel better now?" and lightly kissed his upper shoulders. Only his groin responded.

. . . .

After Mack's call many weeks earlier, Austin could not stop thinking about all of the events occurring in Detroit since the incident on the MacArthur Bridge. He, of course, did not know it concerned the McCants until Mack made his call to him. The media reported that two men were killed on the bridge, then the next day they reported that one of the men survived the ordeal. Weeks later the media reported that the survivor from the bridge was kidnapped from the hospital. Then a few weeks later the victim appeared, unharmed, and was summarily arrested by the police. All of this indirectly involved Robert, since the kidnapped victim was his twin, which is all Austin cared about. Now more than ever he felt the need to ensure Robert was safe.

After talking to Dr. Schultz, he realized the request from the CIA was even more alarming. From McGregor's perspective, it was no mere coincidence that Robert's brother Michael was involved in incidents of that magnitude. Not with the CIA asking about him. The shooting on the bridge, the kidnapping and escape.

"Who in the hell kidnapped him?"

He started his mission to check on Robert earlier that summer and he could not end his quest until he knew Robert was completely safe. He would meet with Dr. Schultz then visit Mack and Robert. He informed his employer that he would be gone for a few days.

The following morning McGregor left his home at 5:00 a.m. CT and drove to Detroit, since he wanted to have his own transportation. The five-hour drive would also give him time to form a strategy.

Four hours into his drive, McGregor passed through Ann Arbor, home of the University of Michigan.

"Why don't I just pull over here and seek Robert out. I don't know where he lives, but finding a history professor shouldn't be that hard."

He smiled and thought, *"Stop trying to be Sherlock and just continue with your plan. Remember. Never deviate."*

He drove straight to the hospital and met with Dr. Schultz. Their meeting lasted about thirty minutes, which left him with the remainder of the afternoon. He checked into his hotel in downtown Detroit and contacted Mack on his job.

Mack was surprised to hear from him, since they had not spoken since Mack's original call two months ago. He did not expect McGregor to drive all the way from Chicago because of his continuous concern for Robert.

"His anxiety last summer about Robert was genuine. Perhaps it was a mistake calling him about the doctor."

"Austin, what are you doing in town? So much has occurred since we talked last August. So, what's going on? Have you found out something I should be concerned about?"

"I have plenty to discuss with you after I finish my appointments for the day. We can talk later this afternoon, say 3:00?"

McGregor gave Mack his hotel phone and room number and asked him to meet him there at the Renaissance Center, locally known as the Ren Cen.

McGregor knew he had to convince Mack he had his brother's best interest in mind.

"I just met with your Dr. Schultz from Harper Hospital. He was indeed Robert's doctor when he was in Germany. The son-of-a-bitch just repeatedly lied to me. He does not know I've been contacted by the CIA. I bet he's involved with them as well. I never understood why Robert went to Germany in '71 in the first place. Schultz's report indicated that he had a special interest in Robert. I never got a report on any soldier like Robert's report the entire time I was in 'Nam. No, Mack, I'm not satisfied with the answers I got from Schultz. I'm going to dig deeper this afternoon. Will you meet me after I'm finished?"

Mack replied, "Of course, I'll meet you at the hotel."

Mack hung up the phone and thought, "*What the heck! Freaken CIA! What was Robert really into? I guess I can't blame this one on Michael.*"

McGregor drove back to Harper Hospital and went to Dr. Schultz's office. The receptionist told him that Dr. Schultz had left for the day. McGregor then went into the administration office and spoke to the clerk at the front desk.

He flashed his old army credentials and said, "Hello. My name is Colonel Austin McGregor, from the US Army Psychiatry department. I was expecting to meet with a psychiatrist by the name of Dr. Karl Schultz, but I've been informed that he's gone for the day. I don't have time to waste chasing this man all over town. If you would provide me with his home address, I can complete my business and be on my way."

The clerk thought, "*Wow, first the FBI. Now this guy.*"

She retrieved Schultz address and gave it to McGregor. He maintained his serious demeanor but thanked her for the information and left the office.

After getting directions from a local gas station, McGregor drove to Schultz's home in Birmingham.

"Very nice community. Too academic for me. Looks like a community of college professors and yuppies."

He walked up to the home and rang the doorbell. Gertrud answered the door.

"Hello. My name is Austin McGregor. Is Dr. Schultz home? He and I met earlier this morning, and since I'm leaving town early tomorrow, I won't have time to see him again. I hate to impose on him at his home, but it is very important that I see him once more."

Gertrud said, "Mister, I'm sorry, but my husband is not home. And I find it most disturbing that you would take it upon yourself to just come to our residence without notice or an invitation. You will just have to delay your plans and see him at his office tomorrow. Good-bye!"

She abruptly closed the door.

McGregor was a little startled to have a door closed in his face. He had no recourse but to drive back downtown and wait for his meeting with Mack.

Around 2:45 p.m. Mack left his office and walked over to the Ren Cen, the newly constructed skyscrapers in downtown Detroit. These new structures completely dominate the skyline of the downtown district. Located on the river, the buildings consist of a seventy-three-story glass-covered hotel, the tallest hotel in the country, surrounded by four thirty-nine-story glass-enclosed office buildings.

When Mack arrived at McGregor's room, he found the door ajar. He entered the room, then left very quickly moments later.

. . . .

Jack continued to follow Dr. Schultz, only now he used a different family member's car each time. He suspected that someone in the house was adept at observation, like he was, so he had to be extra careful. He had been waiting for an hour for Dr. Schultz to arrive home, when he saw a man go up to the house, but not enter. So, he followed the man back into the city. The man drove to the new business complex along the river, parking his car in the basement of the complex. He caught an elevator to the lobby then sat in the lobby of the hotel. Jack replicated his movement, settling into a large leather chair near the hotel entrance. A moment later he could not help but notice the man react to two men, dressed in black suits, who had gotten off the garage elevators and walk to the hotel registration desk. After making an inquiry at the desk both men retraced their steps back to the garage elevators. The lone man, now somewhat rattled, exited the lobby and caught a hotel room elevator.

At 2:30 PM Jack saw one of the men dressed in black step out of a dark sedan and enter the hotel lobby, heading for the hotel room elevators. The sedan pulled up a few parking spots and waited. Minutes later the man exited an elevator and left the hotel, climbing back into the sedan, which then drove away.

Ten minutes later, Jack saw his brother Mack come into the hotel lobby and head directly for the hotel room elevators. He tried to get his attention, but Mack was on the elevator before he could reach him. Mack was only gone for a few minutes before he returned. The look on his face told Jack to stay hidden, so he left for home. He would discuss with Mack what he witnessed later.

CHAPTER TWELVE

Vengeance

The Wayne County Prosecutor was informed that she had a call from the office of the Justice Department in Washington D.C. She accepted the call even though she was unfamiliar with the name.

The caller said, "I understand you have an outstanding warrant on a Michael McCants for assaulting a police officer."

The long pause implied the caller was awaiting a response to the statement, so the prosecutor eventually said, "Yes, we do."

The caller continued, "I understand you arrested him as he exited the Federal Building in downtown Detroit. After he had been interviewed by the FBI. An interview focused on his kidnapping from a local hospital while under police surveillance."

The prosecutor said, "Yes that is true but..."

"Kidnapped! He was kidnapped! From one of your hospitals in broad daylight, and you arrested him after he escaped his

kidnappers and was being debriefed by the F B I! Debriefed about his kidnapping! The media was all over his abduction and subsequent escape, and you arrested him in front of a crowd of reporters. THE SAME DAY HE ESCAPED FROM HIS KIDNAPPERS!"

The prosecutor said, "Well, yes, it did happen that way."

"Hmmm, let me get this straight. This man was deemed dead after being shot by one of Detroit's finest and falls thirty feet into a swiftly flowing river. He survives that ordeal only to be kidnapped while still in the hospital. After three weeks he manages to escape his kidnappers…without your assistance…and you still arrest him and lock him up on a Friday evening after 5:00 p.m. THE WHOLE COUNTRY KNOWS WHAT ARRESTING A PERSON ON A FRIDAY AT 5:00 P.M. MEANS! It means that he will have to spend the entire weekend in jail before the courts open again Monday morning. Boy, I can just imagine you wishing that was a holiday weekend!"

The prosecutor, now feeling very uneasy, tried to interrupt, but was shouted down.

"You locked him up for the weekend without giving him his phone call. You rushed him into a cell so fast you didn't even bother to take his fingerprints or mug shots. No one in his family knew where he was, even though one of your top cops told them not to worry. Everything will be alright. Then on Monday you arraigned him without proper counsel, knowing he was totally unprepared to defend himself. Only to find out you ARRESTED THE WRONG FUCKING MAN! You arrested his twin! A college professor from the esteemed University of Michigan! Imagine if he had been harmed while in your custody. In your jail. I repeat, in your jail! A history professor, with no criminal record, could have been killed IN YOUR JAIL! The wrong man was arrested, and

he could have been killed. Now how were you going to explained that to the world?"

A very long pause followed, then the caller said, "Now, what are you going to do about this?"

Another pause, then, "I highly recommend that you drop these bogus assault charges, an assault that allegedly occurred when the man was a mere sixteen years old, against the very same cop who shot him on that bridge. A cop that you now have under investigation for bribery from the very same man he shot on that bridge along with shooting Mr. McCants. Do I make myself clear?" Click.

The Handler hung up the phone, walked out of the borrowed office, and exited the City-County Building at 2 Woodward Avenue in downtown Detroit. He walked to his car, parked in an official parking space, then drove away.

An hour later all charges against Michael McCants were dropped. No explanation was given.

. . . .

Jack contacted Mack at his home and informed him that he saw him in the Ren Cen. Mack was alarmed to find out that his younger brother was in the Ren Cen lobby and insisted they meet at once. When Jack arrived at Mack's home, Mack called Robert in Ann Arbor. Michael was with Robert, so Robert placed the phone on speaker and informed Mack of his presence.

Mack said, "Robert, I have Jack here as well. I never told you this before, but I met a guy named Austin McGregor. He was your colonel when you were in the service. We met here in Detroit earlier this year during a sales meeting. He recognized me and knew you were my brother. He told me he was very concerned about you because of some shit happening in Chicago or whatever. The point is, we met and discussed your time in 'Nam. That's why I questioned you so heavily after the Packard incident.

"Robert, McGregor came back here today because I called him about a Dr. Schultz."

Robert's brain suddenly went into overdrive. First, he was hearing about Dr. Schultz; now the Colonel. Michael could see his brother's demeanor change and immediately knew who Schultz and McGregor were.

"Is this why that doper called out to me last year? Did he think I was Robert?"

However, he knew not to interrupt Mack.

Robert, getting angry, said, "You called my colonel after you met Dr. Schultz? Why? You met him last summer? I don't recall you mentioning that when we spoke. I don't recall you mentioning him at all!"

Mack was now feeling very distraught. Robert had not raised his voice to him since they were kids. Now he had to deliver distressing news to him.

"Robert, I have some bad news. Your colonel is dead. He was murdered tonight in his hotel room. I found him lying on the floor but left before the authorities arrived. I'm sure it had something to do with that wacko Schultz."

McGregor was still reeling from the abrupt treatment he received from Mrs. Schultz. As he drove back to the city, however, he noticed the same car that was behind him on his trip north to Birmingham, was now behind him again as he headed south to Detroit. He stayed on Woodward Avenue, the center artery of the city all the way to the Ren Cen, a sixteen-mile drive. The car remained two or three cars behind him all of the way. After parking his car in the underground garage of the complex, he caught an elevator to the hotel lobby and waited to see who might also get off the elevator. Minutes later two men in dark suits got off a garage elevator. He knew they had to be the guys following him.

"Those men are definitely after me. They must be a part of the crew that kidnaped Michael. This proves that Dr. Schultz was involved. Why else would they follow me to his house?"

Then he realized, "Mack is headed here. I could be bringing him into a trap. I need to warn him of the danger he and his family are in."

He wrote a cryptic warning for Mack, then caught an elevator to his room.

He placed the note in plain view on his hotel room desk. Minutes later CIA Agent Johanson knocked on his door, then let himself in. He shot McGregor with a pistol armed with a silencer, then left the room, not noticing the corporate binder on the desk.

Mack arrived at McGregor's floor minutes later, finding his room door slightly open. He entered the room, only to discover McGregor's body. He had been shot in the head. He knew it was in his best interest to leave immediately. As he turned toward the door, he noticed a folder propped up on the desk. It was the folder McGregor's team used during the project collaborations they had last year. He opened it, using a pen from his jacket, saw the note inside, jammed the note into his breast pocket, then walked out of the room, making sure not to touch the door with his hand.

When he got in his car, he opened the note. It was written in the mainframe computer code EBCDIC.

E7D6E3D940C6C1D4C9D3E740C9E140C9D540C4C1D
5C7C5D940C7C5E240E2C8C5D440D6E3E240D6C640
E2D6E5D540C9D4D4C5C4C9C1E2C5D3E7

.   .   .   .

Robert, very irritated, said, "You never told me you knew him. What happened? Do you know who killed him? You should have called me first before contacting him. I would not have wanted him involved in our drama!"

Michael was shocked at the level of frustration Robert was feeling. He must have really felt close to this man, even though he had not thought about him recently. He instantly knew Robert was going to avenge his murder.

"Wow. He's going into his 'focus' mode. I may have trouble reading him."

Mack said, "How would I know who killed him? I arrived after the fact. We were supposed to discuss Dr. Schultz, but I found him shot to death. I'm sorry I did not involve you, but this was all about you. Hell, I made the call a day after Michael entered the hospital. You were nowhere to be found. All I did was call him in Chicago to ask him a simple question. I didn't ask him to come to assist us. Merely to give me some information on that psychiatrist. That was two months ago. He came here without my knowledge. He only called me after he'd arrive."

Jack interrupted Mack. "I know who shot him. It was those guys in the black suits. One of them exited the car and got on the elevator. The other one stayed with the car. Minutes later the first one got off the elevator and climbed back in the car. Then they drove away. A few minutes later you arrived and got on the elevator. You were back in minutes. I saw how distraught you were, so I left without bothering you.

"I've seen both of them before, watching Dr. Schultz's house in Birmingham. I bet they're parked near his house right now."

Mack angrily said, "What are you talking about? What do you know about Dr. Schultz's residence? In Birmingham? How could your black ass observe any house in that neighborhood without being noticed?!"

Michael just smiled at the thought since he did it all of the time.

Jack spent the next five minutes explaining how he had been keeping an eye on the doctor ever since Schultz visited Michael in the hospital. Which is why he mentioned the doctor during the family meeting, leaving out his surveillance escapades.

Michael jumped in. "I don't know who this McGregor guy is, but if he was trying to help Robert and me, then we've got to find these guys. When have we ever allowed others to fuck with us and get away with it? Besides, they are undoubtedly involved with my kidnapping. By the way, they grabbed Robert recently. And as you can see, he also got away."

Mack and Jack were completely startled.

Mack said, "What are you talking about? Robert, what is he talking about?"

Jack just remained silent but alarmed. He now realized that he had been taking a lot of chances with his sleuth escapades.

Mack said, "If these guys want you two so badly that they would kill a retired colonel, then none of us are safe. Austin left me a note, written in a mainframe software code. It said we need to get out of town. So, we need to notify mom and dad. In fact, I'm heading over there right now. Can you two meet Jack downtown. I'm sure those two killers have not left town. Their assignment must still be the two of you, so they are probably local muscle. Try patrolling the downtown streets. I may even ask Castanza for help. Better yet Michael, perhaps you should pay him a visit. He seems to have taken a liking to you, which is kind of weird. Only don't break in this time."

Michael was confused how Mack knew about that.

Mack continued, "Castanza's boys may know what's going on. Hopefully he's not involved."

After Robert hung up the phone he said, "Drop me off at the hotel then go visit your amico Castanza. When you are finished you can find Jack and me in the hotel lobby."

Michael could not help but notice that Robert had suddenly become a commander.

He thought, *"He must have been a hell of a lieutenant."*

. . . .

Mack was extremely distraught after leaving McGregor's hotel room. He had never seen a murdered body before, much less one he was acquainted with. He could only feel for McGregor's family. Then he remembered the slip of paper from McGregor's folder. He pulled it out of his breast pocket and read it.

E7D6E3D940C6C1D4C9D3E740C9E140C9D540C4 C1D5C7C5D940C7C5E240E2C8C5D440D6E3E240 D6C640E2D6E5D540C9D4D4C5C4C9C1E2C5D3E7

Mack could not help feeling that Austin McGregor knew his time was short. That is why he took so much time creating this cryptic message, when he could have just gotten in his car and driven away.

He tried to decipher the note, but it did not make sense. Then he noticed an error.

He thought, "EBCDIC does not use E1. This is a common error made by non-developers." He shifted the letters for E1-E8 to E2-E9.

E8D6E4D940C6C1D4C9D3E840C9E240C9D540
C4C1D5C7C5D940C7C5E340E3C8C5D440D6E4E3
40D6C640E3D6E6D540C9D4D4C5C4C9C1E3C5D3E8

The note read, "YOUR FAMILY IS IN DANGER GET THEM OUT OF TOWN IMMEDIATELY"

.   .   .   .

After dropping Robert off at the Ren Cen complex Michael drove east down East Jefferson from the Ren Cen complex, then pulled over to a phone booth at Alter Rd, the eastern boundary of Detroit. The Pointes were just ahead but he did not want to enter this community without Castanza knowing he was coming.

"I don't need trouble from the 'Pigs in the Pointes' tonight."

He called the house from the number he remembered from the night of his visit.

When it was answered he said, "I need to speak to Castanza. Tell him its Michael McCants."

When Castanza answered the phone Michael said, "Hello. Mr. Castanza. This is Michael. Michael McCants. I heard you've been discussing me with my brother Mack. Sir, may I pay you a visit? I'm in the neighborhood."

Minutes later Michael pulled into the long driveway of Antonio 'Little Tony' Castanza.

Four suits walked out into the driveway. Michael barely noticed them since he was too busy marveling at the view. He had been to Lake Michigan numerous times before, while living in Chicago. Somehow, however, the tiny Lake St. Clair looked just as mesmerizing.

The wind was blowing hard in a western direction making the water crash against the rocky shore, creating a roar not heard anywhere in Detroit. The white caps created by the crashing against the rocks contrasted beautifully against the dark blue surface water. On the opposite side of the lake was a dark blue line of horizon, kissing the sky as twilight began. Michael had spent numerous nights sleeping in yacht storage yards on Detroit's east side, but never tired of the beauty of the lake, day or night. Yet even though he was only three miles west of the home, he never recalled hearing this wonderful sound.

One of the four suits summoned Michael, searched him for weapons, then escorted him to the back of the property. Another of the four moved his car north of Eight Mile into a parking lot of a private club along the shore.

"Guess he can't have his neighbors thinking he's slumming. I should have drove my Benz."

Michael did not know how he would be received and was shocked at the exuberant reception.

The three suits left the yard as Castanza said, "Ciao, mio figlio! Hello, my son. Che bello rivederti! Yes, nice to see you again. It's been weeks, but now at least you're conscious. Yeah, I figured that if you can watch me sleep, then I had to repay the favor. So, Michael, what can I do for you? I feel I owe you a favor since you took Busta out for me. Are you here to collect the reward?"

Castanza chuckled, then said, "Sorry, mio figlio. But I've already paid it to that Polack Sumanski," and chuckled again. "Besides, you've stolen so much of my money I believe you owe me! Perhaps I should have you rob NBD once or twice to make up for the moolah you stole from me." He continued to find humor in all of his remarks.

Michael thought, *"I'd never believe he could be so funny. He didn't look humorous that night standing in his kitchen in those silly pajamas."*

"Sir, I'm here to ask a favor of you. My family is again under assault. Only this time it's not your men, but a branch of the federal government. I suspect an illegal branch of the CIA. Their behavior is not what one would expect from the feds. They murdered a man in the Ren Cen today."

Castanza said, "Figlio de puttana! Sons of bitches! I guess I'm not surprised you were involved with that hit. I knew my boys would not do something like that. Who was that guy anyway?"

Michael spent the next few minutes explaining the relationship between McGregor, Robert, and Mack.

When he concluded, Castanza thought, *"Who would have thought a simple ghetto nigger family from Detroit could be in so much intrigue. I have to be careful here, however. Their mother is still connected to New York. I've got to honor any request from my Black son as long as it's reasonable. Besides, I really like these people. They have more soul than that stiff-ass lawyer of mine. And I suspect Michael doesn't even know just how much clout he truly has."*

Castanza said, "Okay, Michael. Listen. Here's what I'm going to do. I want you to return to your family. I'm going to give you a different car to drive. It used to belong to an old employee of mine who is no longer with us. It has a phone in it, and I will be contacting you over the next half hour. Capiche?

"It was nice finally seeing you walking and talking. And the next time we meet I hope it's under more pleasant circumstances. Addio per ora. Goodbye for now."

Castanza stood, shook Michael's hand, then walked into the back door of his home. A minute later one of the suits exited the home and escorted Michael to the garage entrance. He entered the garage and drove out a Black '77 Lincoln, then handed Michael the keys.

Twenty minutes later Michael parked the black boat in the Ren Cen parking lot, where he met up with Robert.

. . . .

Robert went to meet Jack in the Ren Cen hotel lobby. When Jack drove up Robert explained that Michael had already met Castanza in Grosse Pointe. He even commented that Michael had a mobster's car, which Jack found confusing.

Jack said, "I've been driving around the downtown area, looking at all of the hotel parking lots. I didn't see their car anywhere. But I believe I know where we'll probably find the shooters. Jump in."

Jack drove north out I-75 to Eight-Mile, then west to Woodward Avenue. He headed north toward Maple Rd. Eventually pulling onto Dr. Schultz's street.

Just as Jack thought, the two men were sitting in their car.

Robert thought, *"This kid is really sharp. I'm glad he's on our side. And he's only eighteen years old. Far more mature than I was at that age."*

They formulated a plan, then Robert became extremely focused. Jack could no longer read his brother and became concerned about what might happen next. He had heard the stories of Robert's time in the service, but never really believed any of it. Now he was not so certain. Robert exited the car and walked into the nearby park.

Jack drove up beside the suits' car and tooted his horn.

When the driver rolled down his window, Jack said, "I saw you kill McGregor," then drove away.

He led the two men on a short chase, then pulled into the park, jumped out of his car and ran toward some trees. The men chased him; right into Robert.

The first man ran past Robert, who was standing behind a tree. He then clotheslined the second man, causing him to drop his gun. Robert picked up the gun, then shot the man in the heart. 'Poof". The first man, hearing his friend in distress, stopped, took aim at Robert, but was dead before he could pull his trigger. Robert's gun only made two quiet *poof* sounds. He never flinched the entire time. His expression, however, was one of fury.

Robert rifled through the jacket pockets of the men. He found his parents' address on a piece of paper in agent Johanson's pocket. He angrily shot Johanson between the eyes at close range, wiped the gun down, then dropped the gun on the ground. He returned to the road, finding Jack sitting in the driver's seat, engine running. Jack had missed the killings, which was part of Robert's plan. Jack, however, knew the two would never harm anyone again. The two brothers drove away. An hour later a jogger found two bodies in the park and called the local police.

CHAPTER THIRTEEN

Government Reprisal

Jack wanted to drive to Santa Rosa, but Robert insisted on going back downtown. He said he had to meet up with Michael and would return with him. Jack understood the ruse and did not reply. He dropped Robert off near the Ren Cen parking lot, then drove home to Santa Rosa.

Michael was leaning against a black Lincoln as Robert turned the corner. The twins drove the Lincoln to Santa Rosa, arriving just before Jack, who could only smile. After he parked his car further down the block, he entered the house and heard Michael speaking to his parents.

He looked at Jack and said, "Castanza has arranged for us to move to a safe location in Idlewild. I have the directions."

Four hours later a '72 country squire and a big black Lincoln pulled up to a beautiful chalet. After an hour the Lincoln drove back to the city. It would be several more hours before the sun broke the horizon.

. . . .

Castanza called Pierre Bordeaux to get the lawyer's address of his vacation home in Idlewild.

Castanza told him, "You don't need to know why. Just be sure it's empty for the foreseeable future. Capiche!"

He then called Michael on the car phone and gave him the address and directions to a chalet in Western Michigan. He was to take his family there immediately. Then he told Michael that he could not afford to get mixed up with the feds, so they are now on their own. He had done his duty, per the request of the New York Don. Michael was even more confused but did not pry further.

"Michael, those punkasses that attacked your baby brothers are going to be dealt with. Permanently."

Michael understood what that meant and asked the Don not to get involved.

"With respect, sir, you don't want a bunch of White guys killing a group of young Black guys in a hospital, do you? My brothers and I will handle them as the need arises, based on their culpability in the rumble. I do appreciate the offer. Goodbye."

. . . .

A red-headed man, hospitalized in Receiving Hospital, was found dead in his hospital bed. He was strangled with a phone cord. An eggplant with strawberries on it was laying on the foot of his bed. The police discovered that he was not a local person and was responsible for organizing the hit on the McCants boys. They checked on the whereabouts of the McCants and discovered that all of them had left their home the day before the murder. None of the McCants had been seen near the hospital over the past several days.

The assault charges against Horace for rendering one of his attackers unconscious, crushing his face at the supermarket, were dropped. All of the potential witnesses against Horace had recanted their statements.

Sumanski was not happy when he heard about the murder at the hospital.

He thought, "Fuck. Five-grand wasted."

. . . .

The Handler was very distraught and angry. He had lost two men in a park in a northern suburb of Detroit, after eight of his men were seriously injured at the warehouse. He knew it was Robert, their latest kidnapped victim.

He had a scheduled meeting with his lawyer, then a conference call to McLean Virginia. He called his lawyer and informed him that he would not be able to meet with him in person because of a scheduling conflict, but they could discuss matters now over the phone. He was talking to the lawyer when he overheard a conversation in the background. He could not believe his luck.

He thought, *"Hmmm, so that's where those mongrels are hiding. In that Black resort out west. Well, they are finally going to get their just desserts."*

. . . .

Seventy-two-year-old Dr. McCants finally acknowledged that it was again time to reach out to his father for help. His son Horace had informed him that Frank's family was on the run. They had to hide out in the Idlewild resort, at a friend's chalet. Dr. McCants felt extremely bad for his son, especially since they should have been able to take refuge at the family estate near Brooklyn Michigan, thirty miles west of Ann Arbor.

"Hell, I've got a chalet in Idlewild. They could have used mine!"

He picked up the phone and made the call. It was the second call in months.

"Baba, I need your help. My boy Frank's family is in trouble. I think it's our government. At least an illegal wing of the government."

"Okay son. You have to know I've been keeping tabs on the goings on in that city. I'll look into it," and hung up the phone.

．　．　．　．　．　．　．　．　．　．　．

Third week of October 1978

Idlewild was a vacation resort developed by the African American community during the 1920s. At its heyday, before segregation laws relaxed, the resort attracted Blacks from all over the Midwest, especially Chicago, Gary and Detroit. Once it was fully functional, music groups would tour at the resort. It was an oasis for the Black elite.

Bordeaux's chalet was a half mile away from the actual resort, but still regarded as part of the resort. The forest area was extremely thick in all directions. The late fall colors were dazzling, making the area extremely beautiful. The ground was colored in various earthtones of red, yellow, brown, and green, since half of the leaves had already fallen from the trees. Only the evergreens remained full. Birds were gathering for their flights south and squirrels were abound as they began to prepare for winter. The night air was crisp, requiring sweaters for most, especially Frank, with his lean body. It did not help that he was still only wearing a summer T-shirt. Martha, however, did not seem to mind the cool air.

He joked, "All that Irish in you, huh?"

The McCants were unpacked within the first hour so they could settle in for the day. They had never resided in a home this size before, and Frank was humorously showing concern that Martha might get ideas about her future living conditions.

All of the homes at this part of the area were empty, since it was the middle of the week and well past summer vacation season.

After breakfast Martha completed clearing the table with Ervin helping her with the dishes. The house was unusually quiet. The three teens had their own rooms for the first time in their lives.

Frank placed a collect call to Horace. The two discussed how they might protect Santa Rosa during the following days. It was an unnecessary concern. The two always went overboard with their security planning.

Most of the family was able to relax the first night. Jack, as usual, stood guard, not believing the family was completely safe. Seventeen-year-old Horace slept like a baby in the full-size bed, covering the entire mattress with his 6'2", 220-pound frame.

The first two days were a joy for the family. They had never been away from the city as a family. Due to the abruptness of their move only the younger three sons left for the resort. Richard and Louis would join them later after getting their families settled. Mack took both dogs home with him, since neither had ever been on a long highway drive. He knew it would not be wise for him to drive to the safe house for fear of giving away their location. He only called from various phones in his office. He also pondered whether he should place a call per his mother's request.

"Honey, take this card. Please call Commander Cavaletti and inform him of our decision to go underground and the reasons why. He does not need to know where we're going."

Robert and Michael stayed at his apartment in Ann Arbor, waiting for any aggression headed their way. They did not want to bring any violence to the family if the two of them were the intended targets.

Michael was now seeing a side of Robert he had never noticed before. He was no longer the 'bookworm,' but possibly the most dangerous person he had ever known.

"Busta kicked my ass and almost killed me. I suspect Robert would have gone through him almost immediately. He just killed two men, yet he has not thought about it since. And the kidnappers only had him confined for eight hours? Wow. And he slept most of that time. What happened to him in 'Nam? I cannot find any thoughts on his service time since the timeline is so far away. He never ever thinks about it. When I killed Sammy, I fretted about it for years. I didn't lose any sleep over Ken's fate or Busta's death. And Sammy was going to kill me the same as Busta. Yet he died at my hands and that may be the difference. Robert doesn't appear to have any remorse at all. We may be twins, but we are no longer the same. Hell, we may never have been the same. And I was too engrossed in my own life to care enough about his."

· · · · · · · · · · · ·

Cavaletti was pondering the recent killing spree. Two men in a park in Birmingham, both shot with a gun with a silencer attached. One of the men was also armed with a gun with a silencer attached. The same gun that killed a man in a downtown hotel. A man was murdered at Harper Hospital. Someone just walked into his hospital room and placed a phone cord around his neck and strangled him. The same man who tried to kill the two young McCants kids. The word from the other assailants was that he was the one who recruited them for the rumble. They did not know him before and did not know he was planning on murdering the boys. He was just passing out hundred-dollar bills.

One of the men said, "Sir, I didn't know he was going to stab Horace. Shoot, I played basketball on St. Gregory's playground with Horace and Ervin back last August. It was supposed to be a simple beatdown."

The fact that all of the men involved in the fight had been visited by suits very recently only helped with this explanation.

Now he gets the alarming call from Mack McCants.

He felt helpless and thought, *"I promised her I would protect her family. Now what do I do?"*

· · · · · · · · · · · ·

By the weekend the family was finally relaxed. Richard and Louis had arrived and all of them barbequed, even though the temperature was a mere fifty degrees. There was a volleyball net up, with other sports equipment in a shed. Martha was relaxed enough to swim in the cold lake nearby. The boys were amazed that she could tolerate the water, but Frank just laughed.

When Louis attempted to get him to go into the water he said, "No way, Jose, am I getting near that water. Just looking at it makes me shiver. Guess those European genes of hers can come in handy at times," and they laughed.

That evening, after three days of relaxing, Jack was getting anxious again. He sensed trouble brewing but did not want to alarm anyone, just in case he was wrong.

"I'm never wrong about these feelings. Something is going to jump off tonight."

After a nice dinner and a game of monopoly the family began separating into their own quarters. By midnight everyone was asleep. Except Jack.

· · · · · · · · · · ·

At 2:00 a.m. their world exploded. Bullets came flying through every window in the house. Frank grabbed Martha and pulled her to the floor beside the bed. He yelled for the boys to get down, but no one could hear him over the roar of munition rounds crashing in on them.

Martha thought, *"Oh my god! Someone gave away where we were hiding. I knew we should have been more discrete outside of the house, not acting like some fucken rich niggers living it up in their private castles. Grandma, please help!"*

Jack crawled to each room to ensure everyone was down on the floor. Richard crawled into his parents' room and climbed on top of them, attempting to cover their exposed bodies. Louis motioned for Ervin and Horace to crawl into the bathtubs. Both boys had tossed their mattress toward the windows to shield them from the automatic rounds flying through the glass. Some of the rounds even penetrated the interior walls.

As sudden as the firing started, it stopped, as the front and back doors came crashing in. Numerous men dressed in dark-green fatigues rushed into the house. Some of them ran up the stairs and rushed into the bedrooms, screaming, "Get to your feet! All of you! Now!"

Frank jumped up before Richard could stop him. He rushed the man and threw a roundhouse punch to the man's face. The man deflected the punch like it came from a child and hit Frank across the jaw with the butt of his rifle. He fell unconscious to the floor.

Within minutes the entire family was huddled in the living room, all tied up.

One of the men said, "New orders, guys. They don't want them dead. A truck is coming to take them away. They believe they can use them to bargain for that freak son of theirs. The one named Robert."

Martha refused to cry and believed this was not the end for her 'Fighting Sullivans.' She could feel her grandmother for the first time since she left New York. The feeling, however, was not a sense of helplessness. Then she looked over at the arousing Frank and smiled.

'My granny loves me and won't let anything happen to me. Help is on the way."

The first soldier spoke on his walkie, "John-8, where is the truck? It should have been here by now. John-8…John-8…"

He looked at one of the other soldiers and said, "John-4, go down the road and look for the truck. If should have entered the driveway by now."

John-4 responded, "Okay, John-1," and walked out of the chalet.

John-1 called John-4 a few minutes later but got no answer.

He thought, *"It could be the area, but these walkies should work anywhere. Something is off."*

Just to be sure, he walked to the doorway and tried the walkie again. It appeared to be working fine. He could hear the squawk coming from John-6's and John-7's walkie. He looked out to them, but they were not at their assigned positions. He stepped further out and looked around but saw no movement from his men. He walked around the building, then down to the driveway, then back toward the chalet. Now he knew the mission was in jeopardy. He called out to John-2, John-3 and John-5 over his walkie. He got no response.

He rushed back into the house, yelling their names, "Hey Pete! Tim! Where the fuck are you guys!"

It was the last words he would ever speak.

It took thirty minutes before Jack was able to untie himself. He then began untying the rest of his brothers and parents. Frank was still groggy, and his head was swollen. Martha walked into the kitchen and opened the refrigerator, having to step over a couple of bodies, and grabbed an ice tray. She returned to the living room and placed ice cubes on Frank's temple and wrist. Seventeen-year-old Horace, now furious, grabbed one of the dead men's guns, and stormed out of the house, looking for someone to kill. Richard followed him. They only found dead bodies along the yard and down the road. There was also a truck on the road, but the driver was also dead.

Richard rushed back into the house and ordered everyone to leave the house immediately. He instructed Horace to wipe down the gun he was holding. Everyone complied. Jack pulled over his car and Ervin climbed in. Richard pulled over Frank's country squire and Frank and Martha climbed in. Louis drove Richard's car around and asked Horace to join him. He did not trust Horace's temper since he knew Jack and Horace were still at odds.

The three cars drove until they found a rest stop along the road, and everyone piled out and sat on the empty benches, still wet with dew. The air was now very cool, and Frank had to be wrapped in a blanket and hugged by Martha to keep from shivering. He was still suffering from his obvious concussion.

Finally, someone asked the forbidden question.

Ervin said, "What just happened? How did we survive this? Who killed those guys?"

Jack said, "I'm not sure, but I did see one of them. He was dressed in all black. He had a mask on, just like those soldiers had. I don't know why he only partially cut through my rope. That's why it took me so long to get free."

Frank smiled slightly, even though it hurt to move his facial muscles. He, however, did not respond to Jack's comment.

He thought, *"Big brother Horace and his boys came through. But what's with the all black outfits? And why did he leave without untying us?"*

Martha thought, *"Castanza is my hero yet again."*

Jack thought, *"I don't want to give them the wrong impression, but I think Robert saved us tonight. The guy I saw walked just like us."*

The Michigan State Police were summoned the following morning to the chalet. They discovered eight bodies, all with headshot wounds. The Michigan Attorney General received a call before early noon. Ten minutes later the State Police abandoned the site, leaving the taped off area as they found it, bodies, and all. Minutes later a cleanup crew arrived. One hour later no sign of death existed. Just massive destruction.

CHAPTER FOURTEEN

Road-trip

Late spring of 1979

Robert decided not to work the summer months and informed the university that he would be back for the fall semester. That gave him almost four months off. He and Michael decided to spend some time together on an extended road trip. He called their parents to inform them of their plans. His mother answered the phone.

"Mom, I think it's time Michael and I got to know one another again. It's been many years since we've spent any time alone so we're going to leave town and do some extensive travelling."

Martha was taken aback by the declaration and said, "Son, I'm not sure this is the time for you to be leaving home. I suspect you may still be in danger."

Robert said, "Mom, if we are in danger then we need to get it away from you guys. Don't worry. It's been seven months since the Idlewild incident. It's been quiet ever since. We will keep in touch. We don't have any definitive plans. We're probably just going to explore the country. I've got an extended vacation and I want to use it. This will be the first time that we've traveled alone and it's about time. Please tell Dad and the boys we'll be in touch. Make a point of calling Mack to explain. I don't want to talk to him until we're gone. He may try to talk us out of it. Do you have anything you wish to say to Michael?"

Martha, now feeling awkward, said, "Yes, son. Let me say good-bye to him."

Robert handed the phone to Michael, who raised an eyebrow.

He said, "Hello, Mom. Robert explained that we were getting ready to leave and the reasons why. I will take care of your son, so don't worry." Then he paused and said, "Mom, I'm sorry I've put you through so much pain and aggravation all these years. I love you, Mom. Good-bye," and hung up the phone.

Martha could do nothing for a long moment, then burst into tears. Even though she was terrified that he might die after the bridge incident she was still unable to display any affection toward him once he had recovered. In fact, she found it difficult to even approach Robert since the Packard incident last summer. She was back to being the same old mother who could not nurture her thirteen-year-old crying son back in '65.

Michael looked at Robert and said, "If we're going to be gone for four months then we need cash. Lots of cash. Let's stop in Gary, Indiana. I have a stash there."

Robert was confused but decided to go along with it. He was glad, however, that Michael was able to express to their mother his feelings for her.

It was Michael's decision to just leave the apartment with nothing packed. They would get everything they needed as they progressed along the roads. This was extremely difficult for Robert to grasp, but he realized that he may need to relax and let Michael lead the way.

"This is crazy! I can't believe I'm doing this. But I guess I'm lucky to have him with me. He's got experience traveling and hanging out just about anywhere."

The two brothers left Ann Arbor after eating lunch at Paesano, an Italian restaurant on Washtenaw Avenue. Not, however, before pulling into a condo complex in Ypsilanti and parking for thirty minutes. Once they hit the road, Michael took over the driving and three hours later pulled into an alley in Gary, Indiana. He told Robert to wait for him and grabbed an obviously empty backpack and left the car.

He returned twenty minutes later with a huge bulge in the backpack and climbed into the passenger seat.

He said, "We're going to be needing about 10 G's a month to really enjoy this trip. So, I brought 60 G's since we're going to need a new car. I don't plan on styling across America in this thing. I'm surprised you aren't driving a country squire," and laughed.

He then said, "Those guys won't miss this dough. At least not right away. And I didn't leave a note this time," and continued to laugh.

Robert merely grimaced as he pulled away.

After spending time doing light shopping, they spent the night in Gary, then hit the road with new custom luggage and a shiny new '79 black corvette convertible.

· · · · · · · · · · · · ·

Michael pulled the '74 grey Impala into the parking lot of a condo complex near the Ann Arbor-Ypsilanti border. He excused himself from Robert, explaining that he will be back in twenty minutes. He walked onto the short porch of one unit and knocked on the door.

His grandfather answered and said, "Hello, Robert. I am glad to see you have finally decided to visit me again. Please come in."

Michael walked into the living room and said, "Hello, Grandpa. I haven't seen you since I was four years old. I'm not Robert. I'm Michael. We talked as I sat in your car back in '56. You promised you'd visit again, but... Well, here we are."

Dr. McCants was stunned.

His wife, Willamae, looked out from the kitchen, but decided to leave her grandson alone with his grandfather.

"Michael! Oh my God! Well, I guess I shouldn't be surprised, since you are twins. My oh my, I am so glad to finally get to meet you again! I've heard about your trials and tribulations in Detroit and am glad those adventures are over. You look good, so I have to believe you've recovered from your injuries. How is your brother Robert?"

Michael smiled and said, "Robert is fine. He's sitting in the car waiting for me. You will need to give him more time. I'm just glad to see you after all these years."

. . . .

Summer 1979

Both Frank and Martha, driving to a family gathering for their annual picnic, were reminiscing about how wonderful life was when they first met. Their thoughts, however, were their own.

Sixteen-year-olds Martha and Frank were walking through Royal Oak Township, headed toward Horace's home, when one of Horace's neighbors made a disparaging remark about Martha.

She said, "Look at uppity Frank, walking around with his White bitch."

Martha walked up to the girl, who stood a half-foot taller than the short teen and punched her hard in the face. With her hands remaining in a boxer's position, she said in her Harlem accent, "Who the fuck you calling 'White', bitch!"

Martha and Frank had to walk through Ferndale via Nine-Mile Road to get to Horace's home in Royal Oak Township, where Frank was living. A delivery truck drove by them, and someone took a shot at Frank.

"Nigger fucking around with our woman," was all he heard as the truck roared off.

Frank knew Martha felt his anger and frustration.

Frank and his six McCants brothers and their families had gathered annually for a summer picnic for the past twenty years. They loved a certain corner of Palmer Park, a beautiful city park along Woodward Avenue and Seven Mile Road in Detroit Michigan. Large estate mansions lay to the north of the park. Beautifully designed apartment towers to the south. The esteemed Detroit Golf Club to the west.

The family was now huge with some of Frank's forty-plus nephews now married with children. Several of the in-laws were in attendance.

Martha was sitting next to Mrs. Estelle Walters, her brother-in-law Herbert's wife's mother. She had known the woman for over twenty-five years, since Herbert's wedding to Mrs. Walters' daughter Lucy.

She said to Mrs. Walters, "I love to be out here enjoying the sun. It's funny, but my mother used to yell at me to get out of the sun. I knew why she behaved that way back then and to some degree I wish I had listened to her! This sun is death on this pale-ass skin of mine."

The woman responded, "Honey, you should still heed her advice. This sun can be a killer. Hell, you're dark enough. Most of my generation knew you were Black the moment you entered the room. I know I did. It's the soulful way you carry yourself. The way you rock them hips, child. I used to live in New Orleans. The creoles down there gave up trying to pass and just created their own social network. They were more privileged than us Blacks, but they still got their asses kicked same as us, whenever a racial incident arose. Besides, it was very dangerous for them to attempt to pass as White. Those that did pass were so fearful of discovery that they avoided having children. Couldn't trust that they wouldn't deliver a little 'picaninny'."

Both women laughed, each having dealt with such an offensive word.

Martha waved around the crowd of people and said, "I guess Frank was the only one of the McCants boys interested in a 'creole' huh?"

The woman said, "Baby, Frank didn't care how light you were. In fact, all the girls he dated before you were dark, just like my Lucy. Like his mother, that old coot. That woman treats all her daughters-in-law as if they are not worthy of her pedigree.

"Remember, Black men quite often marry women who resemble their mothers. You were the exception. And that could have been because you pursued him as well. If you had just smiled, then went about your business, Frank would have eventually married someone else. Possibly, probably, another dark girl, just like all of us here at this picnic. With the exception of you, dark skin seemed to have been his preference too. I personally could care less. Your boys are just as handsome as my grandsons. And that Michael of yours is something else, child! Oh my, but I loved that boy the moment I first saw him. There was no one quite as precocious as your little Michael."

Martha said, "When I was around six years old, my father brought a new friend to our home. Don't bother to ask me what that was about. She was a caramel-colored lady. You know, that reddish-brown color. I thought she was the most beautiful person in the world. Six months later she had a baby, my dad's kid. She named him William. He was about my boy's color. By the time I was twelve I knew I would only have children that looked like my brother William! I used to pick him up when he was a baby and lightly lick his face and imagine the sweetness coming from him. It's funny, but when my kids arrived, I never did such a ridiculous thing to them. At least not until Ervin, my ebony prince, arrived! Then I started licking again!"

Both women just laughed.

Mrs. Walters said, "Yeah, your Black prince is pretty special too. And he knows it!"

Martha decided to dig a little deeper into the McCants.

"You've obviously noticed there are no girl babies born into this family. What's that about? These fellows only have male sperm?"

Mrs. Walters knew Martha was probing but felt after thirty years of marriage to a McCants, she had a right to some answers.

She said, "I don't believe any of the previous generation had many girls either. It was rumored that Dr. McCants had a sister that was caught on the Michigan campus with a white boy. Her grandfather put her on a ship immediately. Apparently, the eldest rule in that family. That's probably not true, but I have never heard him talk about his sister. Lucy told me that Herbert commented on it once. Horace found out and reprimanded him. Apparently certain family secrets are to remain secret. Even if you are ostracized from the family!

"Don't quote me, but Herb told my baby that all of the female children are exceptionally intelligent. That is why they are sent away. For extensive education, well beyond what is offered here. I really don't know what that's supposed to mean, especially since their clan all lived just west of Ann Arbor.

"Don't tell me you have not noticed that all these males are exceptional. Take a look at your eight. What you see among them exists with all their cousins as well. Exceptionally gifted athletically and academically. Hell, I'd bet there are at least fifteen or twenty of these boys who finished high school and college with 4.0s. And they did not get it from their bitch of a grandmother, not to imply she's not intelligent. Just plain mean!

"You also must wonder why none of them participate in organized sports. None of my McCants grandsons seemed to be interested in them. My other children's kids do, but not those McCants boys."

Martha had taken it for granted that her boys were smart. She had not noticed their cousins were as successful as well. Nor had she considered their lack of interest in sports. She knew that Frank was not involved in football or baseball. He also never tossed a ball around with the boys either. Her sons played basketball, but none of them showed any interest in joining school teams.

A couple of hours after the picnic started a car pulled into the parking lot and a spry older man got out, hopped over a parking block, then marched toward the gathering. Herbert and Frank looked over to see their father approaching them. He arrived three hours later than his usual arrival to the picnic. He usually arrived at the beginning of the picnic and left after a couple of hours, complaining about the long drive back home. That way he could avoid Frank, who also came two hours later than the scheduled time.

All of his daughters-in-law stopped what they were doing and rushed over to him, very happy to see him. All except Martha, who was suddenly feeling apprehensive. She looked around for Frank but could not see him with all of the commotion.

Mrs. Walters was shocked to see the 73-year-old, since he was usually gone by the time Frank and his family arrived. She was aware of the tension between Frank and his father and just waited for their encounter. She also knew why, so she placed her hand over Martha's hand, smiled at her, and nervously waited beside her.

After a few minutes Dr. McCants broke away from his entourage and approached Mrs. Walters, standing to his right, away from Martha. He smiled and greeted her, taking her hand and lightly kissing the back of it.

He said in the most elegant tenor voice, "Hello, madam. It has been a while. You are as fine today as the day I first met you. I hope all is well."

She smiled at him, looked into Martha's eyes momentarily, then said, "Thank you, Joseph. But I was over forty when you met me. I know I'm aging well, but not that well. And how is your wife, Willamae?"

Dr. McCants continued to smile and said, "She is doing, my lady. She is doing."

Then, to everyone's surprise, he stepped in front of Martha and said, "My dear. May I have a moment of your time? I owe you three decades of apologies. I put you through the same hell that I experienced when I got married. I did not realize I was repeating the same terror my family put me through. There was no cause for it to be repeated but it was, to both of our detriment. I hope you will please forgive this decrepit old man for his foolishness."

With this simple gesture, thirty years of anguish within Martha washed away and she started to cry.

She thought, *"You bitch! Don't let this motherfucking, son of a bitch, handsome old fool make you cry!"* She looked over to Frank, then Mack, then Jack, who was staring intently at her, and then just turned into Niagara Falls.

Mrs. Walters placed her arm around Martha, then pulled the woman into her bosom. All of the other women rushed in as they all began to sob. Martha's paleness disappeared in the sea of ink. The men just walked away. They did not need to see their father tear up. Nor did they want to either.

No one seemed to mind the lack of presence of Mrs. Willamae McCants.

.   .   .   .

The twins visited numerous cities along I-65, as they headed south. However, every time Robert mentioned a city nearby that was off the interstate, Michael merely shrugged.

He said, "In due time, brother, in due time. Just want to get to Florida before it gets too hot. I understand it's not very comfortable down there in June, so let's get it out of the way."

After they arrived in Florida and checked into their hotel, Michael indicated that he wanted to visit a friend. He, however, wanted to wait until nightfall.

"It will be cooler once the sun goes down."

Robert knew Michael was up to something. He just hoped his brother was not thinking of something devious, like he did in Gary.

At 8:30 p.m. they got into the corvette and twenty minutes later pulled over at an expensive beachfront sub-division of homes, then waited. Now Robert was very apprehensive. He, however, did not want to imply anything, so he waited. He had forgotten how enjoyable being with Michael could be, since they stopped hanging out over fifteen years ago. He did not want to ruin the mood they had established the moment they left Ann Arbor.

At 9:00 p.m. the sunlight began to fade and the interior lights began shining.

Michael said, "Okay, Brother. I want you to go to this address. When the lady answers the door, just introduce yourself. She will take it from there."

Robert said, "What are you up to, Michael? Who is this woman?"

Michael replied, "Just trust me, Brother. Obviously, I wouldn't have you do anything detrimental to either of us, would I? Just humor me this once."

Robert got out of the car and walked down the walkway, then turned towards a home. He knocked on the door of the home and his mother Martha, having traveled forward fifteen years through a time machine, answered the door.

. . . .

During the two-day-long drive down I-65 and I-75, Michael discussed with Robert a concern he had. He was not able to remember much about his life between early 1971 and early 1973. He knew it was not the injuries because of the fight, because he noticed the loss of memory years before. It was like he fell asleep one evening and woke up a couple of years later. He did have memories, but they did not always make sense. They were convoluted, like in a dream. They did not always match up. There were times he remembered sleeping in a loft, but the loft was in Indian Village, while he was living in Gary and Chicago. His memories had him sleeping in boats along the Detroit River, but he always avoided the yacht clubs in Chicago, since his Black presence was too obvious.

Robert did not understand it. Yet he too had recently experienced the same fogginess. Not, however, to the extreme Michael was describing. He had been reprimanded for missing his lectures for a six-week period and he had no excuse for it, other than that Michael was hospitalized. He, however, knew he would not have skipped his lectures, when a drive to Harper Hospital from Ann Arbor was only an hour and a half, roundtrip. In fact, he remembered doing some lectures, so why did the dean say he was gone a full six weeks. Even the receptionist behaved as if he were gone the entire time.

Michael said, "You have had this happen to you as well? It seems rather strange, don't you think? You were out of the country during my mental absence. I, however, was not out of the country, but in the hospital during your hazy period. Hell, I remember you visited me, so I don't know why you would be blank during that time."

As they mulled over the mental lapses, they pulled into a gas station. Robert walked into the station to pay for the fuel, then returned and handed Michael the keys, since it was his turn to drive. After Michael pumped the gas he went into the restroom, then returned to the car, sat in the driver's seat, then pulled away.

The female receptionist was enamored by the handsome young man driving the corvette. She could not help but remark, however, that he took the time to change his shirt after pumping the gas.

The brothers decided to spend a week in New Orleans. They always booked lodging at five-star hotels, but they also wanted to be near Bourbon Street. Michael decided to go for a walk while Robert unpacked. He met two young ladies working in a shop and took up a conversation with them. He finally asked one of the ladies if she wanted to have dinner that night. She gladly accepted so he arranged to meet her at 8:00. He told the other young woman that his twin brother was with him, and he would ask him to come over and introduce himself as well. Perhaps they could double date.

Thirty minutes later Robert walked into the shop, looked around, and approached the two women.

Robert thought, *"This must be Shirley. She's definitely Michael's type. She fits his description precisely. He loves his chocolate!"*

He introduced himself and explained that he would love to meet the two of them later and the four of them can go out to dinner.

That evening Robert had a change of heart.

He told Michael, "I think I'm going to pass on that dinner date tonight. You go ahead and enjoy yourself."

Michael was extremely disappointed but did not push the matter.

He thought, *"He may still be experiencing PTSD from the war, even though it's been six years."*

Michael arrived at the shop at 8:00 p.m. and apologized to Camille, explaining that Robert was experiencing jetlag. Then he and Shirley went out to dinner, then to her place. He did not get back to his room until 1:00 a.m.

He woke Robert and said, "Brother. I'm sorry you were not able to enjoy your evening, but that Shirley was something special! You go ahead and continue crashing. I'll see you tomorrow morning."

Robert, having second thoughts about his continued isolation from others, decided to call Camille. After Michael fell asleep, he dressed and went down to the lobby and used a pay phone and dialed her number.

"Hello. This is Robert, the fellow you met earlier today. I am sorry to call you so late. I should have been more attentive to you today. My brother and I have been on the road for close to a month now, so all of the driving can be tiresome. Perhaps…"

Camille interrupted him and said, "Look, Mr. Robert. If you're going to waste my time apologizing, then just hang up. Otherwise, get over here in the next ten minutes. The door will remain unlocked for that amount of time. Here is my address."

The following morning Robert walked into the hotel lobby. Michael was sitting in a lounge chair, expecting him.

He said, "Young brother, ain't it way past your curfew?" and they both laughed heartily.

After spending two weeks in New Orleans, blowing their schedule by seven days, but enjoying the sights and the company of Camile and Shirley, the twins headed north, with plans to stop at Grambling State University.

Along the highway they passed a shooting range and decided to spend the afternoon taking target practice. The predominantly White crowd was not amiable to strangers intruding on their range, but the corvette was impressive, so they relented. Michael assumed that Robert had some experience with guns after spending two years in the army but was not prepared for the marksmanship his brother was about to display. Robert rented a long-range rifle for an hour.

"Michael, you're only used to firing handguns. This is a long-range rifle. Watch this."

Robert loaded the gun with four rounds, took careful aim at the target, and fired.

"Pow Pow Pow Pow."

Four rapid shots at the distant silhouette. The rapid sound of the gun was noticed by the other men nearby. When he was able to retrieve the silhouette, he showed Michael the single hole in the paper. Only the size of the hole indicated that more than one round penetrated it.

The men standing nearby moved in for a closer look.

One elderly man said, "If I didn't know no betta I'd sware that boy just put fo holes in that there bulls-eye. Fo holes on top each other. Well I'll be. *Pop Pop Pop Pop*! I'll be dang! All them bullets went through the same god-dang hole! Well I ain't never seen nothin like it!"

Michael was astounded.

An hour later, when they got back to the car, he said, "Aha! I'm starting to get memories of the time I was in the hospital. You were a crack shot in the army, like Mack said. I heard him talking to Horace. He also said, you were injured and had to spend time convalescing in

Germany, under the care of a psychiatrist. He stated that a psychiatrist was inquiring about you at the hospital. Is this the Dr. Schultz I've been hearing about? Tell me, what's going on? Is that why those men kidnap me? Thinking I was you? This is the time for you to open up to me, of all people."

Michael pulled into the next roadside motel they saw and checked into a room.

When he came back to the car, he said to Robert, "We're going to lay everything out on the table. I'm going to share everything that's happened to me over the past fifteen years. And you're going to do the same."

They spent the next two days discussing their lives since '65.

After a couple days relaxing in the cheap motel and pouring their hearts out about their past, the two hit the road again. When they saw signs for the historic Grambling State University, they could not help but stop. They arrived at the sports fields as the track team was finishing their training, so the twins sat down on the bleachers and watched. After another thirty minutes, the track coach called it a day and the team headed to the locker room. Only a few students remained on the field, practicing the long jump.

Robert stepped out onto the track, mischievously thinking, "*I wonder how long we can run out here before they run us off?*"

He said to Michael, "I see you're wearing your Adidas, as am I. I bet I can still beat you in the fifty!"

He pushed Michael away and took off. Michael never caught up to him.

"See I told you I could still beat you!" he said and laughed.

Michael appreciated the joke then walked to the starting line of the quarter-mile track. He told Robert to clock him using the second hand on his wristwatch. He had not run the quarter since he was an eighth grader at Cleveland Jr. High in Detroit.

One of the track coaches was testing his stopwatch, which he had just gotten out of the shop.

"Look at that young man on the track. Should I run him off?"

The older coach said, "Naw, but test your watch on 'em as he sets up at the starting line. He looks fit enough. He might be able to finish in sixty seconds since he's only wearing gym shoes."

The third coach said, "I'll put a dollar on him to run a fifty-seven, gym shoes or not."

"Okay, you're on. A buck it is."

The older coach took the stopwatch and waited for Michael to begin.

Michael took off running. The coach, calling off Michael's splits, said, "100 in 10 seconds… 200 in 19 seconds… 300 in 28 seconds, 400 in 37 seconds, 440 in 41.4 seconds! He just crushed Lee Evans '68 Olympic and world record! In gym shoes no less. I knew this watch was junk! The bet is off."

He tossed the watch into a trash container, then walked back to the locker room.

The other coach thought, *"I don't care what that watch read. That young man ain't even breathing hard. Strange though. He seems to be talking to himself an awful lot. Hand gestures and all."*

As they were preparing to drive away from the school, they saw an outdoor basketball court and decided to stop and shoot the balls lying about the court. The three track coaches happened to notice them again and stopped at a distance to watch. Robert picked up a ball, walked over to the free throw line and took a shot. All nets. He picked up two more balls, placing one by his side, then took a second shot. All nets. Then the third ball. All nets. He continued shooting until he had taken fifty shots.

Then Michael began to complain that he wanted to shoot, so Robert relinquished the court to him. Michael dribbled the ball toward the basket, leaped into the air, and dunked the ball. He grabbed another ball, dribbled toward the basket and performed a 360-degree spin in the air and dunked the ball. He bounced the ball off the backboard, caught it mid-air, and dunked the ball. He looked over at Robert, smiled because he knew Robert could never do that, and began to walk away.

Robert said, "Anyone can do that. Hell, I've seen Ervin dunk a ball."

Michael laughed, then said, "Yeah, but hell, he's 6-foot. He'd better be able to dunk a basketball."

As they drove away the coaches said, "That man is really talented. Fifty free throws in a row, then he dunks the ball. And he's only 5'8" if that."

The older coach said, "Those were more than just fifty free throws in a row. Those were fifty all-nets free throws in a row! No rim, not one single time. Where did this guy come from?"

Then the older coach conjectured to himself, "*Strange, but this young man changed his stride often during that display of excellence. Two entirely different walking patterns. Almost like he was two different people. I'm an expert on body language and if I didn't know it, I'd swear he was switching his stride, from one cadence to another. I've seen the best athletes in the world, and I've never seen anyone doing that. Calm during the free throws, then explosive while dunking. And not just during the dunk but fetching the ball as well. Two entirely different cadences. And he was more animated the whole time he was dunking, unlike during his free-throws.*"

·   ·   ·   ·   ·   ·   ·   ·   ·   ·   ·   ·

They drove to Las Vegas, but after spending just two days in the city Robert realized that he did not care for the casinos. He found it was too easy to merely focus on the various games and win almost every time. When he loss he wondered if the games were rigged. Besides, they were trying to spend the rest of their money, not add to the cache.

The frequent winning was not a thrill for Michael either.

"Hell, I can get fifty grand in just fifteen minutes. All I have to do is drive over to the west side of town. That's an even greater rush, climbing over a roof at night in a new neighborhood."

After three months, the two had been all over the country, excluding the west coast and Texas. They decided to avoid such a large geographic area, deciding instead to return next year and tackle those states. They really enjoyed Montana and spent two weeks staying in Billings, visiting dude ranches, going to rodeos, and hiking and camping out in Yellowstone National Park.

On the last night of the road trip, after spending a week in Minneapolis, Robert and Michael were sleeping in yet another five-star hotel. Robert was thinking how he would never again be able to stay at any hospitality venue that was not rated five stars.

As the two slept soundly, the phone rang. Michael awoke and answered it.

The voice said, "Boi. I hads me a dream ta night. Youse gots a big trip youse gots to be on. Da gon kills yo Doc! Da already kills yo boi McGregor. Youse gots to go to dat land wit da Tag Mahall. Lickety-split too, sho nough! Find yo bra-the's doc in dat deep forest befoes da do. Yep, dem boys coming from dat fort in Louisiana. Bets ta hurry befo dey leaves, too!"

Before Michael could respond to the caller, he heard a dial tone.

Michael looked dazed. He had not heard that voice in nearly twenty-five years. Since he was four years old. Even though he knew exactly who it was, he did not understand what she was warning him about. Only knew it was a warning. Almost an order.

He awoke Robert and said, "We just got a call from family. It was ma's grandmother."

Robert stared at him for a moment, then said, "What are you talking about? Ma doesn't have a grandmother, does she? How do you know ma's grandmother? And how could she get the number to this room? Hell, how could she know what STATE to find you in? You were dreaming. Go back to sleep."

Michael thought for a moment, then said, "Yeah, you must be right."

He looked at the phone again, then realized he had indeed used it. Robert had it last when he called the front desk. He always hung up the phone with the cord on the attached side. Michael always hung it up on the opposite side, which was irritating to Robert.

"I didn't make any calls tonight, yet I've obviously used the phone. Shit, that wasn't a dream."

"At any time did you have an Indian doctor? Indian as in Asia?"

Robert just stared at Michael.

Then he said, "No. Never. I always use brother doctors. The only Indian doctor I've ever worked with was in Germany. One of the doctors at the treatment center in Kaiserslautern. I spent a lot of time with him in '71. He tried to get past my guard but, like Principal Johnson at Post, he never could. I know I must have frustrated the hell out of him. Ha! Sorry, I guess it wasn't really that funny. The man was just doing his job. How do you know about him?"

Micheal ignored the question and asked, "Have you ever been to a military site in Louisiana?"

Robert was now feeling curious. He knew his twin could read his mind, but only for very recent events. He, however, had not seen Michael for over two years after he met Dr. Patel or trained in Louisiana. That was in '71, over eight years ago.

He asked, "How do you know about Louisiana or Dr. Patel?"

Michael got out of his bed and sat at the room desk. He grabbed a piece of paper and wrote down, 'Taj Mahal, Doctor Patel, forest,

McGregor, Louisiana, big trip, India, killing, very soon, great-grandma'. Then he turned off the lamp, letting Robert know the conversation was over. He would address all of Robert's questions in the morning.

The following morning, over breakfast, Michael pulled out the paper he had written on during the night.

"Okay Robert. When I was four I discovered that Ma had a secret stash in her closet."

Robert interrupted him and said, "Yeah, in the back, on the floor. Everyone knows that. Even Ervin. At one time or another we've all discovered it. We just don't talk about it. And we never open anything from that closet. That would be stupid and rude."

"Well, I've been rude most of my life. Anyway, I opened it. I read a letter from Ma's grandmother. It had a phone number on it. It said something to the tune that she had only one chance to call for help. So, I called the number and before I could say anything this old lady said, 'Michael, what are you doing going through your mother's stuff! Hang this phone up now!' I slammed the phone down and wet my pants."

Robert just stared at him. He did not know whether to address the fact that Michael went into Ma's personal belongings, or the fact that the caller knew who he was, or that he wet his pants.

Finally, Michael looked down to his list and said, "I know this trip was supposed to end today, but I think we need to extend the trip and drive to a fort in Louisiana."

CHAPTER FIFTEEN

Castanza's Haven

The week after the Idlewild assault

Martha contemplated what had occurred at the chalet as they drove home from Idlewild. She had never been around so much death, but for some reason she was not troubled by it. She had grown up in violent conditions, having witnessed murders or other levels of violence as a young child.

Frank, on the other hand, was very disturbed by the assault. He almost lost his family and as hard as he tried, he was unable to do anything about it. He blamed himself for relaxing so much, when he should have had the boys guarding the house. Mack could not convince him that they might all be dead if they had resisted.

When they arrived home Frank called Horace to let him know they were back. He still believed Horace was responsible for the rescue and just will not admit it. He told Mack that his uncle Horace probably had gotten an old gang together and just does not want the exposure. After talking to Louis and Richard about the rescue Mack knows no local gang could have possibly achieved those results. Most of Horace's running buddies were over fifty years old and had not been in any type of conflict in decades. Mack believed it was either his brother Robert or the mobster Castanza.

Jack and Ervin did not go straight to Detroit after the assault, but instead drove to Ann Arbor. Ervin wanted to be sure that Robert and Michael were okay. Jack was not at all concerned for them. He believed they were responsible for the rescue.

When they arrived at Robert's apartment, they spent the afternoon discussing with Michael just how close they came to being killed. Ervin considered whether Michael had any involvement. He had seen him in action on the bridge.

Jack wanted to talk to Robert, whom Michael said was at the university. He told Jack that he would bring Robert up to date later that evening when he arrived home. Jack, however, insisted that Michael go get Robert now. He was very dramatic, so Michael relented and left the apartment. Twenty minutes later Robert entered the apartment alone. The two younger brothers understood. After rehashing the events at Idlewild, Robert told the boys to head home because their parents may need them.

As they drove home Jack said, "It was very important that Robert hear what happened firsthand. Telling Michael is not the same as telling Robert."

His brother understood.

Forty-five minutes later the pair was pulling up to Santa Rosa.

· · · · · · · · · · · · · ·

Three days after the assault Martha was immensely disappointed she was not able to talk to her grandmother, but she dared not call. She considered speaking to her sister but decided against that as well. So, she got in her car, telling Frank she was going to canvas a new area on the east side, but instead drove to Eastland Mall.

She walked around the exterior of the mall for a short while, trying to get the courage to make a phone call. She wanted to have a meeting with Castanza. Eventually she walked into the mall and went to a payphone and made the call, having remembered his number from earlier in the year. She decided to take an aggressive approach, since the last time they spoke she was in tears, weakened by the fear of her son Robert being harmed by Castanza's men.

After the phone rang several times, someone answered it and merely said, "Yes."

Martha replied, "Hello. My name is Martha McCants. May I please speak to Anthony Castanza."

Ten minutes later she was making a right turn onto Lake Shore Drive in Grosse Pointe Farms.

After hanging up the phone, Castanza was flustered.

He said to Ricci, his consigliere, "What could this woman want? Has she been on the phone with the Lastanza family? Hell! How did I get myself into this mess? I heard what happened at that nigger campground. I don't have a clue how the feds found them, but I definitely will find out. Perhaps I was supposed to provide protection?

"Did you get ahold of that punk-ass lawyer of ours? I thought I told you to get that fucker here. Where is that French nigger Bordeaux?"

Ricci replied, "Boss, he's not French. His family may be from Haiti or New Orleans."

"I didn't ask you for a history lesson on that nigger. I asked you where he was?"

Ricci said, "Calm down, boss. Just relax. You shouldn't get your blood pressure up. You know what your doctor said."

"God dammit! I asked you a fucken question. Where is Bordeaux?"

"Boss, he should be here any minute. He was in the area. I called him on his car phone."

"Well, he'd better fucken get here before Mrs. McCants does."

Just then Bordeaux pulled into the driveway and parked, then walked into the house. Minutes later Martha also pulled up in Castanza's driveway and parked behind a Jaguar. By habit she touched the hood of the Jag to see if the car had been parked long. The hood was still very warm. She instinctively knew this car was not part of Castanza's or his crew.

Ricci walked out to greet her and introduced himself, then escorted her into the foyer. She suddenly realized by the way Ricci treated her that she had clout. Clout she was completely unaware of.

"Wow. I was not expecting to be treated so formally. This reminds me of how Grandma was treated whenever those Sicilian guys came around. They acted like my granny was royalty, even though they hated her son. I'd better not act like some dumb broad, or I could lose any leverage I may have. I must carry myself as my grandmother would expect me to. I'm here to thank this man, not kiss his ring, and I need to remember that."

Castanza entered the room, saw Martha standing there, and became confused. He did not expect this Italian-looking beauty, which added to his uncertainty. He took a deep breath then walked up to her and introduced himself.

"Salve signora McCants! Io sono Castanza. Antonio Castanza. E un piacere incontrarti. It is a pleasure to meet you." He reached out his hand and she extended hers, palm down. He took her hand and kissed it gently on the knuckles.

"Get a grip on yourself, girl! He's just being formal. And you've heard Italian before! And don't try to impress him by throwing those few Italian

phrases at him that you picked up in Harlem. That would only lead to him continuing the language, one that you cannot speak!"

"I wasn't expecting her to be so elegant, cheap dress or not. She has to be Sicilian. But I can see Michael and Mack in her face. I wonder what her maiden name was. It would be rude of me, however, to ask. This is not the proper time to be so informal."

He continued to hold her hand as they walked into his massive living room. She was now the third McCants to have been in this home.

He said, "Mrs. McCants. I want to truly apologize for the trauma you experienced in Idlewild. I understand it was a life and death situation."

Martha almost lost it.

"Life and death? What does he know! We almost died!"

She decided to take the initiative and bluff her way through the conversation.

"Sir, I want to thank you for the courtesy you've shown me today. I also want to thank you for getting my son Robert out of that mess at the Packard. A mess that your men created. And I want to thank you for setting my family up for the kill in Idlewild! And there was plenty of death as we departed, no thanks to you."

Castanza was beside himself. He began to tremble, then calmed himself. Now he knew she was connected. This was New York style all the way.

"Oh, please, ma'am. That was not what was supposed to happen. I merely wanted you to get to a distant place where your family would go unnoticed. I thought that negro resort was the best place for it. In retrospect I should have sent protection as well. But most of my guys would have stood out at that resort."

"And most of my Black guys are no longer with us."

Castanza paused, then shouted, "Bordeaux. Get in here!"

In seconds a tall handsome light-skinned Black man entered the room.

Castanza said, "Mrs. McCants, this is my lawyer, Pierre Bordeaux. Perhaps you've met before. At any rate, the chalet you were using was his home. I have asked him to come here to explain what could have gone wrong. Pierre, this is Mrs. Martha McCants. She is the mother of Michael and Robert McCants. I believed you once mentioned her son Robert in conjunction with your daughter Carol. And you met her son Mack rather recently."

Bordeaux, accustomed to associating with mixed-Blacks, thought, *"Even though she looks White I can tell she is mulatto. Except she is dressed low-class, which immediately excludes her from our circles. Her hair is not styled to the latest fashion, and she does not sit properly on the couch. Her arms are folded like a man would. No, she obviously missed her debutante ball. She is not a sophisticated lady, by any means."*

He walked over to Martha, bent down, and extended his hand.

She did not stand but shook it and asked, "Your daughter knows my Robert?"

"Oh Shit! This must be the girl he was smitten with back in '68. The one who broke his heart."

"Yes, they had a single class at Wayne State U in the winter/spring of '68, just before the King assassination. I had to transfer her over to Michigan after that."

Martha took note of the way he said 'single.'

Castanza interrupted them.

"Have you been up to your property since the shooting?"

Bordeaux became flushed and said, "I certainly have. It's a wreck! A total mess! They really shot up the place."

Before he could finish Martha blurted out, "Shot up the place? They shot up the place? They almost killed my entire family!"

Bordeaux said, "Yes, of course, I was going to say that next. I'm sorry if I seemed insensitive. That must have been an extremely traumatic night for you and your sons."

Ricci, sensing the added tension in the air, spoke up.

"Pierre, please tell us how anyone could have possibly known they were there. Their whereabouts was not supposed to be public knowledge."

Bordeaux said in a condescending voice, "Unfortunately, once they arrived it became public knowledge."

He looked at Martha and said, "I'm sorry, ma'am, but your family has a certain notoriety. All the way back to that rumble they had in that alley in '65. By your second day at the resort, folks here in Detroit were discussing your arrival. My wife even came home discussing it. I was on the phone with a client when she walked in to inform me."

This little bit of information went right by Castanza and Ricci. It did not, however, get past Martha.

"You were on the phone with a client when your wife blurted out where my family was hiding?"

"Well, I'm sure my client had nothing to do with your assault. He works for the federal government."

Martha was immediately on her feet, leaping at Ricci so quickly he froze in his stance. She grabbed his hidden gun from its holster and performed a full pirouette to face Bordeaux, forcing him to fall back onto the couch. Castanza was stunned.

He yelled, "Dio mio! Oh my god! Mrs. McCants! What are you doing?"

Martha thrusted her left arm toward Castanza, open palm, as she held the gun in her right hand.

She screamed, "You, mother fucker, was talking to the feds about my family's whereabouts! You ratted us out!"

She was now inches away from Bordeaux's chest, her finger on the trigger, her hand as steady as the floor she was standing on. He, however, was trembling with fear, a feeling he had never experienced before.

Ricci thought, "*God damn, she's holding that big-ass piece like a pro! With just one hand! And she's so tiny!*"

Martha said, "It was the feds who kidnapped my boy Michael, ya sadiddy punkass motherfucker! Then they kidnapped my boy Robert. They killed his friend McGregor at the hotel! They may have even sent that pack of wolves to kill my sons at the grocery store! Now, after you speak to a fed, while your bitch-ass wife is gossiping about my family, my entire family is almost killed! THEY FIRED AT US FOR FIVE MINUTES WITH AUTOMATIC WEAPONS! The only reason we're having this conversation is because they got new orders not to kill us, but to bring us in. That sounds like either the mob or the feds. And it wasn't the fucken mob! What the fuck do you think, Monsieur Pierre Bordeaux!?

"Well, my boys are going to get to the bottom of this. And when they do, you had better hope you had no direct involvement in our perilous night. Fottuto figlio di puttana! Ya motherfucken son-of-a-bitch!"

· · · · · · · · · · · ·

At the precise moment that Martha was seconds away from shooting Bordeaux, a middle-aged woman, driving to the grocery store in Wilmington, North Carolina, almost lost control of her car. She had to pull over to collect herself. As she sat in the car, her mind flooded with worry, she realized that someone she dearly loved was in serious trouble. Again. This was the second time in three days she had this feeling. An extreme feeling of trepidation. Extreme level of anxiety. After a short period of time, she finally collected herself, turned her car around, and headed back to her home, arriving fifteen minutes later.

She pulled into her garage, entered the house, and stormed into her grandmother's parlor. There sat a ninety-five-year-old woman, who looked much younger, about to rise from her chair.

The younger woman, now in tears, said, "Grandmother, I just had another awful feeling! Something is terribly wrong, and I cannot comprehend it. Please, Grandmother, please help me with this. It's my big sister, I know it is. I can feel it. It has to be her. I need you to resolve this! I need your help!"

The old lady knew she was being too hard on her family. She was beginning to realize that her rules were much too harsh, and they could only lead to disaster.

She said, "Okay babi-gurl. I does understands. And I's sorry I's been so mean to ya all des yars. But, you can handle dis one yoself. Ya knos what ta do sweetheart. Handles it yoself. I's ain't gon be har forebber. Ya gots ta take dem reins from me and ride dat bronco buc yoself. Now git to it. And hurry! Times awastin!"

She handed her granddaughter a piece of paper, then sat back in her chair, somewhat winded.

The granddaughter left the parlor and headed to her den. She picked up the phone and called the number on the paper. A man answered the phone on the first ring.

He nervously said, "Ciao."

After a lengthy conversation she hung up the phone and dialed her older sister. The sister who lived in Detroit.

When the phone was answered she immediately said, "Frank, where is my sister? Tell me everything is okay."

Before Frank could respond his wife Martha took the phone from him, waited for him to leave the room, then said, "Hello, sis. I've been waiting for this call. Everything is fine. I just had to go 'Harlem' on some gangsters, that's all. Like Granny used to do. But everything is fine now. How is Granny anyway, Dominique? Is she alright?"

What Dominique did not know was that her grandmother had already handled the Grosse Pointe situation. She had already called Lastanza the second Martha pointed the gun at Bordeaux.

· · · · · · · · · · · ·

Thirty minutes earlier

Castanza was frustrated. He does not know his position in the world anymore. He just allowed a woman to threaten his lawyer in his presence, with his consigliere's gun, and was unable to react.

"What power this woman possesses. I don't know any woman here in Detroit that could have pulled that off. She is truly well connected and well trained. She did what I would have done twenty years ago. And that nigger lawyer just sat there trembling. I'm getting too old for this shit."

Ricci entered the room and said, "Boss, he won't tell me who his client is. That 'confidentiality' shit. I think he may be more afraid of his client than he was of Mrs. McCants. One thing's for sure. I bet he's going to lock his office door the next time he talks to a client. No more barging in by his bitch, I'm sure. Punk-ass Frenchman," and laughed.

"Boss, have you ever seen anything like that? That woman leaped through the air and grabbed my gun before I could move! Boss, she leaped over the fucken coffee table! In a mini skirt! And did you hear what she called him? A 'sadiddy punkass motherfucker!' What the hell is a 'sadiddy'? Anyway, he must be one because he sure as hell did not object. We need to hire her. Hire her and those sons of hers. Man, could they rule the westside. We'd have no more trouble if she ran the area. We wouldn't even need both positions filled, Shapatilo's or Busta's!

"I'm not serious, boss. Just trying to get you to relax. And I'm sorry she upset you so. Should I let Bordeaux go home now? And should

I give Mrs. McCants your goodbyes? She's still sitting in the parlor waiting for an answer from Bordeaux."

Just then the phone rang. It was Lastanza, from New York. Ricci handed the phone to Castanza, but before he could place it to his ear he could hear, "WHAT THE FUCK IS GOING ON THERE? DO YOU KNOW YOU ARE JEOPARDIZING MY OPERATIONS HERE IN NEW YORK? WHAT HAPPENED TO THAT LADY'S FAMILY? ALL I ASKED YOU TO DO IS KEEP THEM SAFE! WHAT HAPPENED TO THEIR PROTECTION, YOU MOTHER FUCKER?"

. . . .

Pierre Bordeaux was speaking on his phone to a client when his wife entered the room. She knew not to disturb him when he was on the phone, but she blurted out before she saw the phone to his ear. He angrily waved her off, but not before she had shouted, "Do you know that those McCants trash have moved into our home in Idlewild!"

. . . .

Annette Bordeaux was walking along the Avenue of Fashion on Livernois Avenue between 7-Mile Road and 8-Mile Road in northwest Detroit. The shopping district was once a haven for the rich, with furriers, jewelers, and other expensive clothing stores along a half mile stretch of the nine-lane avenue. It still attracted shoppers and various cliques in the upper-class northwest community who still met to dine among the various niche restaurants.

Annette met a couple of her sorority sisters as she headed to her car. One of the women hugged Annette and said, "Girl, I just heard you sold your home in Idlewild to those ghetto rats, the McCants. You know the ones that are always involved with those drug dealers. My daughter Shirley told me the oldest boy even tried to date your daughter Carol. She had to leave Wayne State U to get away from him. And now one of their boys was even shot by the police after he killed that drug kingpin Busta on the MacArthur bridge. Well, now we have them as neighbors! How could your husband sell your home to them? They had to have used drug money to afford your chalet. I thought we had a covenant not to sell to trash. Well, there goes the neighborhood!"

. . . .

Dr. Joseph McCants got a phone call well after midnight and leaped up to answer the call in the living room. He had been waiting for a response to a request he made earlier in the week and did not want to be disturbed by his wife.

He said, "Yes, Baba."

The response was, "Everything has been taken care of. Your son's family is safe."

Joseph said, "Thank you, father. Thank you so much."

The caller hung up his phone, then said to his great-grandson, who was sitting across from him, "Looks like you were busy tonight. I see your jacket is cut. Did a blade get to you?"

The young man said, "No, sir. It merely caught my fatigue. I got there a little late, but everything went smoothly."

CHAPTER SIXTEEN

Fort Polk, Louisiana

August 1979

The last week of the Road Trip

Fort Polk, in Louisiana, is a major training facility for the US Army. It was used primarily during the Vietnam war for boot camp. The recruits were then sent to Advance Infantry Training, depending on their success in boot camp. Robert McCants spent over three months in 1971 training at these two facilities.

The McCants twins arrived at Fort Polk after nightfall. After driving around the outskirts of the facility they decided not to approach the gates until they had devised a plan. So, they settled at a nearby restaurant parking area.

Michael said, "I should have no problem getting inside the base. The security on the rear looks weak, even though the fence is electrified. But I don't know why we're here so I don't know which of the many facilities I should be entering. You say you were here in the spring of '71? What do you suggest?"

Robert was somewhat confused. The warning Michael relayed to him from their supposed great-grandmother was very vague. He was still not certain that Michael had not dreamed he received a call from her. Michael did, however, know facts and people he should not have known about. Even if he could read his mind.

"Your guess is as good as mine. I cannot imagine what our mission is. We need to get inside and look around. Perhaps we can find some evidence of a mission involving Dr. Patel. That might be our only lead. I've got an idea. Why don't you sneak in and look around? See if there is an outstanding order implying a trip to India. Also, if you can steal me a uniform of a captain or other high-ranking officers, then perhaps I can go in as well in disguise. I'll of course, need credentials."

Michael said, "Those are two dumbass ideas. Granny should have been more specific."

"Let's not talk about 'Granny' right now. Let's focus on the task at hand that she's given us. It's late evening. First, let's go into the restaurant and eat."

They enter the restaurant only to find uniform soldiers sitting at most tables.

Michael whispered, "You didn't say this place would be full of storm troopers."

"What did you expect? We're right outside a military base. I never left the base while I was here. I ate all of my meals on the base."

"Perhaps you should stay with the car. I'll order for both of us. We don't need you to be recognized by any of these soldier boys."

Robert looked at him incredulously and said, "Dummy. We're identical twins, remember? I'm looking in a mirror right now!"

Michael smirked at him as Robert walked back to the car.

He settled into a corner booth, ordered two carryout meals, and just observed while he waited for his food. After ten minutes the waitress brought the food. He paid her and headed for the door. That's when he noticed an older man do a double take his way.

"*That guy knows me. Or he knows Robert. Shit,*" and turned his head away as he exited the door.

The man thought, "*Damn, I must be seeing things. I just saw Robert McCants walking out of that door.*"

He got up to check, leaving his plate of food unattended. He walked into the parking lot but did not see anyone standing around. He glanced at all of the cars, then walked back to the entrance of the restaurant.

He glanced around one more time then thought, "*Guess it was just wishful thinking.*"

He walked back inside to finish his meal. After paying his check he headed to the parking area. A car pulled up and the driver got out to open the car door.

The driver said, "Did you enjoy your meal, Dr. Schultz?"

· · · · · · · · · · · · ·

Michael had jumped off the restaurant porch and was hiding in the shadow of the building. He suspected the man might follow him and he did not want him to see the car he was headed for. He was right. After the man went back inside, he walked to the car and climbed into the driver's seat.

He said, "I think we may have been spotted. I'll pull around to the area over there so we can see who leaves the building. It's an older man, not in uniform. I personally don't recall having ever seen him, but I was not stationed here. Perhaps you can ID him."

Robert knew to take his brother seriously. Michael drove out of their parking spot and pulled into a spot near the entrance, killed the engine and waited. To Robert's surprise, after a twenty-minute wait, Dr. Schultz walked out of the restaurant.

"I guess Granny was right. There is something going on here and it can't be good. That's the psychiatrist that worked on me in Germany. Twice. He's the guy Jack's been following. In fact, according to Mack, he checked on you during your first day at Harper. I would not be at all surprised if he was involved with our kidnappings. Those two goons that killed Colonel McGregor were sitting near his house in Birmingham, at least according to Jack."

"The two you had to kill, huh?"

Robert just looked at him and said, "Let's not bring up my very necessary deeds. I don't like rehashing them."

Michael did not reply and totally understood.

"Sometimes I can say the dumbest things."

That night in their hotel room the two discuss their options.

Robert said, "In the morning we'll sneak onto the base and steal two uniforms. One needs to be an officer uniform, and the other non-commissioned. Now let's get some sleep."

The next morning Robert woke and found two uniforms at the foot of his bed. Michael was sitting on a chair reading the newspaper.

"Michael, where did these come from? I know you didn't go onto the base without me."

"No. Of course not. That would be foolish. I've never been caught, but if I had, you wouldn't know where to find me. Instead of going back to the fort, I went into town and broke into a couple of cleaners. The second one had uniforms. The officer's uniform is for me, since the other one is too small for me."

"Who are you trying to fool. We're the same size."

Michael laughed and said, "You wish! My chest is bigger than yours."

"No one saw you return here with them, did they?"

"No. I was not followed."

A moment later someone knocked on their room door. Both men froze. Michael got very quiet. Robert became very focused.

He said, "Who is it?" just as the door burst open.

Four uniformed men burst into the room, followed by Dr. Schultz.

Schultz said, "Well, I knew my eyes were not deceiving me. It was you I saw last night. Which one are you, Michael or Robert?"

Michael looked around the room but could not see Robert anymore. Now he was confused.

He thought, *"What the! What happened to him!"*

Then he relaxed and said, "I'm Michael. Who are you guys? What do you want?"

Dr. Schultz said, "That's good enough for now. I knew I saw you last night at the restaurant. So, I had the base on high alert. I even had MPs working in the town, trying to find you. They witnessed you entering two alleys and coming out with clothing. Must have been these two uniforms. I don't know why you picked two, since there is only one of you. So, tell me. Where is your brother?"

He smiled at his question, for he thought he knew the answer.

"Of course he's not here. Only one at a time."

Michael's expression went from confusion to normal.

"You assholes just missed him. He went down for ice."

"Fine. We'll accept that answer. Let's go. Be careful with him. Lock those handcuffs tightly. We don't want anything to happen to him. We can add him to our collection when we get back from India."

Sergeant Jackson said, "Doc, we won't be leaving for another eight days. What do we do with him until then?"

Schultz said, "That's your job. You figure it out. I'm just glad we got Michael and not his brother. You might have had to kill Robert."

The sergeant said, "Are you saying this is not the one who shot up my men?"

"No. This one escaped because I allowed him to escape. It's Robert who's extremely dangerous. We're lucky it was Michael who is dominant now."

Michael believed the doctor was nuts.

"He sounds like that little punk-ass that had me confined for those three weeks. Asking me to produce Robert, like I'd swallowed him or something. I've got to find a way to get out of this. I'm just glad Robert left the room when he did. I'm sure he knows by now what's going on here. And what did he mean they let me escape? Hell, I did that all on my own, didn't I?"

Sergeant Jackson was also confused, but never understood the highest level of detail about this assignment from the start. His men loaded Michael into a Jeep and drove away. Ten minutes later they pull into Fort Polk. The MPs stopped them at the gate and asked about Michael and Dr. Schultz. Dr. Schultz realized that this was a different set of MPs than was here the day before, so he pulled his papers out and handed them to the driver, who displayed them to the MP. They explain that Michael was a prisoner that they caught trying to break into the fort.

The MP said, "He tried to break into the fort? And you didn't notify us? Turn off your engine. I've got to make a call. We have strict orders not to allow any unauthorized personnel on the base. We are on high alert this week. Something about a special task force."

When the driver did not comply, the MP said, "I said, kill that engine, Corporal!"

The sergeant started to have the corporal resist the order, but Dr. Schultz placed his hand on the soldier's shoulder and said, "Relax. It's just a formality. Let the boy do his job."

He looked at the MP and said, "Son, we are that special taskforce. That is why we were watching out for intruders as well."

The MP heard the comment and the 'boy' reference struck a nerve.

"I may only look eighteen, but shit, I turned twenty last week. And I'm standing here with a loaded gun on my hip. Who's he calling 'boy'?!"

Three minutes later the second MP returned and whispered into his partner's ear.

The MP then turned back to the car and said, "Our orders are to detain anyone attempting to break into the fort. Will you please step out of the vehicle and turn him over to us?"

Dr. Schultz was now furious. He had a special containment facility for duals on the base. Only soldiers assigned to him by The Handler were allowed in. These MPs were not a part of their operation and therefore cannot go into the facility.

He said, "Soldier, I have special orders on this base! Please call this number and get this cleared up immediately!"

The second MP wondered, *"This doesn't make any sense. Why would these guys want to detain this guy for trying to break into the fort? These are Rangers. I bet they do work with that strange unit in the back of the base. If this guy gets taken there he may never surface again."*

He whispered into his companion's ear, "Let's get this guy out of there. If they have rights to him, which I doubt, then they can take it up with the general when he returns to the base this morning. He's scheduled to be here at 10:00 a.m."

The first MP smiled, still offended by the 'boy' comment.

He turned back to the Jeep and said, "I'm sorry, Doctor Shitts, but this 'boy' must follow orders from his captain. I suggest you take it up with the commander later this morning. He will arrive at 10:00 a.m. Now you, soldier, step out of the vehicle and hand over the prisoner."

Dr. Schultz began to scream, "WHAT THE FUCK IS WRONG WITH YOU TWO IDIOTS? DO YOU KNOW WHO I AM? GET THE FUCK OUT OF THE W..."

The sergeant glared at the doctor, then said, "We're sorry for any misunderstanding. Of course we'll turn the prisoner over to you. Corporal Brown, please step out of the vehicle and release the prisoner to the MPs."

The soldier behind the driver got out of the car and grabbed Michael by the arm, pulling him from the Jeep. Michael struggled somewhat to step out because his hands were handcuffed behind him. After walking Michael around the car and handing him to the MPs, the corporal climbed back into the back seat of the Jeep.

Sergeant Jackson said, "We will be in touch with the commander once we get back to our offices. Please secure the prisoner at the brig. Try and keep him away from anyone being detained there. I'll bring the orders required to release him to me as soon as we finish speaking to the General. Again, sorry for any confusion."

The second MP called over two additional MPs, who had gathered near the gate, and instructed them to take Michael to the brig. The first MP just smiled.

Thirty minutes later Sergeant Jackson appeared at the brig with orders to release Michael to him. An MP at the front desk called over a second MP and gave him the order. A few minutes later he returned with Michael. The sergeant noticed something was off about the prisoner, but he could not put a finger on it. He thanked the soldier and walked Michael to his Jeep. One of the soldiers in the back seat climbed out. He sat Michael inside and the soldier joined him. Now there was a man on each side of Michael.

They pulled away, drove to the back of the base, then stopped in front of a newly constructed facility.

Michael thought, "*Wow, this is a prison, brick, mortar, and all. Once I'm in there...*"

Jackson jerked Michael out of the Jeep, then noticed what was different. His special cuffs, which he had personally placed in back of Michael, were now in front of him.

"*And where did he get that leather jacket?*"

Before he could call his man over Michael dropped down to the ground, kicked his feet out, knocking the sergeant to the ground. He then hopped back to his feet, and kicked the sergeant in the head, rendering him dazed. The other soldiers ran around the Jeep, but Michael jumped on top of the vehicle, and off the other side. He then ran directly forward, believing they would not shoot at him. They chased him across the large open area, then around several buildings. Michael saw the outer fence and questioned whether he could jump it.

"*Well, there's only one way to find out.*"

He waited for the soldiers to pass his hiding place, then jumped out and ran full speed toward the fence.

Other soldiers saw him and began shouting, "There he is! Get him!"

The fence was 100 feet away, but Michael sprinted directly toward it, knowing there was no way out if he did not clear the fence. As he got closer to the barrier a Jeep drove parallel to the fence, attempting to block his path. That proved to be a big mistake. Just before he reached the fence, the Jeep stopped in front of him. He jumped onto the hood of the Jeep, flung the jacket upward to the top of the electrified fence, then bounded to the top of the twelve-foot barrier, reached up to clasp the top wire, then over the top, leaving the jacket behind.

Now the soldiers were trapped inside the fence. Michael continued to sprint directly away from the fort. Four minutes and a mile later he was out of sight. The Jeeps could not get around to an exit point before he disappeared into the woods.

Michael continued to run, knowing the soldiers would have trouble pursuing him through the woods.

"I've got to get back to Robert. He may try to find me at the fort, but I have to believe he knows that I will escape on my own. If he leaves the hotel, I'll never find him."

Ten minutes later he arrived at a university, stole a car, then drove back to his hotel. Robert was coming out of the room, having waited beyond his tolerance.

He said, "Hey, what's going on? Did I get knocked out or something? Where have you been? And why do you have handcuffs on!? What the heck happened?!"

Michael was somewhat confused why Robert was confused, since he remembered Robert left for ice just before the soldiers arrived.

"Wow. That's the confusion we were discussing during the trip. Well, we can't worry about it now."

Michael said, "Dr. Schultz happened. That's what. Let's get out of here. And get these handcuffs off of me."

Michael was an expert on emergency evacuations, so he knew to just grab his backpack, leave the luggage, hop in the corvette, and hit the road. The two men were gone just minutes before a jeep pulled into the parking lot.

Once they were on the road, Robert said, "Wow, now I remember. I went to get ice and when I returned you were gone. So, I sat on the bed and waited for you. I kind of figured someone had taken you and that you would manage to escape. That's why I stayed here instead of looking for you."

Michael said, "I'm just glad you left the room when you did."

Robert looked at him then said, "Yeah. The ice machine on our floor was down, so I had to go onto another floor."

· · · · · · · · · · · · ·

Sergeant Jackson yelled, "What the fuck just happened? How did you let him clear that fence? Why would you stop in front of a twelve-foot fence? You gave him a platform to clear it! Get into the truck and let's go!"

They drove to an exit but before they could get back to the exit point Michael was nowhere to be seen.

Jackson said, "We'll never find him in these woods. You guys head over to the road. And contact the local police. Tell them we have an escapee and need an APB out on him. Feed them the necessary physical description."

The soldier said, "Sir, I never saw him. What description do I give?"

He yelled, "5'8" 170 pounds! African American! Medium to light brown complexion! Small afro! About twenty-five-years-old! DO YOU WANT ME TO DRAW YOU A PICTURE!"

He drove back to the office to meet with Dr. Schultz, mumbling to himself all the way.

"How do I explain that we let his subject escape? He's going to freak. I thought he was losing his mind at the entrance gate. He should not have insulted that Black M.P.

"Michael was able to escape because he got his cuffs reversed. I had his arms behind his back, yet when he returned, they were in front of him. How he did that I'll never know. And that stolen jacket helped him clear the electric fence. He must have grabbed a rubber mat from the brig and hid it under the jacket. Boy, he planned this whole escape! Probably had it all planned out before we even entered the base."

As expected, when the sergeant explained to Schultz that Michael had escaped, he went ballistic.

The sergeant thought, *"Now I have to deal with The Handler. Well, that will be easier than dealing with this German asshole. Michael wasn't even a part of our plan. We shouldn't be wasting time chasing him. We have a mission and I'm going to stick to it. We have to be in the air in seven days. Fuck Schultz and his Michael."*

.   .   .   .

After dark the twins drove back to the fort. Robert could see what Michael was referring to about the entry gate or any side entrance. MPs were patrolling all along the perimeter, especially upon hearing of Michael's escape. He now knew it would be extremely hard to breach the front or sides of the fort.

Michael said, "Those MPs were really sharp. We have a better chance going through the back way, since they are not allowed back there."

To his delight, He was right. As he expected, Special Forces were not as adept at security as the MPs are and no one took the jacket off the fence. The rubber mat was still insolating the electric current. Michael hoisted Robert up to the Jacket, then jumped up, grabbed the jacket, and flipped over effortlessly. They were able to move about in the shadows of the building until they came across a crew loading an airplane. They walked inside the containment area and hid. Minutes later two pilots emerge, discussing their flight plans.

Robert thought, *"Jackpot! This is definitely the plane heading for India. All we need to do is get on board."*

Before Robert could say anything to Michael, he heard a crash and saw crates falling nearby. The loading crew rushed inside to find several crates laying on their sides. They picked up the crates then returned to load the remaining supplies, then closed the cargo hatch. Robert just smiled at his brother as they hid behind loaded crates.

One hour later the plane began taxiing for takeoff. No one knew the plane had 175 pounds of extra cargo aboard. No one except Dr.

Schultz, who witnessed the twins climbing the fence. It was under his instructions that the jacket was left on the fence.

Twenty-four hours later, they landed in India.

CHAPTER SEVENTEEN

Dr. Patel

Dr. Sekar Patel was born in Madras India in 1929. His family lived in a neighborhood not far from The University of Madras, having settled near the university over six generations ago. Sekar dreamed of attending the school, an idea that was viewed with humor among his family and friends. For Sekar to think he would escape his destiny was frustrating to his father, who wanted his son to get his head out of the clouds and focus on his metallurgy studies, like his other two sons had. Like his father and uncles had. Sekar would then be able to bring home a fourth family income, creating jewelry for the local jewelry stores. Just as all of the men in the Patel family had for the past six generations.

When he was twelve years old, a professor at the university found him staring into the gates of the school and asked him what he was daydreaming about. Sekar was about to run off, but instead he boldly said in Tamil, with a heavy Gujarati accent, "One day I will teach in this school."

The professor's associates began to laugh.

One of the associates said, "Well little man, first you must learn to speak proper Tamil!", laughed some more, then walked away.

The professor, however, found nothing humorous about the little boy's dreams. He had once lived in a shanty town near the university over fifty years ago. A British professor found him standing in the same location and took him under his wing. Now it was time for the professor to pay it forward.

Ten years later, at the young age of twenty-two, Sekar Patel became Dr. Sekar Patel, associate professor of psychiatry at the University of Madras. It was 1951. He was viewed as a savant in the field of psychiatry. He was assigned a task of traveling the country to study the new nation's shaman and report back on the various methods used throughout the country. The shaman of India were held in high esteem until the British arrived. They were still highly regarded among the masses, but only regarded as charlatans by the English-educated doctorate of India.

After spending ten years studying the methods used by shaman, the head of the university's psychiatry department became concerned for his savant. His reports slowly became less critical and more favorable of shaman's methods. The other deans of the university also feared Dr. Patel was becoming indoctrinated by the shamans. So, it was decided that he needed to begin studying in the West and was transferred to Cambridge, in England. They were hoping to clear his mind of the influences of the Sramana. He worked and studied under the western Freudian method for the next decade. It was while working with the British in London that he was loaned to the US Army and stationed in West Germany. Six months into his stay in West Germany, he met Robert McCants. His life soon began to unravel.

January 1972

Dr. Patel made an appointment with the head of the Cambridge Department of Psychiatry. He entered his office and was met with a very warm greeting.

"Dr. Sekar Patel. It is so nice to have you back from Germany. I hope you were of good use to the Americans and helped them with their special projects."

The dean's smile slowly dissipated as Patel explained his future plans.

"Sir, I am very grateful for the opportunity to have worked under you and your excellent guidance these past ten years. However, after working in Germany I have decided to return home to my beloved India."

He decided not to explain his reasoning. He did not want it to appear that a nineteen-year-old man-child from America had impacted him such that he would forsake further experience in the West.

The dean attempted to persuade Patel for over an hour. Once it was obvious that Patel had made up his mind to return home, they both said their goodbyes and Patel returned to Madras. However, he did not go back to his old university. Instead, he headed to Sundarbans Park, seeking out his monk. He wanted an explanation for what he witnessed in Germany, or he would never be able to return to western psychiatry. It took him months before he finally found his guru. He settled down with him and threw himself into his studies.

However, after four years of living a spartan life, and with his savings depleted, he knew it was time to move back to civilization. He decided, however, not to return to Madras, not wanting to appear as a failure. Instead, he moved to Madurai, seeking employment at Madurai Kamaraj University.

It was while working at the university that Patel discovered he was the target of a US government search, and he suspected he knew why. He had heard of abductions of Duals by the US government while studying under his Sramana. Once he heard that Dr. Schultz was among the men seeking him out, he knew they must be looking for him because they had issues with the lieutenant. So, he fled his home and never went back, fearful of being caught. Instead, he headed back to the Sundarbans.

. . . .

The flight was long, boring, and exhausting. The ride was also rough at times. Both Michael and Robert had trouble getting comfortable, even though the plane had knapsacks for the troopers which they took advantage of.

Not long after the plane was in flight from Louisiana, Robert began to ask Michael some tough questions.

"Michael, what happened back there at the fort. I remember talking to you then I found myself outside of the room getting ice cubes. Then I was back in the room as you walked in. But the timeline is wacked!"

"Yeah. I kind of know what you mean. One minute we were talking, then the storm troopers crashed in, then I remembered that you had left to get ice. Funny thing though. We didn't need ice. I'm just glad you left when you did. It made it easier for me to escape. I didn't have to drag your slow ass along with me."

Robert contemplated how they managed to board the plane. He did not believe they were able to get back into the fort so easily.

"No way they left that jacket on the fence. It would not have been easy to remove it, considering the fence is twelve feet high and they would have to cut the power before removing it. Perhaps they figured no one would be foolish enough to try to enter again. However, I have no doubt someone wanted us to sneak back in. At least Dr. Schultz would."

As he thought about how easy their re-entry was, he began to inspect the cargo. What he found was alarming.

He walked back to Michael and said, "They have restraints for a dozen people. Enough automatic weapons for a platoon and enough rations for two months. Medicine, flea and mosquito spray, spare foot gear. The type of gear one needs in a tropical terrain. Like what we used in Vietnam. The camouflage gear is tropical as well. They wouldn't need this type of gear in India, unless they are not going to urban India. But Dr. Patel would be working from a university, so why would they need jungle stuff?"

Michael said the obvious. "Your doctor is no longer in urban India. He must be hiding in a tropical area. I suspect they know exactly where to find him. Too bad they don't have any of their plans on this plane. We either have to find him first, wait until they arrive and steal their plans from them, or follow them to him."

Robert said, "It'll have to be option one. We cannot afford to try to handle a platoon of Rangers. I've been through that training. Those guys train daily, every day of the year. Now they have a week to focus on this mission and the right training environment at Tiger-land."

Michael said, "I don't think they're in Tiger-land anymore. I heard the pilot mention flying to Mangrove Forest in Florida for a final week of training."

Michael sat motionless for a while, reading Robert's thoughts, then said, "You really shined at this facility didn't you."

Robert just glanced at him and said, "What have I not shined at? Let's get some more sleep. I believe we're going to need it."

That night Michael decided to sneak up closer to the pilots to find out if they knew anything about the mission. He could only hear minor details through the cockpit door, but the name Dr. Schultz and Dr. Patel kept coming up. It became obvious to Michael that Dr. Schultz's only mission was to find Dr. Patel. As he was moving back to the rear of the plane, he noticed a folder labeled TOP SECRET and could not resist opening it. It was sealed and he knew he would have to be extremely careful to break the seal and later repair it. Then a realization dawned on him, and he ripped the seal open.

"With all this thrashing of the cargo, they can't expect this folder to remain undamaged. Besides, their mission is a go, whether or not someone discovers its so-called secret."

What he read had to be from a science fiction novel.

After he read the entire manual he took the folder back to Robert. He needed Robert to explain quite a bit of it to him. He did not know what the reference to 'Dual Persons' meant, but it was beginning to bother him.

"Why were these guys so interested in Robert and me?"

He found his twin sleeping so he woke him up. Robert responded as if he was enjoying a dream and did not want to be disturbed.

"Come on. Wake up little brother. I think you'd better read this before we land."

Thirty minutes later Robert's focus was on again. Michael could sense something was terribly wrong.

Robert said, "We don't have much time. We've got to find Dr. Patel. His life and many others may be in the balance. For whatever reason, our grandma wanted us to save these Duals, and we're going to do just that."

• • • • • • • • • • • • •

February 1979

Six months after the bridge incident

Six months before the flight to India

Commander Cavaletti continued to ponder the recent murders in the city since he had gotten involved with the McCants family. Like most cities, Detroit had its share of domestic and drug violence. Petty crimes of home invasion, domestic violence, robberies, and car theft. Drug murders and occasionally a mob hit. He, however, did not recall the last time there were so many murders over a large geographic area that appear to be linked together. He summoned the captains of all the precincts to a meeting. They were given the impression that the meeting was merely an individual review of their quarterly reports. None of the men expected to find the others present when they arrived.

The 10th precinct captain walked into the headquarters at 1300 Beaubien and noticed the captain of the 12th precinct.

He approached him and said, "Hello, William. Didn't expect to see you here. I've got a meeting with Peter. Who are you here to see?"

William did not care for Ralph Baker, the 10th precinct captain. He believed he ran a loose ship, trying to fit in with the BMOC Sumanski.

He smiled at Ralph and said, "I'm meeting with Peter as well. My meeting is scheduled for 9:00 a.m. What time is your meeting?"

Ralph looked surprised, then noticed the captains of the other precincts beginning to arrive. It was 8:50 a.m.

He said, "I was given the impression this was a personal meeting. I wonder what's really up."

William continued to smile and said, "I guess we'll find out soon enough," and walked over to greet the other captains.

At 9:00 a.m. Cavaletti walked to the back of the conference room and closed the door. He had already instructed the secretary that only the mayor or the chief of police were allowed to enter the room.

He began by saying, "Gentlemen, I'm glad to see all of you. And on time too."

The men merely chuckled. All except Ralph, who was feeling somewhat uncomfortable. He knew he was the only captain present who had a lieutenant under investigation.

Cavaletti continued, "Guys, we have an anomaly occurring here in the city. In fact, it goes beyond our borders. There have been an unusual number of crimes recently that I believe are related. A visitor from out of town is murdered in his hotel room. The weapon had a silencer on it. Two men are found dead in Birmingham. One of the two was armed with an automatic and silencer. Both were killed with the same gun as our hotel guest. A young man being held at Harper Hospital was killed in his hospital bed. We later found out he was hired to kill two teenagers. Did you hear what I just said? The young man, who was from out of town, was hired to kill someone in our city.

"A car was forced off the road on the Lodge and the two occupants died in the crash and subsequent fire. We found a shotgun in the car that had been recently fired. We still don't know their identities."

· · · · · · · · · · · · ·

Richard and Louis were driving home on northbound Lodge Freeway after visiting their brothers at Receiving and Harper Hospital. It was a traumatic evening for the entire family. They were still upset that someone would attack their younger brothers and wished they could have been there to help.

Richard said, "I guess we can no longer call them the 'little-kids'. Especially since they are so much bigger than the 'big-kids', from

Mack on down to you. And today proves they are true McCants warriors. Do you think this was their first true rumble?"

"Probably. And they've been grown since that night they went after Busta's cars back in '70."

Richard gave Louis a curious look but did not ask him to explain. He remembered the two of them loosening hubcaps on Busta's men's cars. The drivers of those cars spent some time in the hospital after the cars crashed. He also heard about Mack's assault on Busta's men two nights later. He knew nothing, however, about the 'little-kids' involvement with Busta.

Suddenly a car pulled up next to them and the passenger in the car shoved a sawed-off double-barrel shotgun out of the window and opened fire. Richard reacted quickly by slamming on his brakes, causing the shooter to miss striking the car. He then swerved hard to his left, striking the rear right corner bumper of the car. The car spun clockwise, passed in front of his car, then hit a stalled car under the Linwood Ave bridge abutment, and burst into flames. Both the driver and the shooter were trapped inside. Fortunately, the owner of the car had already walked away to get fuel.

Richard slowed down for the briefest of moments, then floored his accelerator. He drove all the way to the Meyers exit, bypassing his usual exit at Livernois, just in case they were being followed. They were going to visit their parents one last time before calling it a night.

Louis, still gripping the passenger door handle, could only say, "Wow! What was that all about!"

After a short visit with their parents, Louis retrieved his car and they both drove home to their respective families.

Both men slept well that night, knowing their younger brothers would be safe from harm. Neither man experienced any remorse from their involvement with the crashed car.

. . . .

Cavaletti continued, "Last year a young man was kidnapped from Harper Hospital. A man who was hospitalized after being shot by one of ours! He was kidnapped from right under our noses, since we once had him under guard. Worse yet, we arrested the kidnapped victim after he had escaped his kidnappers and was debriefed by the FBI! I've found out later there was a hit out on him in the prison. Fortunately, his family found protection for him within the prison. And it turns out we arrested the wrong man. I know his arrest was intended to get him killed while in lockup, because he was not even fingerprinted! Just thrown into a cell.

"I believe all of these crimes and mishaps are connected somehow. Even the assault in western Michigan last October. They found eight bodies on the scene. The home was severely damaged, but we don't know who was staying there at the time, nor if anyone was injured. Then that investigation was suddenly shut down by the attorney general of Michigan."

There was a light murmur emitted by the men. None of them knew about the killings in Idlewild.

"I want to find the strings that tie all of these incidents together. That is your charter. You are to work your precincts, doing the leg work yourselves. I don't want any of this assignment to get outside of this room. No one is to know about my suspicions. Do I make myself clear? You are not to share this discussion with anyone on your staff. Just gather whatever data you have and report back here in three days. Nine o'clock sharp. Any questions?"

The room suddenly became very quiet. Only the sounds from the exterior of the door could be heard. Then William spoke up.

"Sir, I completely understand and will be prepared to report back here at 9:00 a.m. Thursday morning."

The commander then said, "If there is nothing else then you are dismissed. And one more thing. Do not share your data with each other either. I'm the only Dick Tracy here for the time being. So, let's get to work."

Once the conference room was clear the commander got up from his chair and walked through the headquarters. He went into his office and changed into a business suit. Then he walked over to Michigan Avenue, then up Michigan to Cass Avenue, entering the building on the south side of Michigan, west of Cass. He entered a coffee shop in the lobby of the building and met with two men. The same two FBI agents that questioned Dr. Schultz last September about the McCants kidnapping. The three men sat down and discussed their mornings. They, however, were only interested in the commander's morning.

Special agent Hamilton said, "Are your guys going to cooperate?"

Cavaletti said, "Cooperate? They have no choice. We have the evidence. Now we need to see who attempts to hide any. I plan to get to the bottom of these crimes and to get rid of any involvement my police force has in it.

"The ledgers that were found at the 12th precinct indicating Sumanski's payoffs also had top cop's names on it. And some politicians as well. I will focus on Detroit. I need you to focus on any national connections, no matter how high up it goes or who tries to tie your hands. Something stinks fellows. Let's find out what. There may not be a connection to all of these incidents, but we won't know unless we look further into them."

Cavaletti concluded, "We cannot meet like this again anytime soon. I suspect the problems we have here in Detroit are just the tip of the iceberg. The fact that you were told to drop your investigation into Dr. Schultz means that someone extremely high up is pulling strings. If I'm right, then none of us are safe if word gets out of what we're doing. Understood?"

Special agent Stewart nodded to his partner, then both agents got up and walked out of the shop.

Cavaletti waited until the two men left the shop. Then he headed back out to Michigan Avenue.

He thought, "*The FBI trains their agents well. But they also rely on a high level of patriotism. Good versus evil shit. So, they leave their training as naive as when they start. But I know better. Years in Army Intelligence taught me there is no such thing as good versus evil. Sometimes, rarely, there is just plain evil. And it can exist just about anywhere. Especially in our beloved government agencies.*"

· · · · · · · · · · · · ·

The young enlistee was most impressive to his trainers. His test scores were near the top of the class. He had a four-year degree from a top American university as well as having played football for four years on scholarship. He was definitely Intelligence material, so his trainers recommended him for a position within Army Intelligence, and he was immediately transferred to Washington.

Twelve years later he resigned his position so he could settle down and raise his family away from the political machinery of D.C. He interviewed at the Detroit Police Department and was hired as a police captain at the police headquarters, reporting directly to a commander. He moved his family back to Detroit, his hometown, and settled on the northeast side of the city. When his commander retired five years later, he was promoted, over men with more seniority, to the commander position, reporting directly to the Chief of Police.

Cavaletti was now in a position to launch a secret investigation that he believed could be national, and perhaps reach the highest levels of the American government. He was certain the CIA was involved but did not know to what level. His background, however, made him aware just how great the risk may be. His life, and perhaps the lives of the special agents, depended on total secrecy.

.   .   .   .

There was a long layover in Germany. Michael wanted to get off the plane to get some proper food, but Robert dissuaded him.

He said, "Hell, man, you ate that restaurant food last night and had breakfast this morning before we went into the fort. You can fast until we arrive in India, I'm sure. Then you can have all the mangos you can find," and laughed.

Fortunately, no one felt the need to reinspect the cargo.

The plane landed in India eight hours after leaving Germany. Both brothers had fallen asleep and were not prepared to disembark the plane.

Michael aroused first then woke Robert and said, "It's time to vamoose little brother. This plane will be pulling up to some loading dock any moment now."

What they did not know was the plane had landed in a clearing area, at night, in the middle of a tropical forest.

Both twins grabbed their gear, which they had pilfered from the cargo, and peered out of the small window in the back of the plane, waiting for the right moment to jump out.

Michael said, "Shit. It's dark as hell out there. I forgot about the 6 hours backward we would be going."

Robert said, "It's nine and a half hours forward, not backward. It's probably past midnight. We left Germany before noon. And the landing was rough, suggesting we landed on grass, not pavement."

Just as the plane came to rest Michael said, "Okay Mr. Smartypants. Let's go."

He jumped from the door and stood ready to close it again. Robert, however, hesitated for a moment then ran back to the cargo area, to the surprise and frustration of Michael. He returned two minutes later, stepped out of the door, then ran into the brush. Michael closed the door and followed him.

Once they were certain they were clear of any observing eyes Michael started to ask him why he lingered, then realized he already knew. The reason was recorded in Robert's mind.

Michael just smiled at him and said, "Okay, little brother, let's find your Dr. Patel. Since you like being the point man, lead the way."

CHAPTER EIGHTEEN

Sundarbans Park

Mangrove - a tropical tree that has roots which grow from its branches and that grows in swamps or shallow salt water.

Webster

The Sundarbans is a forest area in the eastern region of India and the newly independent nation of Bangladesh's western border. It has mangrove trees along the ocean edge. The forest is home to a variety of birds, monkeys, saltwater crocodiles, dolphins, and a large variety of reptiles and various aquatic animals. The Indian government has recently proclaimed the area a protected park, patrolled by park rangers. Penalties for poaching are extreme.

It is also the home of the Bengal tiger, known in this part of the world as a man-eater.

. . . .

Robert and Michael spent the next two days walking through the forest. After the first six hours Robert had become tired of Michael's complaining.

"Man, its freaking hot out here. I can't believe your Dr. Patel lives in this god-forsaken place. He must at least be in a village nearby. So why did that plane land next door to a jungle?! That last mosquito was large enough to airlift me away!"

Eventually they come upon a paper wrapper from a military rations package.

Robert thought, *"I knew it. Just as I thought. We've been walking in circles. We can't get our bearings because we have no focal point. We're spinning like a top, going around and around. And Michael is a litterbug. We need a guide, or we will never find Dr. Patel. Hell, the only reason we're looking in this god-forsaken place is because the stupid plane landed here. I think we possibly would have been better off using option two."*

Michael looked at Robert and said, "I think you're right little brother. Only it wouldn't hurt for you to speak aloud. It's just the two of us, and I've realized we were lost yesterday. And I believe you dropped that particular wrapper."

He thought, *"Dummy. I guess I could have gotten a compass from the plane. Not that it would have done any good. We don't even know what direction to move in."*

The constant chatter of the monkeys was becoming nerve racking. The tiny flying insects buzzing around them was very aggravating. Especially the mosquitoes. Walking in knee-deep water, then thickets, and seeing crocodiles, and having to sleep in the trees, was driving Michael insane.

"Hey, Grandma, why did you sign me up for this?"

Robert, however, did not seem to mind.

An hour after they realized they were walking in a circle the chatter of the monkeys began to grow. It became louder and louder.

Then it stopped. No sounds from the trees at all. Not even the birds were chirping.

Robert suddenly halted and said, "Michael. Stop. Something's wrong."

He began to focus on the vegetation straight ahead.

Suddenly Michael was unable to read his brother.

"Shit, he's gone inside himself again. I guess he doesn't want me to cheat and grab his thoughts."

Robert was not concerned with Michael reading him. He was too busy looking as far as the human eye could see, considering the vegetation coverage. What he did see alarmed him. Two pairs of eyes looking directly back at him through the dense trees. Nothing else. Just two sets of eyes. Not just any set of eyes either. Two pairs of feline eyes, 100 meters directly ahead. Michael could only see the thick tree coverage, not between each individual trunk.

Before Robert could warn him, two twin 600-pound Bengal tigers came bounding toward them. Robert no longer needed to warn Michael. He was already climbing the nearest tree.

As Michael reached for yet another branch, he suddenly realized that Robert was not following him. It occurred to him that Robert could not climb as quickly as he was able to, so he looked back and was completely startled at what he saw. Robert was frozen in his spot! His arms were in front of him, palms open, fingers pointed upward, as one does when under attack from a big yard dog. They had faced off with big dogs many times before. Only this was no Doberman. That would explain why Robert had wet his pants.

Michael yelled out, "Bro, get out of there! Hit the trees! Move, Robert, move!"

Robert, however, was unable to move. He could not move because he was experiencing a new emotion. One he had never imagined, and until now, could never comprehend. For the first time in his life he felt fear. Fear and terror! Utter terror!

"Oh. My. God. I can't move! I am feeling a totally new sensation. I am utterly afraid, like I've never been before!"

One of the tigers rushed forward then stopped fifteen meters in front of him. Then it quickly moved to within eight meters of him, stopped, and began smelling the air. He sensed danger ahead, then saw Michael in the tree. He bared his fangs for the whole world to see, and Michael did not miss the show. Then he emitted the mightiest of roars, causing the fabric of Robert's clothing to shiver. The second tiger stepped forward, slowly ascertaining the environment. He could see Robert in front of him and also Michael in the tree. He sensed their fear, which he interpreted as a potential meal. The alpha tiger took a menacing step toward Robert, closing the gap from eight meters to four meters, while the second tiger took over his position eight meters away. It never took its eyes off of Michael.

"They're measuring the distance it will take to leap upon me. I've got to move!"

Instead of backing away, however, he remained frozen in his spot. His bladder was now nearly empty. He suddenly realized that he could die. He had faced off with dozens of enemy soldiers and never felt the anguish he was now experiencing.

He closed his eyes preparing for the attack, then suddenly, slowly, the anguish began to dissipate. Before he realized it he began to feel the cats! To sense the cats! Both cats. So, he did what only Robert could do. He began to focus on his adversaries. He knew he had to focus harder than he had ever focused before. He gradually began having a feeling of tranquility. As if the cats meant him no harm. A new relationship was beginning to form. He pushed his focal point directly toward the cats' minds. The cats' menacing glare began to change. The lead cat took a second step toward Robert. Only that step was not a menacing step. More of a curious, relaxed step. Robert pushed his focal point further into this cat's mind. The cat relaxed even more and took yet another step forward. Now it stood a mere two meters away. He could feel the beast's breath on his soaked pants.

Michael stood on a branch ten meters up, in utter terror for his beloved brother. He began to wave his arms and yell at the beast, but the tiger was no longer interested in him. Only the person directly ahead.

Michael was unable to read his twin, so he did not realize his brother was no longer afraid.

Robert pulled his left arm back to his side and extended his right arm toward the tiger, palm still out, but with his fingers now reversed downward, his right elbow locked. The tiger took two more steps forward, licked his mouth with his tremendous tongue, then emitted the most beautiful sound Robert had ever heard. The giant male cat chuffed.

· · · · · · · · · · · ·

The night of the landing

The pilots had begun unloading the cargo from the plane. They wanted to be back in the air before daybreak. They did not mind flying at night, but they did not like landing or taking off in the dark. Their liftoff point was more uncertain when they could not see the tree line. Yet they could not afford to be seen. Otherwise, the hidden cargo could be pilfered.

Bob, the lead pilot said, "I don't know what these guys want here. This is tiger land. And I don't mean the one at the freakin fort either. These are real beasts. They've got man-eaters here. We should have had some locals to meet us here so they could watch our backs."

Dick, the co-pilot, said, "Yeah. And help us with the unload? Like they won't see what are cargo is, and report our presence to the park rangers? Not a good idea.

"I noticed the cargo door signal light came on as soon as we landed and stayed on for about two minutes. It was probably that rough landing of yours."

About fifteen minutes into the unloading, Bob noticed that some of the cargo had been opened. He initially assumed that the rough ride caused the crates to burst open. Only the breakage was not random but controlled. Like the wood was pulled out, not broken out.

"If I didn't know any better, I'd swear we had company during the flight. I thought I heard noises back here. That could explain the cargo door light you saw."

Dick thought, *"What's the matter now? Why did they make him the lead pilot? He's always imagining things."*

Bob said, "When we get back, I'm going to report my suspicions. After all, there was an attempted break-in at the fort just days ago."

. . . .

Michael was still frightened, but also astonished.

"Did that big-ass cat just purr at you?"

Without turning his head, Robert smiled and said, "It's called a chuff or prusten. Big cats don't purr. They can't due to a buildup of cartilage…"

Michael cut him off and said, "I don't give a fuck what it's called! I'm calling it a freakin purr! Did it not just purr at you?!"

"Yes. He's beginning to relax. Please be still for the next few moments. And lower your voice. Don't distract me. I'm trying to communicate with him. And I need to keep my focus on his brother as well."

The two cats continued to occasionally glance at Michael in the tree, but only looked up briefly. They wanted to keep their eyes on Robert. The second cat walked closer, then the lead cat took two final steps toward Robert, then rubbed his head against Robert's extended hand. This brought his brother all the way in. Both cats nuzzled each other as they took turns licking Robert's hand. Robert could suddenly feel the love coming from the animals. As a child he had never gotten close to the family pets. Now he was regretting not relating to the dogs.

"This is what the little-kids were experiencing with Prince and Klaw? This was why they liked hugging those dumb German Shepherds."

Robert crouched down, tears flowing down his face, reached out to the lead cat as the animal moved in, and hugged the huge beast. The other cat came upon his open side, wanting to be hugged as well. The cats' eyes closed, their haunches dropped to the ground, and both of them took turns lightly licking Robert's tears away.

Robert now knew instinctively that the three of them were bonded for life.

Finally, Robert said, "Okay, big brother. You can come down now. We have new friends. Only don't make any sudden movements. Not just yet. They both love me, but I don't know how they feel about you," and smiled up at Michael.

Michael realized that Robert was no longer focused as before. However, he was still unable to read him.

He said, "I didn't know you could deliberately block me. I don't know if I like that. I've always relied on it."

"I'm not blocking you; I'm just tied to our new friends. And yeah, now you know how I feel. I've never intruded on your thoughts. Anyway, I don't know what's going on between our four-legged friends and me, but please come down."

Michael slowly descended from the tree. He could now smell the bengals. One of the tigers glanced over toward him but did not approach him. It just continued to be caressed by his new friend. Robert was now down on one knee. He stroked the long back of the felines.

Finally, the lead tiger stood, turned around and took a few steps back toward the dense coverage he had emerged from. His brother followed. When Robert did not move, the first cat stopped, walked back toward him, grabbed his left sleeve in its mouth, then gently pulled Robert toward him, then released him. He then turned back around and slowly walked toward the coverage. Both tigers disappeared into the foliage. Robert finally stood up and followed them. Michael, not knowing what to do, followed Robert.

"I can't believe we finally get a guide and it's freakin man-eaters!"

The four of them soon entered a dense leaf coverage, attached to dozens of vines. They had to move the vines as they proceeded forward. The men had a tough time making progress because they had to bend over frequently. Michael began to raise his machete, but Robert advised against it. The tigers just weaved through the coverage, like nothing was there. After an hour of walking in the confining terrain, having covered only a kilometer, they came to a small clearing. Now they knew why they thought they heard voices minutes earlier.

Directly ahead of them stood several men and more tigers, surrounded by huts with thatched roofs. All of the men were looking towards Robert and his brother as they burst out of the thicket. Some of the men appeared to have their own personal four-legged companion. Except one older man whom Robert recognized immediately. He was Dr. Sekar Patel.

· · · · · · · · · · · · ·

On the return trip back to the States, the plane landed at an American base in Geilenkirchen, Germany, near the border with Netherlands. Bob, the pilot, instructed Dick to handle the plane's refueling, while he entered the base. He placed a call to Fort Polk and asked for The Handler, who he knew had arrived at the fort after word that there was an intruder.

After the phone was answered he said, "Sir, I believe we had passengers on the plane, at least from Germany and possibly from Fort Polk. The cargo was disturbed, and I don't believe it was by accident. We had noticed the cargo warning light on but dismissed it due to the rough landing."

The Handler said, "Thank you for the call," and hung up.

Bob, having worked with The Handler before, was not surprised at the abrupt ending to the call. It was still, however, somewhat unnerving.

The Handler thought, *"This is perfect. I was wondering how we would get those two into India. We can now capture them and the others during the same trip. We just have to be very careful with the Robert twin. I don't want him killed. That is, if he doesn't get eaten first by a tiger."*

He made two phone calls, first contacting his command sergeant, then Dr. Schultz, waking both men from a sound sleep.

He said to the sergeant, "Our extra cargo made the trip on their own. Let's move up the launch date."

Before he could hang up the phone the sergeant said, "No. We will not move up the launch. We have concrete training plans, and they must be completed. There are too many new personnel here due to the losses we've sustained recently. This is not negotiable," and hung up the phone.

The Handler was not surprised at the sergeant's push-back. That is why he liked using him. He was very precise with all of his assignments, something he respected and admired.

He then called Dr. Schultz and said, "You have bungled this assignment, as usual. But luck was on our side. The McCants are in India," and hung up the phone.

Dr. Schultz hatred for his handler was steadily increasing.

"How dare he speak to me this way. I have given his organization excellent work all of these years. It was his ineptness that had Michael kidnapped from the fucking hospital, not mind. And I don't know why in the fuck he tried to kidnap Robert. He knew how dangerous Robert could be. It was my initiative that helped the boys get back into the fort. He's a moron and I cannot wait to be rid of him. I have never killed anyone, but if I get the chance, he'll be the first."

His bravado existed because he did not know his handler was inside the fort complex with him.

. . . .

Cavaletti gathered the reports from his captains. Most of them had nothing to report. Those with reports were summoned individually.

The captain of the 12th precinct, located on Woodward and 7-Mile Road, reported a car accident on northbound M-10 where two men were trapped in a burning car. Witnesses said the men had just fired on a sedan, then lost control of their car and slammed into an unattended car near the bridge at Linwood Avenue. Upon impact the car burst into flames. No one could describe the victim's vehicle, since it immediately left the scene. When asked why he listed this incident he replied, "No particular reason. It just happened the same day those young boys were attacked at the supermarket. That occurred in Ralph's 10th precinct, but it may be related. I'll exclude it if I cannot tie the two incidents together."

The Southwest Precinct captain sited a report of automatic gunfire not far from Zug Island. The employees in the area stated the gunfire lasted for several minutes. Later they reported seeing multiple white vans enter the area soon afterward but left before the police arrived. This occurred the following morning after that U of M professor, Dr. McCants, was released from Wayne County Lockup.

The captain said, "You know the case where they arrested the wrong twin. That very night a shootout occurred in the very area his brother, Michael McCants, said his abductors had held him hostage. I know it's not conclusive, but you said anything that might relate to the collection of incidents we've had lately."

The captain of police headquarters reported he had communicated with the State Police about the shootings in Idlewild.

"Everything is hush hush about that night. And the Attorney General has squashed the investigation. Said it was a federal matter."

The captain of the 13th Precinct had very little to report about the Michael McCants' abduction. The lone security guard only stated that men in suits had McCants and when he attempted to stop them, he was assaulted. No one else reported seeing the abduction. The captain further stated that he personally did not believe it unfolded quite that way, but it really does not matter. The abduction still occurred.

Finally, when Baker arrived, he reported, "We heard there was a teenage rumble at the Farmer Jack supermarket. When we arrived, we detained the ten men who were responsible for the attack and called for ambulances for them and the three McCants teens."

Cavaletti said, "Ralph, that's historical. I want to know how you tied the incident itself to the other incidents."

Ralph had nothing more to report, even though the McCants live in his precinct.

Cavaletti said, "Nothing about a car crashing into a telephone pole two blocks from the McCants' home? Or one of your prisoners from the rumble getting killed in the hospital?"

Cavaletti knew all of the details of the supermarket attack and knew it was no rumble. He knew Captain Baker, a personal friend of Sumanski, was lying about the ambulances. The ambulances had been called before the police had left the station, like the police knew they would be needed. The fact that the McCants' boys drove themselves to the hospital seemed to be excluded from his report. Most of the attackers of the McCants were teenagers, not men. Most of the cops hanging out in Sumanski's driveway were known to be Baker's friends. Cavaletti also knew Baker was complicit in the payoffs involving Sumanski's case. His name was on the bribery list, he just didn't know it. No one except Sumanski had been approached by Internal Affairs by Cavaletti's orders.

Later that day Cavaletti met with the Special Agents Hamilton and Stewart. Only this time they met in the garage under Kennedy Square. He worried that they would not know how to investigate crimes that they were told were not in their jurisdiction. When they had nothing to report he knew he was correct. There was no reason for him to continue to meet with them. If they persist then they could be killed, like McGregor. No one kills a retired Army Colonel in a public place unless they are serious players with plenty to hide. He would have to go it alone, using his Army Intelligence contacts. He just had to be extremely careful.

Before he drove home he stopped by the McCants house on Santa Rosa, even though it was on the opposite side of town from his home. He wanted to see how the three sons were doing and if they were having any more problems with the street thugs. At least that's what he told himself.

Martha greeted him on the porch.

"Hello officer, I mean, Commander. Everything's fine."

"This Sicilian cop does not know about my meeting with Castanza. I don't need him to know I pulled a gun on that ass-hole lawyer. I'd better keep it that way."

"I'd invite you in, but my husband Frank isn't home. He's visiting his brother in Pontiac. And the boys are also visiting friends."

Cavaletti understood. Most men of his generation were like that.

"I guess I'm the same way. No men in the house if the man-of-the-house is not home."

The two talked for a few minutes. She assured him that everything had gotten better since Michael was safe. She let him know that Michael was living with his twin in Ann Arbor and there had been no new threats against her teens. He then checked his watch and realized he was late for home. So, he told her again, for the tenth time, that if she ever had a problem, she had his number. He gave her a warm smile, then walked to his vehicle and drove away, heading north to 8-mile, then eastward home.

The female neighbors on both sides of the street gave a collective "un-huh!"

After the long day Cavaletti arrived home in time for dinner. It had been a while since he had spent any time with Judith and their son, so that night, they enjoyed a movie on his new VCR player and consumed plenty of pop and popcorn. Then, after the house was settled, he made love to her. Possibly for the first time in weeks. They held each other for a short while, rolled over, and fell asleep, their backs compressed against one another.

He entered RIM and dreamed of the loving moment and that he was making love to his lover again. Then he whispered his lover's name.

She, however, laid awake reminiscing about the moment. She appreciated his attentiveness. Then, as her eyes began to close, he spoke his lover's name. She opened her eyes and thought, "Who's Martha?"

CHAPTER NINETEEN

In Search of Patel

The men in the compound surround Dr. Patel as Robert and Michael approached him. Robert could not help but notice that all of the men with beast had a twin standing near them. Two identical men, dressed slightly different, with one four-legged companion. He understood that the men do not know him, so he initially must be cautious. He instinctively placed his hand on one of his tigers.

Dr. Patel recognized Robert immediately. He said, "Kadavule! Oh, my god! Lieutenant McCants! Kadavule! It is true. They are searching for me. Are you working with them? How did you find me?"

"Hello Dr. Patel! You remember me? And no, I am not working with anyone. I have been told by my great-grandmother to find you. She believes you are in great danger. That is why my brother and I are here."

Robert looked directly at Michael. That simple glance made Patel's brain explode with exuberance. The doctor finally realized why

Robert was so confounding to him! Why he was forced to quit his profession after twenty years of Freuden work. The confusion without an explanation suddenly became crystal clear to him! He was dealing with a Dual! A man who had special Dual talent. Superpowers that other beings don't possess. In Robert's case, he had an extraordinary ability to focus!

Dr. Patel could not control his excitement. He started jumping up and down and spinning around on his heels. The men just looked at him in amazement.

He finally settled down and said, "That's it! You are a Dual! Kadavule! Robert, I cannot see your brother, but believe me when I say that I know he is there next to you! We must talk. You said your grandmama sent you? How strange. Robert, all of these men are Duals. Like you they have a twin."

Robert was confused, for he can obviously see the doubles.

"Why is he talking as if he cannot see Michael?"

Michael said, "Why doesn't he look at me?"

Robert began to feel strange. A feeling he had never experienced before. Then he fell unconscious and Michael disappeared.

. . . .

An hour later Robert awoke and found himself inside a hut. A couple of men were helping him to sit up.

He wondered, *"What happened? Where am I? And where is my brother?"*

Dr. Patel walked around the cot Robert was laying on.

"Robert, are you alright? Do you feel light-headed, or can you sit up on your own? For the past hour or so you have been mumbling about your past. Your childhood. Your parents and your brother Michael. I now understand everything about you."

"What just happened and how did I get in here? And where is my brother? What have you done with my brother Michael?"

Kirsh began to reply, but Dr. Patel raised his hand and said, "Fellows, let me handle this initially."

He looked down at Robert and said, "Your brother is fine. He is in a safe place. You need to relax and trust me. I am about to educate you on who you truly are. The fact that you just passed out is an example of the restrictions you placed on yourself many years ago. If you think you are ready, I shall begin. Robert, are you ready?"

"Am I ready for what? And where is Michael?"

"Doctor, what's going on? Okay. You win. You've been trying to get pass my psyche since we first met. You are not the first. But now I'm confused, so please explain what you did to me. And where is my brother Michael?"

Dr. Patel, his Gujarati accent getting heavier, said, "I'm sorry Robert. But only you can call upon your brother. I have to be very careful with how I explain this to you. Are you relaxed and opened minded?"

Robert, now tired of the mind games, said, "Doc, I really don't feel comfortable sitting here, wet pants and all, so please start talking."

Patel said, "Okay. But please be open to new possibilities. First, when you arrived here weren't you curious how you could survive those big cats out there? Why you were able to bond with them? I must say, I have never seen any Dual who could connect with two bengals, Chanakya and Brijesh. One yes, but not two! Only the shaman has the ability to connect with multiple felines. Aren't you curious why you can focus so sharply on things? Things that others cannot focus on. Not even your brother Michael. And what about your brother? Why can he read your mind? You can't read his, can you? Nor can he read anyone else's mind. Why is that, Robert? Why did your parents also stop you from speaking of Michael when you were a child? As if he were not truly there. I'm going to explain all of this to you, but only if you think you are ready to hear it. Because if you are not, you could lose your mind. And as a psychiatrist, I don't mean that loosely. I'm deadly serious Robert. Are you prepared to hear the truth about who and what you are?"

. . . .

Frank and Martha were starting to relax in their home after a very traumatic year. They had not heard from Robert but were not too concerned. As long as he had Michael with him, they knew he would be okay.

Frank said, "Baby, you were right when you wanted to get our second born son help. But somehow we managed to survive without it. His SPD has not hindered him, and I personally have grown to accept it. It was extremely difficult during his adolescent and teen years. But Michael proved to be a great asset to the family. Even Mack has grown to accept him. Do you know what Mack told me recently? That when he came home that fateful day of the King murder, the reason he did not bring the car home was because he was chased by that cop Sumanski. That cop was going to beat him, but Michael arrived just in time and saved him. Perhaps even saved his life. That is why Sumanski hates Michael so much. And you were right. We don't know which of the two is the real deal. As far as I'm concerned, they both are. I truly love them both."

Martha could not help but begin to cry. Her husband came to her and hugged her gently.

"I've been feeling that way since the incident at the Packard. Something my grandmother said, about needing to take care of them. She told me to take care of Michael. That she would take care of Robert, which she did.

"Michael stopped Busta, our nemesis. Our sworn enemy. He risked his life to stop Busta. That was Michael who was lying in the bed upstairs. And in that hospital bed. Not Robert. So yes, I do love them both. Even though life with them is so confusing sometimes.

"I don't want to think about sending them to a psychiatrist ever again. Think about it. They were so brilliant that they fooled every school official they ever encountered. Hell, Michael got himself enrolled in the freaken kindergarten!"

The two of them just held each other.

Then Martha said, "Do you remember when I said I would not keep secrets from you ever again. Well, I have something to tell you. And you cannot get mad, either. Please don't get mad."

Frank pulled back from his wife and said, "Okay. What is it?"

Martha said, "I paid that Grosse Pointe mobster a visit the week after we got back from Idlewild."

. . . .

Dr. Patel brought Robert outside of the hut, but insisted he remain seated in a chair.

He said, "Do you see this gentleman here and his brother next to him?"

Robert, not wanting to cooperate with Patel, whom he did not trust, looked sternly at the two men.

"Yes. I see them."

"Where are they in relation to where I'm standing?"

Robert indicated their positions near Patel.

"I am going to touch Kirsh on the shoulder."

He reached out and placed his hand on Kirsh.

"Now I'm going to walk through Tanvik."

He turned and walked directly through Tanvik!

Robert was shocked and bewildered all at once. He started to pass out again.

Kirsh, speaking in Bengali, said, "Sir, begging your pardon, but you must slow down. That was very dangerous! You are not experienced enough in the required training methods. Most of us never needed training. This gentleman is not ready for this news. You may lose him completely."

Dr. Patel understood Kirsh's concern but also knew of Robert's immense intelligence. Therefore, he continued.

"Robert. I'm going to come out and just say it. There is only one human body standing next to me. It is both Kirsh and Tanvik. They were born twins, just like you and Michael. However, they occupy the same human body. Just like you and Michael."

Robert tried to stand up but almost fainted again.

Kirsh rushed to his side, but Patel cautioned him to stay away. He knew how dangerous Robert was capable of being and did not want Kirsh caught up by what Robert might do next.

He was right. Robert became furious.

He shouted, "Do you think I'm crazy! You've been trying to get in my head since we first met. Of course there are two men standing there. I can see them and touch them. See?" Robert reached out and touched both Kirsh and Tanvik. "I'm holding both of their arms!"

Dr. Patel said, "Yes, your brain is telling you that you are touching both of them. In fact, you are only touching Kirsh. Place my hand on your arm then move my hand down your arm to Tanvik's arm."

Dr. Patel walked over to Robert, who then grabbed Patel's hand and placed it on his. Then he ran Patel's hand up his arm to Tanvik. When it got to Tanvik it suddenly went straight through! Robert was now freaking out!

"What the fuck are you trying to do to me! This is not happening!"

He began to rotate, first counterclockwise, then clockwise, back and forth, shouting at the top of his lungs. The men standing near him became alarmed. Finally, he stopped and dropped to the ground, whimpering and looking bewildered. He feebly said, "Where is my brother Michael?"

Chanakya and Brijesh became aroused and began to roar. The other bengals, uncertain of their behavior, began pacing the compound. It took Tanvik and the other sapiens partners to calm them down. Only when Robert quieted down did his charges relax. Then both beasts left the compound. They would not be seen again for several days.

Patel, witnessing Robert's frailty for the first time, was no longer frightened of him. However, he was not showing the proper sensitivity or concern, which troubled some of the men. He was truly confident in Robert's ability to handle the revelation.

He said, "Robert. You must have been confused all of your life as to why Michael always left the area when others came around. Why you were never with him and your other brothers. Your memories have been managed by your brain to ignore this anomaly. But it's true."

Kirsh, continuing to speak in Bengali, said, "Okay, sir. I think we should end this discussion and pick it up tomorrow, after Robert has been able to sleep on it. I suspect he cannot reach out to his brother right now. I don't see him either, even though he was here when they arrived. If we're not careful we could lose the other brother forever. Even Chanakya and Brijesh have left the compound. Our shaman has told us to go lightly with new duals. This gentleman is from the West so he has far more restrictions on what he will accept and will not accept. Besides, since the two of you have a troubled history, I can't see him trusting you anytime soon. So, we are going to end this session for now. I will take over his care. We can pick this up in the morning. Also, I'm going to send for our shaman. He is far more experienced in indoctrination of new duals. Do you appreciate what I'm suggesting, Dr. Patel? You too have become too western. So, let's start again tomorrow."

. . . .

As her husband sat next to her, Martha explained what happened when she went to Castanza. When she finished all Frank wanted to know about was the lawyer.

"So, you put that punkass e-lite in his place? Do you think it was mere coincidence that he gave away our position?"

Martha paused for a moment, then said, "Yes, I do. I think he is an honest but greedy man. He is too honest to do anything corrupt. But he is also greedy. Why else is he representing a criminal like Castanza. I have no doubt that he's on retainer. And Castanza treated him like his personal lapdog.

"Frank, I suspect my grandmother's connections in New York extend all the way here. Hell, as kids Pops claimed that his father was some Sicilian gangster. Grandma, however, acted as if this was just braggadocio talk, since Pops envied them. She would know if that were true, and she never acted as if it were. I even heard that she was dating a Jewish fellow before Pops was born. Only she knows who Pop's dad was.

"A few minutes after I pulled that gun their phone rang. One of his lackeys came running into the room and said, in front of everyone present, that a Lastanza was on the phone, and he was hopping mad! I was escorted into their parlor but could still hear Castanza referring to me while responding to the caller. How could he know I was in the house? How could he possibly know what was going on in that house unless Granny called him."

Frank was now confused. It sounded to him as if her grandmother had psychic powers or something.

She noticed his troubled look and said, "No baby. She is not clairvoyant. She, however, is a practitioner of Voodoo, an African religion. My sister Dominique is as well. I learned early on to never question what Granny is capable of doing. Hell, it may have even been Dominique who called New York. She can be pretty tough too when the occasion arises."

Frank still was not convinced but decided to let it slide. This was the second time Martha talked about her family. Now, however, she is being far more specific. His parents had given him a practical education, even enrolling their sons into schools outside of the Pontiac Public School district, to ensure they got the best education possible. He went to plenty of schools where he and his brothers were the only Blacks and had to put up with a lot of hazing. They lived with both Blacks and Whites and were well prepared for the real world. No way was he going to now start believing in hocus-pocus.

She said, "Anyway, I left the house before Castanza got off the phone. I tried to behave as my granny would want me to. Like I was in charge. And you know what? It worked. They were kissing my white-looking ass all the way out of the driveway! By the way, it's time to upgrade your car. No more squires! No more freakin station wagons! We're going to a new car dealership tomorrow, even if I have to pay for it."

. . . .

After the difficult introduction of dual existence by Dr. Patel, it was decided that Robert would be educated by the shaman. Over the next three days he spent his entire time in the shaman's remote temple. A translator was provided to assist in the communication between the two. Dr. Patel was not allowed in Robert's presence.

It did not take the shaman long to realize just how powerful Robert was, which enthused his desire to ensure Robert had a good transition.

He spoke to Kirsh and Tanvik, "There is far more to this man than mere Romani genetics. I sense an extraordinary connection he has with an elder relative. I also suspect he has yet another powerful ancestry that even he may not be aware of. That could very well explain his powerful physicality and extremely sharp mind."

Tanvik said, "Michael said his great-grandmother instructed them to come rescue Dr. Patel and the rest of us duals. Who is this woman that she could possibly even know of our existence? And rescue us from what?"

No one had seen Michael for the past three days, which is a clear sign that Robert was still struggling with his indoctrination. After the third day Dr. Patel became worried. Tanvik and Kirsh had been updating him on a regular basis on their Shaman's progress with Robert.

He told them, "We don't really know the damage his parents did to him as a child. Most of you never had such restrictions placed upon you. Your parents understood duality and did not hinder your development. All of you were born in the four corners of India, none of which are as culturally restrictive as the West is. However, Robert and Michael were born in a western society. Their parents obviously viewed, and undoubtedly still view, their son's dual identity as Multiple Personality Disorder. They obviously attempted to hide the condition from the rest of their society, which caused Robert and Michael to also hide. Actually, they had to hide in plain sight, since both of the men still lived full lives! When you think about it, that was amazing! To fool the world as an infant, as a young child. And continue to fool everyone to this day!

"What I never expected was what could happen if one of the twins was isolated from the other. Robert was drafted and Michael was not. Robert was transported across the US then over to Europe then Vietnam. For two years he was not able to return to the location where he last saw Michael. Therefore, Michael was in effect lost for two whole years! Their control center had to place Michael in limbo for two years!"

On the fourth day Tanvik reported to Dr. Patel that they witnessed Michael in the temple. The indoctrination was a success with Robert. Now it had to be performed on Michael. Fortunately, the shaman will have Robert to assist in convincing his brother.

By week's end two mentally exhausted Americans were finally accepting their duality.

. . . .

Frank said, "Martha, I married a moll?" and laughed. "No, wait. I married a wise-guy's kid? Oh wait, wait, wait. Your pops was a procurer, not a wise-guy."

Frank continued to chuckle, then got serious when he noticed Martha was not amused.

He said, "Honey, you're not making this stuff up, are you? Okay, I'm not making fun of your dad, sweetheart. And I know it must have been very traumatic when he died. But now I want to meet this grandmother of yours?

"You have concluded that our sanctuary was lost in Idlewild when that e-lite lawyer's wife's gossip about us while he was on the phone with a client. That's quite a stretch. And we still don't know who saved us do we? It most certainly was not those punk-ass mobsters from here. And Horace said he had nothing to do with it. That only leaves two alternatives. Either your grandmother said, 'Abracadabra', or my father did."

Martha knew not to joke about her grandmother.

"I'm glad you find my father's lifestyle humorous. Let's get serious. You might want to call your dad. I don't know what he could have done, since all of his sons have admitted to not having any involvement."

Frank looked at his wife and said, "I'm not laughing at your dad. I'm laughing at the fact that I thought I had married a sweet, sheltered, little girl, not someone more street-savvy than me! Honey, you've shared your life story with me, but I only told you mine from my parent's perspective. I need to share with you what I do know about my dad's dad. It's quite a story. Goes back more than a century."

They talked until it was bedtime. Then he continued in the morning.

CHAPTER TWENTY

Final Resolution

Robert was finally able to trust Dr. Patel. He now understood that Patel was not trying to control him, but merely to help him. In Germany Dr. Patel did not understand Robert's skills. It was only after Robert left Germany that Patel begun to doubt himself. He did not understand Robert from either the indigenous pagan perspective or the Western Freudian/Wundtian perspective. Which is why he resigned from the western world's psychiatric society.

With the shaman's permission, Dr. Patel asked Robert and Michael to join him outside of the temple. He had several other dual twins join him as well.

Dr. Patel started by again demonstrating that he could only see one twin, not both.

"Robert, I cannot see Michael."

Michael responded, "Sir, I'm Michael. Robert is standing next to you."

Dr. Patel blushed then said, "Michael how many men, excluding Robert and me, do you see standing before you?"

Michael replied, "I see eight men standing in front of me, not counting you or Robert."

Dr. Patel asked Robert, whom he assumed was there as well, "Robert, how many do you see?"

Everyone heard Robert reply, "Eight."

Except Dr. Patel.

He said, "Michael, I only see four people around me, plus of course, you. I also did not hear Robert's response, but I can tell by the reaction of the others that he did respond. I cannot see or hear both Duals, only the one in control of the engine, the body. Just as your parents or brothers could not hear or see both of you at the same time. Michael, I'm not trying to fool you. This is factual."

Robert said, "Doc, it's me, Robert. Michael is now standing near you."

The other Duals smiled in unison.

Robert said, "I see all of them. I find it incredible that you cannot."

There is a murmur among the men as they all began to talk at once.

Then Kirsh said, "Robert and Michael. It is considered rude to switch in Dr. Patel's presence without letting him know of the transformation."

Both Michael and Robert understood and apologized.

Michael thought, *"I guess I can't have any fun with that anymore."*

Robert continued, "Doc, why could I not see Michael until recently?"

Dr. Patel said, "Okay Robert. I believe you are ready to hear the full explanation of duality. You and your brother, as are the others here, are actually Siamese twins. Only you don't share a double set of body parts. However, you still have separate brains. Actually, your brain is no different than mine. But it has the mind of two people.

It also has, and I need you to open your minds to this next topic, a central processing unit, much like a computer has. It is the CPU which maintains who is in control of the body. When you 'freaked out' last week, and I as a psychiatrist can use that term, your CPU shut down your switching abilities. This is my understanding of how it works, keeping in mind that I'm being clinical. It became dangerous for your sanity to allow you to open up to your brother. If you had, it's possible he would have been even more confused than you and we could have lost both of you.

"It works like this. If Michael needs to go somewhere the CPU gives him control, but bookmarks where the separation occurred. This allows Michael to return to that geographic location so you can continue where you left off. You don't want to be eating breakfast and two hours later you're sitting in a classroom, do you? No, if one of you leaves the other at a table, then you need to return there. And you do without even knowing why. Because the CPU is directing you there without you realizing it. The CPU attempts to provide memories to either of you, based on past experiences, so you will not realize the full loss of time. Also, I suspect that this loss becomes the norm for you, and you possibly believe that everyone has these losses. It is perfectly normal to you.

"You also have to avoid depression. That shuts down the CPU's switching function and you won't be able to switch until the depression is gone. You've probably already experienced that. Your CPU also uses existing memories to create new ones using the data from the old memories. However, they are not real memories, so they seem very vague to you. The longer the isolation the more convoluted the memory bank will be. Michael, I can only imagine what your memories were like when Robert was in the Army. Two years of isolation! Your CPU must have been on overdrive!"

Dr. Patel continued. "Your daily existence required you to go places, then switch to the other, so that individual can have his time with the engine. Then you will return to that spot and switch back. In other words, Robert may go the library, then switch to Michael who will leave the library and go about his existence. Then later during the day, the CPU will understand the need for Michael to return to the library so Robert can continue with his existence. Robert will not know that the engine was not sitting in the library but running about all over town. Michael will not know why at a certain time he had to return to the library and return control back to you or even join you on the next leg of your journey."

Michael thought, *"Shit, is that why I can't recall much from '71 to '73?! Or after Robert said he didn't want to be my twin anymore. Did he become depressed after I walked away? Is that why after I ran away from home my memories became so fragmented. Is this little man on to something?"*

Robert thought, *"Those six weeks Michael was in the hospital or detained by that Dr. Little are a blank to me. I remember visiting him once in the hospital, but the school said I was absent for over six weeks. Was I lost because he was unconscious for so long. Then when he came to, I was able to re-appear for a short while until the nurse came back into the room? What is really going on here?"*

Patel said, "You two can dissect this some more later. One more thing. Your brains are able to get sleep when the other persona is active. That is why your body is able to go 24/7, not worrying about sleep. But again, if the one in control is isolated, then the CPU will not permit the other persona to assume control. Then your body does need sleep the same as everyone else.

"Your whole existence was probably the two of you making switches throughout the day. If you were having dinner, then one of you would eat, then leave the room, then the other persona would enter the room to eat. The CPU may even control the amount you consume to prevent you from over-eating. I'm only guessing here. Your family, of course, knew what you were doing and were forced to tolerate it. Others would not know and may not have noticed that the two of you were never present at the same time. With all of those children moving about, others would probably not pay much attention to the absence of one or the other. Your parents may have even avoided taking full family pictures to avoid outsider's questions."

Michael felt the need to clarify Robert's army years one more time.

"Are you implying that when Robert went into the military for two years, I was lost?! Is that why my memories of those two years were so fragmented?"

"Exactly. That was probably the first time in your lives that you were separated. Michael, you cannot go to Robert, if others cannot go to him. Your brother Mack was unable to visit Robert in Vietnam, and neither could you. Your brother could visit Robert on his college campus, and so could you. The danger is if you go somewhere that only one of you can go, then the other becomes dormant until you return to the previous location. Air travel would be a problem. Prison would be an even bigger problem. I would suspect you know this which is why your CPU would never allow you to book tickets on a plane. And you never gave it much thought, most likely. You just reasoned there are other ways for transportation. I can just see you now booking tickets on a train, then one of you running to the bathroom when it was time to present tickets!"

Robert said, "So if Michael has the engine, leaving me elsewhere and he is unable to return to me, then I am in limbo. However, If the two of us are together, such as now, and the engine gets locked up in jail, then both of us are still together. Correct?"

Patel smiled and said, "Yes, that is correct."

Michael said, "But I remember spending four days in Detroit AFTER Robert went into the military. It was around the 4th of July. I remember because I made phone calls to a gangster. I also remember seeing a dead man getting buried in an empty lot."

Robert said, "This was during my training in Louisiana. I did leave the base since we had a four-day holiday. This may have been when you re-surfaced. I must have travelled to Detroit where we were together last. That makes sense. Wow, we are being controlled by a brain alien!"

Michael did not find this funny, nor did Robert mean it as a joke.

Dr. Patel continued, "The duals here do not need to behave that way. They also avoid going into crowded cities. But they were never trained to not be present at the same time, unlike you too. Your parents did you great harm when they trained you to hide one persona or the other. Of course, they also undoubtedly saved you from western medicine, since the authorities would have concluded you were suffering from Multiple Personality Disorder. I know I would have drawn those conclusions early in my career.

"One more important factor. The Duals here have Romani genes. They are from the original clan of Romani, some of which migrated out of India. Their ancestors remained in India and eventually moved to Bengal. I suspect you two are part Romani, possibly from your mother's side, since according to Robert your father showed little or no signs of having any European genetics.

"I have discovered that this dual trait only occurs when a Romani woman, pregnant with twins, loses one due to the child being still-born or stolen. It only occurs with Romani women that have the mystique of duality in their gene pool. It will only surface/develop when one of the twins is lost."

Michael knew their mother lost one of her twin babies during the first night after delivery. It's that lost child's position that they were able to explain Michael, since they never reported losing a child. Michael knew this because he overheard his parents discussing it many years ago.

Robert said, "Are you suggesting that our mother has Gypsy blood in her? How is that possible? She's Black." Then he paused and said, "Never mind. I understand. We obviously know she has European ancestry, therefore, some of those ancestors must be Romani. And I guess I should not use the term 'Gypsy'. I get the feeling it is a racist term. I don't see the linguistic connect to Romani."

Dr. Patel just smiled, realizing that the twins were grasping the facts.

Robert said, "When Michael was being interrogated by the F.B.I. I was able to be present, since Michael drove his own car downtown to the hospital and picked me up there? I was a little confused why I was at the hospital, since my last memory was of visiting him and now he was picking me up while driving a car."

Dr. Patel said, "That is correct. Gentlemen, I don't have a full understanding of the limitations, since your cases are quite unique. All these guys were raised by parents who understood duality. They have never had to be separated. They always take into consideration the problems with separation and therefore, avoid it. You never were trained from birth how to interact with your environment, to avoid creating an extremely volatile situation. I have no doubt, based on what Robert did share with me in Germany, that the extreme difference in your behaviors were due to the forced isolation placed on the two of you by your parents. That they were very harsh with Michael, because of his precocious behavior. Don't get me wrong. You would have had different personalities regardless of duality. But I can only imagine your parents must have been terrified when you, Robert, persisted in speaking of Michael. And Michael actually surfacing time and time again with so varied a personality. And you, Michael, I feel extremely bad for you. I hope your parents have been able to express their love for you since the bridge incident."

Robert looked at Michael, but Michael looked away. Robert could not read his mind, but he could read his face and Michael preferred that he did not at the moment.

Robert said, "Doc. Explain the talents we have. I can focus extremely well. Michael is like an acrobat, without having any training. And will he get one of my tigers?"

Both men heard laughter from the others.

Kirsh, who has an academic degree, spoke up.

"Michael, based on what you've shared with us so far, I might be able to explain. Michael, you are an acrobat because your vestibular and proprioception sense are magnified. Robert you are such a marksman because, your vision and tactile senses are magnified. In fact, your hearing, taste and smell may temporarily shut down to increase your other senses even more. Your CPU controls the entire process, deciding which senses to magnify. This is not really unlike everyone else, just at a higher magnification.

"And to answer your other question. Don't I wish I had a tiger! Only Tanvik has a pet! Only one of us can control the beast. Fortunately, the beast sees, hears, and smells all of us! They obviously know we are part of the other, so we are never in danger. Not all tigers, just the ones born in the Sundarbans. Guys, don't mess up and go into a zoo and climb into the tiger cage! And it is remarkable that Robert can have this symbiotic relationship with two tigers! I have never seen that before!

"One more thing guys. Only with harmony and peace of mind will you be able to maintain your symbiotic relationship with your pet. They will not relate to an evil mind. They may leave you and never return. Robert, they were very disturbed when you were struggling a few days ago. They actually left the compound and are now just returning."

Michael said, "I can go up to that humongous pussy and pet him and he will respond to me?"

Tanvik said, "Yes, he would love the attention from both of you, whether you are in control of the engine or not. But he will only respond to Robert's commands, engine or no engine. Robert, they will kill and die for you. Even over their own kind. And by the way, you have no reason to fear any tiger in the compound or in this forest. They will all sense your duality, even if you cannot communicate with them. I still would suggest you take at least one of them with you whenever you're traveling in the forest. He is a great protector from other apex predators. He, however, will never leave the forest, so taking him into a village will never happen. He is a man-eater, and he knows that going into a village is a death sentence for him."

Michael jumped into the conversation.

"We went riding horses this summer out west. Robert had a real mean horse, at least according to the staff at the ranch. They labeled him a ten! Very hot! But as soon as he got near the horse, it relaxed and treated him as if they had been riding together forever. While he rode, I was unable to read him, which was a very strange feeling for me. The same seems to be happening with his beast here as well."

Tanvik looked amazed and said, "It appears the shaman was correct about the two of you. Your powers extend beyond ours. However, he is still confused why. He thinks it has something to do with your great-grandmother or possibly even your father's people, since you said he has no European heritage. He believes your great-grandmother is most powerful.

"You need to realize that Chanakya and his brother Brijesh have never attempted to bond with any of us before. They only relate to the shaman. Robert, you are the first. I believe they were waiting for someone as powerful as you."

Dr. Patel said, "You have separate talents. And they are extreme. All of these Duals have special talents that make them different from the rest of the world. Tanvik never needs to sleep. His brain does not require it. Samay over there can sing the most melodic sounds. His brother Bankor sounds terrible!"

All of the other Duals laugh heartily, including Bankor.

Dr. Patel continued, "Okay guys. I think you need to go back inside with the guru to complete your training. He will be leaving as soon as you are completely trained."

Michael had one more question.

"Doc, if we are the first duals you've encountered that have to behave as we do, then how come you know so much about how our CPU works?"

Patel responded.

"Because I'm a genius. You were in with the shaman for five days. I had you figured out in three," and smiled.

Robert could really appreciate his reply.

As they approach the temple Robert turns to Michael and said, "You know what this means don't you?"

Michael, confused, said, "No. What does it mean other than the obvious!?"

Robert smiled at Michael and said, "It means that you are NOT my older brother. We are the same age!"

As the Duals began to walk away two men walked into the compound. One of them approached Dr. Patel and with tears in his eyes said, "Baba, they have killed my baby! She is gone!"

CHAPTER TWENTY-ONE

Invasion

Late August 1979

Three days before deceased tiger was discovered

Castanza was having trouble sleeping. He had just had a nightmare about the evening Martha McCants left his home in an uproar. Worse yet, he had not gotten the nerve to address his poor treatment by the Don of New York.

"He screamed and yelled at me then hung up the phone. That was last year, and he still has not apologized or asked me my side of the story."

He got out of bed and walked downstairs, half expecting to find Martha sitting in his kitchen. At 7:00 a.m. he finally got up the nerve to call New York.

He said, "Lastanza. It's Castanza. I know it's early, but you've got to explain to me what's up with this McCants woman. Who's kid is she? Yours?"

Lastanza could tell Castanza had a bad experience involving the woman.

"I've got to be careful with this old fool. Shit, that was last October, and he hasn't been the same since. He's over seventy-years old and he seems rattled. I probably should not have yelled at him until I knew what was going on. I'm letting that old witch run my affairs!"

"Tony, that was almost a year ago. But okay Tony. Tell me what really happened."

Castanza said, "You didn't even listen to me. You just started yelling and hung up on me. Lastanza, the lady took my guy Ricci's gun from him and almost shot my nigger lawyer, that's what happened! In my fuckin house no less. I have never seen a bitch act that way. It came out of nowhere!"

Castanza began explaining all of the events occurring in Detroit, culminating with the day she arrived at his home.

He finally said, "She was this close to pulling the trigger. I didn't even have a piece on me to stop her, not that I would've tried. Why would I be carrying? I'm in my own fuckin house with plenty of muscle here, for crying out loud! Lastanza, I thought she was going to pull the trigger. And you know what? The look in her eyes told me she's capable of pulling the trigger. I think she is capable of being a stone-cold killer, without any afterthought. No fucken remorse. What kind of Nigger-Italians are you guys creating in Harlem anyway?!"

Lastanza was startled by that remark and said, "Her daddy was Black but looked just as white as you or me. Her grandmother as well. You're telling me she also can pass? Well, no one should be surprised at that. I was just getting my feet wet, understand, but I remember him. That fucking pimp only used high-yellow bitches, No White ones or brown or dark Blacks. Primary ones that could pass for White. Like the Cotton Club performers. So…look. I'm sorry you are going through this. But that changes nothing. She is 'hands-off.' You didn't hear this from me, but you've got to treat her as if she was a made-woman. Period. Now take your old-ass back to bed and let me get some sleep."

· · · · · · · · · · · ·

Pierre Bordeaux was having trouble sleeping. He had been having bouts of sleeplessness since the day he encountered that crazy woman at Castanza's last October. At 7:00 a.m. he called his daughter Carol and asked her to come over for breakfast. When she arrived, no breakfast had been prepared.

"He calls me out of a sound sleep and invites me over. Now there's nothing on the table. I know he does not expect me to fix breakfast for him."

She walked out of the kitchen looking for her dad and found him in his study. She walked over to him and kissed him on the cheek. He had not shaved or showered yet.

"Dad. What's going on? I thought we were having breakfast. Where's mother? And what's troubling you?"

He looked at her. She was even more beautiful than her mother had ever been. More beautiful than his mother.

He said, "Baby, closed the door. We've got to talk."

She walked back to the door, closed it, then noticed it had a new knob, one with a lock on it. He motioned to her to have a seat.

"I met your friend Robert's mother last year in Grosse Pointe. You know, that kid you were hanging out with at Wayne back in '68. I need to find out more information about their family. What can you tell me about that McCants kid?"

· · · · · · · · · · · ·

Cavaletti was having trouble sleeping. He had been tossing and turning since last week, when he finally got a chance to review his findings with the chief about the incidents that occurred last year. He was disturbed by the lack of interest displayed by his boss. The chief said that the information was almost a year old and so much more has happened in the city since then. The Sumanski investigation had stalled due to a technicality, even though Cavaletti had presented evidence that Sumanski may have paid a hit man to kill one of the McCants teens. At 7:00 a.m. he walked downstairs into the living room and pulled a folder from his briefcase, then settled down at his dining room table. The report he had received from his connection in D.C. was most troubling, but also straight to the point.

He read the short, bullet-point laden report aloud, hitting only the major items, knowing no one was around to hear him.

"Secret agency working inside the CIA. Group performing biological research. Launched during the Second World War. Hands-off from the highest level of government, including Army Intelligence. Has access to its own special army rangers' unit. Possible cabinet positioned connections. All datafiles marked 'Access Denied'."

He then read the final line, written in pencil. "Peter, stay away from this one. Others who have tried paid for it with their lives."

He knew the last personal remark was from his friend, even though there was no signature.

"He must be referring to the colonel from Chicago. Robert McCants colonel. Now I know why Tomaski is shutting me down."

.   .   .   .

Frank McCants was having trouble sleeping. He had been staring at the ceiling a lot since the day his wife explained her trip to Grosse Pointe Farms. So, at 7:00 a.m., he got out of bed and dressed, then left the room.

"She actually almost shot a guy! I'd never would have guessed she had it in her. What else don't I know about this little woman?"

He grabbed his car keys, looked in on Martha, who was still asleep, then headed to his car. He was going to visit his family. Instead of heading north to Pontiac, however, he drove west out I-94 to Ypsilanti.

He knocked on a door he had never visited before, having called ahead to ensure everyone was awake. His father, Dr. Joseph McCants, answered the door and welcomed him in. After sitting on the couch, Frank got straight to the point.

"Baba, I know you had something to do with our rescue last year at Idlewild. I assume you called your father, who got his posse together. I've met enough of my cousins to know they have extensive military training. I plan on visiting my grandfather very soon to thank him for saving all of our lives."

"Son. I don't go visit the estate without an invitation. And I have not had an invitation since your mother and I married over fifty years ago."

Frank looked at his father and realized for the first time that Father-Time was finally catching up to him. He could see his own face beginning to age just like his father's.

"Dad, that was a mistake on your part. I've made that same dumb mistake with you, but not anymore. Unless you tell me they have armed guards at the gates, I'm going to visit. And I'm taking my young ones with me. Just the three innocent ones. I'd take my wife Martha, but she's been somewhat of a firecracker lately."

Dr. McCants could not imagine what his son meant by that last remark but left it alone.

The two men talked for the next hour then Frank prepared to leave. His mother, who was in the next room, never came out to greet him, and he did not ask about her.

After he left the apartment, she approached her husband and said, "I don't know why he wants to meet your horrible family. If my people were still alive, they would reach out and…"

Joseph said, "Shut up woman. Enough already. Not this morning. Go read your bible."

Then he got up and called his mother to prepare her for a potential surprise visit.

. . . .

Dr. Schultz was having trouble sitting still. It was 1:00 p.m., and he could not wait until the plane landed in Geilenkirchen, Germany. He was excited to be going back to India, which was not how he felt last September, during his first trip to India. This time he knew he would find Dr. Patel.

He walked around the military base for an hour, since he had never been to Geilenkirchen before. After playing tourist for the full hour, he returned to the plane. The sergeant and co-pilot were unaware of his presence and continued to discuss matters pertaining to their operations in Detroit.

The co-pilot said, "I still can't believe he ordered the hit on that army colonel. I believe in top secrecy too, but now we're killing Americans?"

The sergeant replied, "Yeah, I don't like it either. But hell, we lost the use of eight men at the warehouse, the two hitters we hired from Chicago that killed the colonel, then half of my remaining squad of men in Idlewild! All eight of them are dead! Some of the men from the warehouse may never walk right again. A couple of them lost fingers, for Christ's sake! I know that freak Robert McCants killed the men at that Black resort, just like he messed over my boys at the warehouse! Hell, the crazy Dr. Little didn't even get a chance to ask him a single question. That freak of a doctor had to be placed in a straitjacket. So,

I'm looking forward to getting to India. I couldn't have been happier to hear that he and his fucken brother were already there. These quacks can experiment on that Michael character all they want, but the first chance I get I'm going to kill his twin Robert."

Schultz was aware that the twins were in India.

"I'm not surprised they were able to pull that off, after using that jacket on the fence again. These dummies had Michael on the run at the base and let him escape. The way the sergeant talks, my MPD patient Robert must be at the hidden compound with the other so-called Duals, since we're not going near any urban areas. I still don't know how Patel was found.

"I cannot believe my moronic handler killed that colonel. He would not have been any trouble. He didn't even know anything. So fucken what if he knew where I worked and lived! These Americans are imbeciles. Especially The Handler!"

The plane left Germany two hours after landing at the Air Force base and arrived at the secret landing strip in India the following morning. The sudden change in time-zone was hard on all of the men, but especially the older Schultz. Sleeping on the plane was of little help, since the ride was so turbulent.

The original mission called for a dozen men. They were not expecting Dr. Schultz to be joining them. The Sergeant was not happy to have the doctor along. He believed he would only slow them down.

"What was The Handler thinking sending that old kook along with us? He obviously has to stay with the pilots. He won't be of any use to us until we return with the captured men. And he won't be happy when he finds out that Robert McCants is dead! He's going to have to be satisfied with his brother Michael."

While the rest of the men pulled their personal gear from the plane, Sergeant Jackson walked over and examined the stowed away cargo. It was fifty meters away from the runway, in the shade of the trees.

He said, "Everything looks fine. Move the cargo from the plane and place those crates next to these crates, then setup camp for the night. You guys look like you can use a day off. We'll leave at daybreak. And Jim, check on the grenades, then separate them from the rest of the cargo. I don't want any assholes placing heavy gear on top of them."

Jim walked over to the storage area and searched for the grenades. He found them but noticed the top of the crate had been tampered with. One of the top boards had been removed then replaced.

He yelled out to Jackson, "Hey Sarge. This here grenades crate has been messed with."

The pilot heard the remark and said to the co-pilot, "See, I told you someone had messed with more than just gear. And you might want to tell the guys not to be yelling so loud. Sound travels quite a distance out here."

The sergeant thought, "*Why would the McCants bother with our crates…*" then he remembered that Jim was searching for the grenades.

"If it was the crate with the grenades then don't bother it until I can examine it."

Jim yelled, "What did you say? Don't bother wha…"

Suddenly Jim began sprinting as fast as he could. Several seconds later all of the men experienced the loudest blast they had ever heard. The bright morning sky turned red, then blue, then black. Wood particles flew over 300 meters per second in all directions. Metal fragments followed the wood. The subsequent concussive air propelled most of the soldiers backward from the storage area. Even the back of the plane was displaced a foot away, with the left wing almost touching the ground, before the plane rocked back onto its right wheels. A cloud of smoke rose 40 meters into the sky. When the smoke cleared the men rushed over to the explosion site and found a small crater where the crates were stored.

Jim caught the blunt of the tremendous blast. He was blown fifteen meters toward the plane and had severe burns to his back. Two of the other soldiers, standing closest to the blast, were also seriously injured.

Jackson screamed, "Medic! Check out Dietrick!"

He looked around at the rest of his men. Most of them were in a daze. Dr. Schultz was trying to get off of the ground, having been shielded by the plane, which knocked him down.

He was somewhat delirious and said, "What happened? What caused that explosion? Am I hurt? Will someone come examine me? Am I bleeding?"

Twenty minutes later Jackson had a full accounting of the damage caused by the explosion. He also knew he was going to kill Robert McCants if it was the last thing on earth he would do.

He said, "They did not teach that trick at Army Ranger School. He must have learned that trick in 'Nam. Probably from those southern Gook sergeants assigned to him. He could have killed all of us."

He spoke to Jim as he waited for the Indian Tiger Corp.

"What did you see in that crate that made you run?"

"A note, sir."

"What did the note say, soldier?"

"Only one word, sir. 'RUN.'"

· · · · · · · · · · · ·

Robert was resting on the plane when he noticed the labeling on a certain crate. He checked inside and realized his concern was warranted.

"They brought grenades to a tropical forest? What the hell for? The most opposition they might meet is an occasional tiger. Or a few lightly armed rangers."

When the cargo plane landed, he decided to destroy the crate, so he tied a string to one of the grenades, then to the lid of the box. Then he wrote the word 'RUN!' in bold letters on a sheet of paper and placed it on top of the explosives, then placed the lid back on the crate, ensuring the nails lined up correctly. He assumed, incorrectly, that the man who opened the crate would be able to outrun the blast.

.   .   .   .

Sergeant Jackson radioed to a nearby village for his local contacts. The four Indian rangers, whom he had bribed months before, responded to the request for medical evacuation of his injured men. An hour later the rangers arrived in two range rovers and removed the three injured soldiers and Dr. Schultz back to the village. They were later escorted to a small community with a hospital.

Once the rangers were gone, Jackson ordered his men to begin to move out. He had already informed the pilots, who were just completing their inspection of the plane, to fly to Diego Garcia, a large American military base in the Indian Ocean, and await further orders. The men marched for the remainder of the day, then set up camp for the night. Guards were posted with instructions to alternate shifts every three hours until daybreak. Jackson, however, would not sleep that night. He could only think of Jim and worried about the severity of his burns. He was now down to a few regulars.

Jackson was forced to include new recruits to his team due to the recent losses of so many of his men. He had just met them last week, when they accompanied him as he left for Florida to finish their preparation for this mission. Which is why he was so adamant to not leave earlier, as The Handler requested.

Halfway through the night, one of the new recruits, assigned to guard duty, thought he saw eyes staring at him from the forest. Terrified, he opened fire with his M-16. All of the men were now on their feet, guns ready. The sergeant screamed for everyone to hold their fire. He walked out to the site the guard was firing at and saw blood on the ground, but no carcass. It was obvious the soldier had merely wounded an animal.

He walked back, looked at the dazed soldier, then said, "I think you may have hit Bambi. Change rotations with Oscar and grab some shuteye."

He then sat back onto his bedroll and closed his eyes. He, however, would not sleep.

"That deer had a huge paw print."

CHAPTER TWENTY-TWO

Retribution

Retribution – Ret-ri-bu-tion – punishment imposed for purposes of repayment or revenge for the wrong committed.

Webster

The belief that the righteous will prosper while the wicked will suffer.

Ancient Near East and Old Testament

Qisas – Arabic. Accountability, following up after, pursuing or prosecuting. Retaliation in kind.

Quran

The act of taking revenge on someone in retaliation for something harmful that they have done, especially in the next life.

Hindi

. . . .

The entire dual compound was now aware of the news of the dead tiger. All of the men were very troubled by the death and summoned their tigers to their side. Robert noticed their concern and called out to his charges as well. Now the compound had only nine large felines walking among the nine Duals. However, two of the nine now belonged to Robert.

Michael said, "What could have happened? Do you think the military has already arrived?"

Robert asked Dr. Patel to translate for him.

"Ask him how far away did he find his tiger? Also did it appear if his tiger was shot?"

Patel asked the man several questions. They continued to talk for several minutes.

Then Patel said, "It appears he was seeking out his cat, because he could tell it was under duress. When he got within a half a kilometer of the cat, he could no longer sense his baby. It took him two hours, but he found it lying in a thicket. It had indeed been shot. He is most distressed, as is his brother. We are unable to console them."

Robert paused, in deep thought.

"*This must have been the strange feeling I was having a couple of hours ago. I could sense that Chanakya and Brijesh were disturbed, but I was too busy with my own issues to investigate why. I must do better.*"

Dr. Patel looked at Robert and said, "Robert, these men are not soldiers. They will be helpless if this compound is found."

Michael said, "Sorry Doc. It's me, Michael, Robert just walked over to be with the two men. I understand your concern. I'm of the opinion that those men must never reach this compound. How they knew where to begin looking should be of concern to you. Someone from here may have tipped them off. Or perhaps the forest rangers? Do they know of the compound?"

Dr. Patel said, "Michael, I know you don't realize yet the confusion you create for me when you switch with your brother, but please place this scarf in your shirt pocket when you do. It will make it easier for me to communicate with you. Please tell Robert to remove it when you switch. All of the other duals do the same, just so I can communicate better.

"To your first question. There is no way any of these men would betray us. Once we are discovered their way of life ends. They will lose their tigers, which is everything to them. They have been here most of their lives, since their beast are not welcome in their home villages for obvious reasons. Could the forest rangers know of our location? I suspect they know there is a compound here. The nearby villages are aware of duality. It is possible they may have inadvertently shared our existence with the rangers. You have to understand the possibility of duality is not so strange to the followers of the shaman. They have seen far stranger things than twins occupying a single body. Or controlling a Bengal. This includes the park rangers.

"My country, like some many other countries, has a problem with bribery. It would not take much of an offer to get a ranger to assist an outsider.

"Your final comment is true. We cannot afford to have any outsiders find us. I know that the western governments have been seeking Duals since before World War II. I've been able to find out that over the past decade Duals have been disappearing in Europe.

"Well, I must talk to the shaman. He will decide what we should do next. We cannot allow the outside world to find us."

For reasons he was yet to understand, Michael was becoming more and more furious. He appreciated the pecking order of the compound. He, however, never concerned himself with hierarchy. For the first time in his life, he had a mission that did not involve his family. He would talk to Robert, but he was sure that the two of them were going on a hunt. Alone if necessary. His grandmother commanded it.

Michael approached Robert, who was still with the grieving men, and said, "I believe I know where to find the soldiers. The question is, what do we do when we find them? They are armed. We are not. Since the shaman won't move his camp, we have to make sure they never arrive here."

Robert said, "If they want to maintain their freedom then they are going to have to fight for it. These guys may not be trained warriors, but these tigers most definitely are. They are going to have to accompany us to confront the soldiers. Where do you believe they are? Where do we begin?"

Tanvik looked at Michael, waved an outstretched hand to Robert, and said, "Hold it guys. Don't worry. We will find them. However, you cannot take your boys with you. Chanakya and Brijesh were very close with the deceased tiger. They tracked together, which is rare. I'm sure you can feel their anguish as well. You are not trained well enough to totally manage them yet, and we need complete control over them during this important excursion. I don't know how much control I can maintain of my own pet if matters get out of hand. We could have a tremendous loss of life, on all sides. Robert, please command your charges to remain with the shaman. He can control both of them and will need some protection while we are away."

Robert understood and complied. Michael was awe-struck.

He thought, *"I cannot believe he's taking orders from this little man. Hell, Robert is a better man than I am. I've never taken orders from anyone. Maybe that's why he's been so successful."*

Robert did not need to be able to read Michael's mind to know what he was thinking. It was written all over his face.

· · · · · · · · · · · ·

At daybreak the sergeant checked his map and resumed the march. Based on the information he had, they should arrive at the designated site in two more days, even though they were only traveling a kilometer an hour. He most certainly did not want to attempt to travel at night.

He believed that the animal shot during the night was not a deer, but a Bengal tiger. Deer do not have massive paw prints. He had no desire to kill cats but would kill every one of them if it meant he could reach Robert McCants. After the explosion he no longer cared about their mission. He would let Dr. Schultz worry about it. He was also glad to get rid of the old German kook.

None of his men understood the purpose of the mission. Even Jackson was somewhat in the dark. That is why Dr. Schultz was brought along. They knew they were on a 'seek and capture' mission for some indigenous men, but they did not know why. They had also been given strict instructions to capture at all costs. No shooting, unless provoked. Some of the men were as angry as the sergeant because of the recent losses that had occurred at the landing site. He was concerned that he might not be able to control them when they did encounter the targets. He had seen how tired, angry soldiers could get out of control, after spending time in Vietnam and Central America. He was also down to his least reliable men, since his most experienced soldiers were either dead or convalescing back home.

After three more days of hiking without reaching their destination, Jackson realized they were lost. Daylight was just beginning, and the men were exhausted, since they did not have proper water. Five days of marching through this terrain was difficult for the most experienced men.

"We should have been there by now. How could we have missed their camp? Unless these maps are wrong."

Then he got a troubling impression. He instructed one of his men to climb up into the tallest tree.

He said, "It's dawn so the sun will begin to rise soon. I want you to point out where due east is, based on the position of the sun. Do you understand recruit?"

The young soldier looked at Jackson somewhat angrily and said, "Of course, Sir." He then began climbing, scattering birds and monkeys, until he could see the horizon. Ten minutes later a glow began to appear. Then a red-yellowish ball began rising over the horizon.

The soldier yelled down, "Sir, the sun has surfaced. Due east is in that direction."

Jackson looked at his compass then threw it on the ground and stumped on it. He ordered one of the other men to give him their compass. It too was inaccurate by ninety degrees, the same as his compass! North was pointing to the east! They had been walking in the wrong direction! He examined the compass, and soon realized that it had been tampered with. He checked four other compasses. All were precisely off by the same ninety degrees.

He said, "Okay men. We're off track, but I now know what we have to do to get back on track. Recruit, get back down here."

After Michael had reviewed the mission orders, he noticed the collection of compasses. He immediately decided to sabotage their mission by trying a trick he learned from a watch-smith in a repair shop in Hamtramck, Michigan when he was a kid. After forty-five minutes all of the compasses were adjusted. North was now indicating East. Which is why he believed he knew where the soldiers were.

Jackson had the men switch direction and began following the 'southwest' indication on the compass.

By noon the men were exhausted, having to hack their way through the tough terrain, or walk in knee-deep water. The mere seven days of training in Florida did not prepare them for this forest. A lot of their food and water was destroyed during the explosion so they were extremely famished as well. They entered a small hilly clearing, with no water and minimal trees, to their relief.

Jackson said, "Okay guys, take ten."

The men began stripping off their outer gear and laying them on the ground.

Thom, one of the two soldiers near the rear, said, "The Sarge is a real hard-ass. I've never worked with him before and hope I never have to again."

Jonny, the other soldier, said, "That's why they call him 'Stone-ball'."

Thom said, "I don't get it. Why 'stone-ball'?"

Jonny said, "Don't you know his first name? It's Andrew. Andrew 'Stone-ball' Jackson," and smiled.

With only a ten-minute break, Corporal Bakersfield tried to relax. However, he could not take his eyes off the vegetation ahead. He knew he was getting delirious due to a lack of water.

He said, "Sarge, maybe it's my imagination but what happened to all the monkeys? They've been following us since we arrived, picking up our garbage and even stealing our stuff. I can't help but notice that they've been really quiet for the past ten minutes or so. Even before we hit this clearing. I don't see nary a one."

The sergeant had noticed the quiet as well and was becoming concerned about it. They had seen numerous crocs and pythons during the past two days, yet this area seemed clear of them. He had hoped they might run into a wild boar, so they could roast some pork.

"There must be a bad-ass apex predator around here to keep even crocs away."

He said, "Probably just a predator these monkeys have to worry about. A single tiger perhaps since they usually travel alone. Or even a giant python. Nothing for us to worry about."

Corporal Jones patted his M-16 and said, "With these babies, we are the top dog in these here woods."

Bakersfield continued to gaze at the vegetation, some sixty meters ahead. Suddenly, he noticed movement within the brush.

He said, "Sergeant, I'm not sure if my eyes are deceiving me, but those yellowish bushes straight ahead are moving in unison. In fact, they seem to be coming directly towards us."

However, Bakersfield's eyes were not deceiving him.

Jackson said, "Those are not bushes. Everyone, freeze!"

Directly in front of the men stood the most magnificent sight they had ever seen. It was also the most terrifying sight for all of the young men. 200 Bengal tigers of various sizes were slowly walking directly towards them. Shoulder bones were heaving upward then dropping downward, first left shoulder, then right shoulder, over and over in slow motion. When the ambush of felines got completely into the clearing the alpha Bengal stopped. It was Tanvik's charge. They were a mere forty meters from the soldiers, stretched out for approximately 200 meters. They were so close that the soldiers could not see both ends of the formation.

All nine pairs of eyes were now on the felines. All cat eyes were on the sapiens.

Jackson whispered, "No… body… move. And don't make a sound. Slowly lower your head toward the ground. Do not look at them. Look at the ground. And for Christ-sake, lower your weapons."

The men understood and dropped their gazes. For the next five minutes all sounds seemed to cease. No birds chirping, no insects squeaking, no leaves rustling in the wind. Then the most incredibly frightening sound began as the mightiest of roars was articulated. All of the tigers called out at once. All of the men, both soldiers and Duals grasped their ears, trying to stifle the tremendous sound. Some of the soldiers began to cry. Others panicked and began to run. One soldier tripped on the foliage, dropped his M-16, then jumped up and continued to flee, leaving the rifle behind.

Jackson yelled, "Fools, don't move! They will run you down! We'll all be killed!"

This, however, did not stop the flight, and soon all eight men were running back into the forest, leaving the sergeant alone. He glanced up at the ambush and noticed them slowly advancing toward him.

"I only have a single clip in my gun. And I cannot possibly outrun them. God dammit! They are not supposed to gather together like that! This ain't Africa and these ain't lions!"

The alpha cat began to move well ahead of the mass. He approached Jackson, who was now shivering uncontrollably, and began to smell him. Then he showed his canine and incisors, raising his head directly upward toward Jackson's face. He reared up slightly and placed his front paws onto the soldier's chest, then pushed him backward, causing the soldier to fall onto his back. The beast then stepped over the fallen soldier, foot to head, then continued to walk forward. The sergeant would have seen his massive testicles, but his eyes were now pressed shut. The ambush followed the alpha, walking past or over the shaken sapiens. No paws ever touched his body.

Tanvik stood at the base of a giant tree, out of sight of the fallen soldier, extremely focused, and smiled broadly. He was extremely proud of his boy.

"That was good control, my love. Now walk back into the forest, taking the masses with you. Do not harm anyone and I will have a treat for you all."

Michael and Robert merely stood in utter amazement. The other Duals smiled and nodded their heads. Kirsh was especially proud and slightly jealous of his brother's success. Only slightly.

The bewildered soldier eventually got off the ground and headed into the direction of his fleeing troops. When he found them, he ordered them to reverse course. Their mission was over.

· · · · · · · · · · · · ·

That night the band of Duals arrived near the military camp, leaving their charges behind. Michael had decided to seize on the moment and harass the sentries. He instructed Robert and the Duals to hang back and lay down on the ground. He then circled around to the opposite side of the camp and tied a vine to a low-hanging branch, walked thirty meters sideways away from the branch, then, after lying down on the ground, began jerking the vine, causing the branch to sway back and forth. One of the sentries noticed the movement, and like the previous night, opened fire in the direction of the motion. All of the other soldiers, with their nerves now shredded, opened fire as well. The sound was tremendous, but short-lived. When their clips emptied, they attempted to reload, only to find that all the spare clips jammed in their guns.

Jackson yelled, "Cease fire you ass holes! Cease fire! You're spooked by the sounds in the forest. There is nothing out there that can harm you. This fire will keep the tigers at bay!"

Jonny said, "This tiny-ass fire ain't scaring shit! They're going to eat us all!"

Bakersfield said, "Sarge, my rifle is jammed! None of the extra clips will fit properly. I believe they have been tampered with!"

Mathew said, "My clips won't fit either and I've tried three different ones. If all of the clips are damaged, then all we have is our sidearms. What are we going to do if those tigers come back?"

· · · · · · · · · · · ·

*After the cargo plane left the air base in Geilenkirchen Robert
waited for Michael to fall asleep, then began opening crates. He
found the crates with the rifle clips and altered them such that
they would not properly fit into the gun housing. Now he knew
that the only effective clips the mercs would have would be the
ones in their personal supply, which was against regulations.*

· · · · · · · · · · · ·

After the men calmed down the sergeant posted new sentries. An hour
later Robert and Michael took out those sentries. Then the Duals
brought their seven felines into the camp. The completely exhausted
soldiers were sleeping fitfully, especially Jackson, who appeared almost
unconscious. The Duals had each tiger stand over a soldier then emit
a tremendous roar at once. The men awoke, completely petrified. The
roaring went on for two minutes as the beast stared deep into the
men's eyes. Saliva drooled into their open crevasses. A few of the Duals
struggled to control their charges, since they were natural man-eaters,
however, none of the men were injured.

The seven men evacuated their bowels and bladder. Even those
that did not have a beast above them wet their pants. The malodorous
smell was very obvious. Then the tigers slowly walked away from
the camp. Not, however, before they marked the men. The soldiers
could do nothing but sob. All of them knew they would never enter a
forest again.

After the men composed themselves, they began stripping off
their clothing and changed into their spare set. They even used up
the remainder of the water supply trying, but failing, to wash out the
urine in their hair. It would be weeks before they would be able to

wash away the odor. It would be months, however, before they would be able to wash away the memories.

They started packing their gear, completely ignoring their commander. The profanity was legendary. The sentries returned to the camp, having been awaken by the roars.

One of them said, "Sarge, somebody hit me. What the fuck is going on?"

Bakersfield said, "These freaken tigers are playing games with us. Like cats playing with mice. They plan on eating us after they have their fun. Well, I don't know about the rest of you, but I'm getting the fuck out of this freaken hell tonight."

Mathew said, "You can't see shit, dummy. You'll just walk right into one. We have to wait until daybreak. And it took us three days just to get here, not counting the first two days. And our water supply has been ruined. So, yeah, we're getting out of here. But we have to go about this just right or we will perish. Not by the tigers, but by the jungle itself."

When dawn arrived, Sergeant Jackson radioed for the plane to leave Diego Garcia, even though he knew they were at least three days away from the evacuation point. After the soldiers packed what gear they planned on maintaining they began to move southeast, based on their defective compasses. For all of two minutes.

Suddenly Bakersfield exclaimed, "Oh shit, look over there! And there! Oh My God! They're everywhere!"

The huge ambush had the men surrounded on three sides. Then the tigers behind them began to march forward. The men were forced to move west. The tigers continued to herd the men away from the direction they had chosen for escape.

They continued to push the soldiers forward, keeping them corralled in a tight bunch. However, by days end the forced march the men had to endure brought them to a clearing, and to their surprise, their plane was in plain sight.

Bakersfield said, "Well, I'll be! We were heading in the wrong direction. Those cats pushed us out of the jungle and back to our plane!"

Sergeant Andrew Jackson looked over at the cats, but suddenly began to notice men standing among them. Then he saw a mirage. Lieutenant Robert McCants standing among the beast! He rubbed his eyes, shook his head, then looked again. The image he thought he saw was gone. The ambush slowly began walking away.

Jackson approached the pilot and said, "As soon as we're aboard I want you to take off."

The pilot said, "Sure, but what happened to your captives? And man! You guys smell just awful!"

Corporal Bakersfield said, "Look punk-ass, get us the hell out of here. Now!"

The co-pilot said, "Okay, Okay. I'll just need to do a final inspection."

Jackson screamed in his face, spital bouncing off of his nose.

"Fuck your inspection! You've been sitting on your asses for days now! Get this God-damn MF plane in the air immediately!"

Jackson knew he would be resigning from the force as soon as the plane landed in Louisiana. He had forgotten about his desired vengeance toward Robert McCants. He just wanted to forget forever the magic he had just witnessed in the Sundarbans.

Five minutes later the plane was air-borne.

· · · · · · · · · · · ·

Dr. Patel found Dr. Schultz in a local jail cell, joined by two of the injured American soldiers. Jim, with serious burns to his back, was still hospitalized. The soldiers had been pressured into informing on the four Indian Rangers, who were now imprisoned alongside them. The police commander had already contacted the American Embassy about the group of men, but the embassy denied having any knowledge of troops in the area. So, Dr. Patel had to use his limited influence in the area to get Dr. Schultz released into his custody.

Dr. Schultz spent the next month living in a thatched roof hamlet on the outskirts of Coimbatore, Tamil Nadu, India, after Dr. Patel spirited him south to avoid prying eyes. Few of the occupants of the shantytown spoke English. They shared their meager food with him, humbling him after decades of western comfort. He soon learned to enjoy his meals without meat or western eating utensils. After another month Schultz was back on a plane to Germany, using a doctored passport, with a final destination for Detroit Michigan, USA.

Dr. Patel knew it would be extremely dangerous for him to keep Schultz within the city. He was aware that the three remaining American soldiers were found shot to death the night Dr. Schultz left the jail with him. The killers missed their fourth victim by mere hours.

CHAPTER TWENTY-THREE

Thanksgiving Dinner - 1980

The state of Michigan, in mid-western USA, is surrounded by some of the most beautiful freshwater lakes in the world, rivaling the Great Lakes in southeast Africa. With all that water around the state, however, the city of Detroit, the largest city in Michigan, has no lake frontage; only a strait, erroneously called the Detroit River. Windmill Point Lighthouse, located on the city's south-east corner border, sits on the eastern edge of the strait. This strait connects Lake St. Clair to Lake Erie at the Michigan/Ohio state borders. Lake St. Clair, the closest lake to the city, appears to be a huge body of water, but it is extremely small compared to the five North American Great Lakes. Yet once a boat is in the center of the lake, land cannot be seen in any direction.

. . . .

Early December 1979

Dr. Schultz could not believe how his life had taken a turn for the worse since the day he met Michael McCants. He had been to India twice in a twelve-month period, each time attempting to find Dr. Patel for the American government. Then during his second trip, albeit an illegal entry, he was locked in a prison cell. The irony of all ironies is that his rescuer is none other than the man he had been pursuing. Dr. Patel saved Schultz's life at the risk of his own.

When Schultz entered his home, using the hidden key under the doormat, his wife was completely shocked, almost falling to the floor. He did not bother to find out why, but merely walked past her to his bedroom and closed the door. He remained isolated for the next seven days, only leaving his room when necessary. He could hear Gertrud on the phone almost non-stop that first day, but he did not care. She never visited him in his room, which he was thankful for. He just wanted to be left alone.

After lying about for a week he came downstairs and sat in a chair across from her in the kitchen, wanting to talk about his experiences over the past three months. She, however, was not the right person to discuss his problems with. So, he did the one thing he had not done in many years.

He said, "We haven't been out for quite a while. Let's go out to dinner."

Gertrud was surprised at the invitation and accepted it. She was not looking forward to his coming home, any more than he was to being home, but she could not refuse an offer to dine out.

As they drove toward a marina restaurant along Lake St Clair, he began to cry. The tranquility of the lake compared to the harsh surroundings of the Indian shanty town he was harbored in, was a shock to his system. Also, he needed to have someone to discuss his traumatic experiences with, and that person was not sitting next to him. He had been married to this woman since 1946, yet he felt empty in her presence.

"I'm sorry I'm being so emotional, but I've had the most trying experience."

"That's too bad. But keep your eyes on the road."

He was not surprised by this remark since she never connected to him emotionally.

"I've been gone for over two months, and I bet you didn't even notice. I've just gotten back from India. You don't know this, but I'm still partially tied to the American government. They asked me to accompany some soldiers to a forest in eastern India. However, everything that could go wrong, did go wrong. I have a moronic boss, called The Handler no less, and he continues to arrange the most asinine missions. They always fail! That kidnapping of that McCants kid from my hospital was his idea. Even though I told them not to pick him up until I returned to the States from India. That man who visited me at my office that was later killed in the Ren Cen was his doing! He murdered a retired army colonel! He is a komplett versager, a total fuckup!"

He continued to rant on and on about The Handler for the next ten minutes, to Gertrud's dismay.

Finally, she had heard enough.

She began to scream, "MISTER BAIER, you are the komplett versager! All you were asked to do was accompany your men to the Dual village and identify Dr. Patel! But a little explosion and you shit your diaper and drop that one responsibility. Hell, I heard you weren't even seriously injured! The slight movement of the plane's fuselage knocked you over! You are not a man, but a little boy. I have had to live with a little boy for thirty years. And you are so dumb, you don't even know who Agent X is! You don't even know who The Handler is!"

Schultz was dumbstruck. *"How does she know so much about my work? About Agent X and The Handler? And my real name! Has she been working for them as well all these years? Did they arrange our marriage? Did they arrange for me to marry this horrid creature? Oh Mein Gott! I had three children with this thing! My god, the control they've had over me all of these years. They planted a monster in my home!"*

Gertrud continued screaming, "You're even a lousy lover! I can't believe I've sacrificed my youth for this mission to find Duals, and you still don't even know about them! Robert and Michael are one and the same. But they are not suffering from DPD or MPD or SPD dumbass! They are Duals! Even Dr. Little knew that much. Like the other Gypsies we've found in France. PhD my ass. No wonder your country loss the war!"

Schultz looked over at his wife but did not recognize her. Gertrud's face was changing before his very eyes.

"You bitch! You terrible bitch! How long have you been spying on me for the agency? Since the beginning of our marriage?"

The pitch of her voice began to deepen.

She replied, "Spying on you? Spying on you? My God! You are the dumbest man in the entire world. I have not been spying on you, stupid! I am your boss! I … am Agent X! I … am your handler! I am The Handler!"

Dr. Schultz entire life was summed up with that simple declaration. His eyesight began to fail him. He could hear his heartbeat in his ear canals. He looked at this monster sitting next to him and knew this was the end. Thirty seconds later his car was floating toward Canada. His last thoughts were, *"I once said if I ever kill someone The Handler would be the first. She won't be handling anyone else ever again."*

The coast guard found the location of the car in the lake after sighting a floating wig on the surface.

· · · · · · · · · · · · ·

Cavaletti got a call from his friend in D.C. They spoke in code, but the message was clear.

"Did you get the love letter you asked me to advise on? Well, good, just follow that advice and you will do fine. And tell your wife I said hello," and hung up the phone.

Cavaletti knew this was a second warning. He had not expected it, since he had already stopped the investigation after the first warning. He finished his work for the day and drove up Gratiot Avenue to his home.

He pulled his car just past his driveway, then backed into the driveway. A car pulled up in front of his house as he was backing his vehicle into the garage. He noticed the car and, after closing the garage door, walked back down his driveway.

His wife was looking out of the kitchen window and noticed four men sitting in a car. The driver of the car and the man sitting behind him got out and crouched down in the street beside the car.

She yelled, "What in the hell!"

She ran to the side door and yanked it open.

"Baby, look out! They've got guns!"

He reacted just as the driver opened fire. "Pop, pop, pop!" Cavaletti dropped to one knee and squeezed off a round, striking the man in the throat. "Pop!"

He then yelled at his wife, "Get back inside and call 911!"

Before she could turn around the second shooter began firing at Cavaletti with an automatic. "Bam bam bam bam bam bam bam bam bam!" Cavaletti dove to his left, landing in his neighbor's front yard, and returned fire. "Pop pop pop!" All three rounds hit the man in the chest, knocking him down. As the man struggled to regain his footing, the front seat passenger, seeing both of his friends go down and very exposed to Cavaletti's glare, slid behind the wheel and drove away. Cavaletti ran to the sidewalk, looked down the street at the fleeing car as he aimed at the struggling man lying on the pavement, yet still holding the AR16, and shot him once in the head. "Pop!" He never took his eyes off of the car as he raised his arm and fired eastward toward the fleeing car, "Pop, Pop", paused for a moment, then fired one final time. "Pop!" The car veered off the street and crashed into a neighbor's tree. The two occupants died immediately, the driver from two gunshot wounds to the back of the head and the backseat passenger from cranial injuries after crashing through the windshield and impacting the tree.

Cavaletti could not help but whisper, "Punkass should have been wearing his seatbelt."

Judith, carrying a loaded shotgun, ran to her husband and they embraced. She was thankful her son was not home to witness his dad's close brush with death. Neighbors all over the block could only stare in wonder.

When detectives investigated the shooting, they discovered that all of the men were from out of town. The driver of the car had made a large deposit, the week before the shooting, to his bank account. They soon surmised that someone had paid the man $9, 900.00 to kill Cavaletti.

A week later Detroit Internal Affairs, while investigating Sumanski's bank accounts as part of the re-opened bribery investigation, discovered that he had made a recent withdrawal of $9,900.00. Further investigation revealed the date of Sumanski's withdrawal matched the date of the deposit of the shooter. They summoned Sumanski to discuss the recent withdrawal, but he did not respond to the request.

Internal Affairs decided to send a squad car to his home to bring him in. He did not answer his doorbell, yet his car was still parked in front of his garage, covered with a light coating of snow. His neighbor said she had not seen him in over a week. It was very unusual for him to leave his car in his driveway overnight. So, the police got a warrant and entered his home. They found Sumanski lying on his back on the living room floor, his feet under the living room side window. He had a single gunshot wound to his forehead. The window was slightly opened, with a straight-line bruise on the bottom of the wood frame. Two slight impressions were still in the carpet, indicating he was on his knees peeping out of the window when he was shot. He had been dead for approximately a week, matching the time of the shooting at Cavaletti's home. They examined the lead bullet, along with tiny bits of wood, lodged in his brain. The metal bullet matched Cavaletti's gun. The wood matched the side window frame. They also found a note taped to the side of his refrigerator. It read, 'The Handler 703-555-1234'. Cavaletti was not charged in the shooting.

One of the IA detectives thought, *"What irony. He paid for a murder and got his money's worth."*

When Cavaletti got word that he would not be held responsible for killing Sumanski, he thought, *"Dumbass should know not to peek out of his side window during a hit. He makes too good of a target."*

· · · · · · · · · · · · ·

Captain Ralph Baker was arrested the week after Sumanski died. He was brought up on charges of aiding and abetting in the attempted murder of Commander Cavaletti. Investigators also found investigative material in Sumanski's house pertaining to the Harper Hospital murdered victim. The material implicated Sumanski in the hiring of the man to come to Detroit to murder two McCants teenagers. Only the captains under Cavaletti were in possession of this material. It is believed Baker provided his lieutenant with the investigative material.

. . . .

Trigger, Busta's right-hand man, eventually made it back to Mississippi and started taking adult education classes. He would never sell drugs again. He still got shivers when he heard the name McCants or saw short, slim, dark-haired White women. Unfortunately for Trigger, there are plenty of families in Mississippi named McCants as well as short, slim, dark-haired White women.

. . . .

A month after visiting his father, Frank McCants made the hour-long drive to the forbidden valley. He was accompanied by six of his sons. He had told his father that he would not take his wife along. He lied. Martha's soulfulness charmed the entire household.

. . . .

Dr. Patel continued to travel through the Romani community in Europe trying to warn them about the CIA. He did not discuss the incident at Sundarbans Park.

. . . .

Michael and Robert eventually returned to the United States after spending six months in Sundarbans Park with Dr. Patel and the shaman. They would miss Chanakya and Brijesh. It was Dr. Patel who managed to get them back home as merchant marines on a Sri Lankan freighter. Most of the crew were Indian or Sri Lankan Tamils and knew of Duals.

Robert resigned his position at the University of Michigan, believing it was most unfair for them to employ him when he knew he could not properly commit to a professor's schedule. Michael, of course, would never have to work, especially after experiencing working on the freighter. He still had over eight figures of stashed money of Castanza's hidden throughout the city.

After almost losing their sanity, both Robert and Michael were now fully trained Duals. The twins only regret was that they had to leave their kittens behind. They planned to return annually.

. . . .

The Fourth Thursday of November 1980

The McCants were finally able to get back together for a family dinner. Mack and his family had arrived first and were lounging around the small living/dining room. Ervin, Louis, and Richard were playing pool in the basement. Jack and Horace were sitting at the dining room table with their nephews. All of the wives and Martha were gathered in the small kitchen.

Frank, talking on the phone in his bedroom, heard a knock at the door.

He yelled, "Someone get the door!"

However, the buzz in the house was too loud and the knock continued. So, he said his goodbyes to his brother Herbert and left the room to answer the door. It was Robert.

He said, "Hey, Pops," and reached out to hug him.

Frank returned the gesture. He had come to accept his son as he was and knew he could express love to him regardless of which persona he presented.

Frank said, "Come on in, son. Almost everyone else is already here. Have a seat if you can find one."

There was a happy cheer when everyone looked up and saw it was Robert.

Mack thought, "*I see he decided to enter as Robert. How long before he makes his switch to Michael. That persona switch is still so confusing. And I've experienced it all of my life! Hell, Linda still thinks there are two of them.*"

The annual dinner was potluck as usual. Most of Martha's sons preferred their wives cooking to Martha's but dare not say so in her presence. There were so many different pots and bowls on the kitchen table that some of the food had to be placed on a card table on the back porch. Both dogs, now old, were confined to a corner in the living room until the food on the porch was gone.

Horace and Ervin, having grown up with a pool table in the basement, had gotten fairly good at the game. However, they still could not match their father's game and realized his pool hustling days were not yet over.

While Richard, Louis, and their families were eating their dinners, Frank pulled Mack away from Linda. He said, "Mack, let's play a game of pool."

Mack knew this meant his father wanted a private moment with him. They entered the basement but walked into the adjacent room, wanting total privacy.

When he thought he could talk in private, Frank, still unaware of duality, said, "I notice Linda doesn't seem to know the family secret. Are you ever going to tell her about your brothers Robert and Michael?"

Mack sighed heavily and said, "Pops, I don't know what to tell her. She knows that Michael almost got killed a couple of years ago. She believes Robert was away in Ann Arbor or on a business trip or whatever. Which is why he never visited Michael in the hospital. At least not while we were there. I'd just as soon leave it at that. You've seen how freaked out Ervin and Horace were when they realized they had been left out of the loop. I still don't know how Jack figured it out. That boy continues to surprise me."

"Mack, she's your wife. You can't have secrets from her."

"Dad, that's your code of conduct, circa 1950. And besides, I don't have secrets from her. Robert's mental health is his personal business. I doubt if Richard or Louis have told their wives either. You still have not told Horace, Herbert, or any of my other uncles, have you? Or your father! Man is he going to flip out if he ever finds out. And your grandparents might disown us again! Ha! Your dad has gotten really close to Robert and Michael. You don't think Michael will still be able to fool him like he does everyone else?"

Frank said, "Mack, you and I can't tell which one is which, so 'yes'. My dad will never know. It's not like they are trying to fool anyone. They, Robert and Michael, truly believe they are unique individuals and therefore never make mistakes. If I can call it a mistake. Michael has pulled off an extraordinary presence his entire life. He even fooled the US government after being drafted. They never pursued him, which was strange."

Mack said, "Dad, they walk differently, they talk differently, they fought differently. Robert truly believes Michael is not in his head but is a real person! So, I'm going to leave that alone. No, I don't plan on talking to Linda. Hell, what happens when Robert wants to get married and have kids? Wow! Just hope he doesn't have twins!" and laughed out loud.

Frank pondered the comment and began laughing as well.

Mack said, "Pops, we keep talking about what Robert wants. What about what Michael wants? As mom says, we don't know which one is the real deal. Anyway, I've learned to love them both."

· · · · · · · · · · · ·

Martha had been bothered by an incident she was involved in during the late summer of '78. She was unaware who initiated the request and really needed to know.

So, she waited for Michael to arrive, then approached him and said, "Son, please meet me in the backyard. I have some questions I want to ask you."

Then she walked out the back door and down the porch stairs, pulling her sweater tightly around her. Michael knew what the topic was before he got off the porch.

Martha said, "Some time ago I received a package with a note in it. It also had a large sum of money in it. A very large sum of money. The instructions directed me to drop off the money at the home of that dead cop Sumanski, the one who shot you. Son, I have to know, was that a payoff for killing Busta?"

Michael said, "Mother, I have no relationship with Officer Sumanski, even though he may have unintentionally saved my life when he shot Busta. Remember, he shot me as well. And I would never involve you in a payoff scheme, especially involving murder."

Martha felt this was not a clear denial and said, "Hold it, son, you may think you know the streets. But I grew up in Harlem. One day we will discuss my father, but I can tell you his middle name was 'Street.' As was my mother and grandmother, so don't bullshit me boy!"

Michael said, "Ma, I wouldn't bull…"

Martha interrupted him and said, "Son, don't try it! I asked you a question and you gave me an answer that may be true but left plenty to be desired. Okay, let's say you want me to maintain deniability. I just want to know if it was one of my sons who left that package and instructions or some asshole on the street who is using me for their personal gains."

Michael paused, smiled, then said, "Mother, I did not leave $100,000 in your closet with a note that read *'Send Unearned Money*

And Never Spend or Keep It' to ensure the money was left with Officer Sumanski. I didn't even know you had a secret stash in the bottom of your closet, where you keep all your secrets. Nor have I ever dialed a number written in the box or spoken by phone to your grandmother. I also have not met your mother, so I don't know that she is doing fine. Or that she lives in a senior citizen's complex in Florida, after selling her mansion in Chicago and her vacation home in Miami. I don't know that she is living large. Now, I understand it is very important that you maintain an ability to deny any involvement with Officer Sumanski. His death was a godsend, as far as I'm concerned. Anyway, I think it best that we change the subject."

He then smiled at her, leaned over and kissed her cheek for the first time in his life. He turned and walked up the porch steps, into the house and down the basement stairs, leaving his mother standing in the yard.

Martha waited a few minutes, pondering how her son had just outfoxed her, then walked up the porch stairs and into the house, meeting Robert as he walked out of the basement.

Robert said, "Hey, Ma, did you make German chocolate cake for dinner?"

· · · · · · · · · · · · ·

After both twins finished eating, they managed to find time alone in the alley behind the garage. Michael said, "Little brother. I think I've solved our transport problem. I'm going to study flying, then buy a Lear jet."

Robert laughed and said, "Yeah. Right little brother. Make sure it's a custom Lear, model 35 with the two TFE731-2-2A engines. This model is over a foot longer that the model 25."

Michael said, "I wouldn't know a .25 from a .45. I just know I'm going to start taking flight lessons. I think our CPU prevents us from flying together on commercial flights. In fact, I think both of us should learn. Hell, I've got an even better idea. You can learn, and I'll just sponge off of you! Ha!"

Robert replied, "Like when we were in school, huh? You sound serious. Well, how are you going to pull that off. You will have to go legitimate. Start a business to pass Castanza's money through. It will take several years to establish a business large enough to fool the IRS. You did think about them, didn't you?"

Michael said, "I don't have to. You just did!" and laughed heartily.

Jack unexpectedly joined them.

Michael looked at him and said, "I was just trying to reflect back when you little kids used to jump off of this roof. Back in '65. You probably don't remember when we moved onto this block, do you?"

Jack said, "Robert, you don't have to bury yourself in Michael, or whatever you guys do. I know you communicate together when we're not around. Stop doing that, at least in my presence."

Robert looked at Michael and said, "You heard him. This is the brother who sees all. I wouldn't be surprised if he can see me now."

Michael said, "Okay, Jack. You think you know us. Did you just hear Robert talking?"

Jack said, "No, but I can tell by your reaction just now that he said something. I would prefer if you would change in front of me, so I can talk to both of you at the same time."

Michael said, "Jack, we don't flip back and forth, so that ain't happening."

Jack said, "Okay; fine. Anyway, Mom and Dad need a new house. It's obvious they have outgrown this one. If I convince Mack, Richard, and Louis to pool together some money for a down payment, do you think you two could match it?"

Michael looked at Robert and said, "The big fellow just revealed my second topic. I've been scoping a house on Parkside, north of Six-Mile. Next door to Principal Johnson's home."

Robert looked incredulous and said, "No, brother. Don't ruin that man's life."

Jack heard both remarks because the Duals switched right in front of him. For a moment he had trouble handling it.

He said, "Whoa, dudes, slow down. That was… Wow. I was not expecting that. You actually switched right in front of me. Your expressions and voices changed! I think you'd better keep that talent to yourselves for a bit longer. You're not suffering from Multiple Personality Disorder, are you?" Jack made this remark as a statement, because he somehow knew the answer.

Robert, now in control, said, "No, Jack. We're not. Let us explain."

For the next thirty minutes, they attempted to educate Jack on duality. Robert even made his point by calling Klaw out of the house. Michael did a handstand on the neighbor's back fence, then backflipped onto the roof of the garage.

Jack said, "Okay. Enough for now. Michael, you can come down now. I just hope none of the neighbors saw what you just did. Let me take some time to wrap my head around this. Otherwise, my CPU might erupt."

Both Duals laughed at that remark.

Robert said, "Okay. No more current viewing for now. And don't attempt to explain this to the others. Just leave matters alone. We can discuss this further, all right Jack?"

Jack just smiled, nodded his head, then turned and walked back into the yard. Then he looked back one final time.

"By the way, Michael. I saw you each and every time you came around our schools during the '60s. Peeking around corners, over cars, or from that rooftop over there. But we can discuss that further as well."

. . . .

Robert got up from the dinner table, danced around his father to get past the crowd of bodies, then walked into the kitchen. He could not help but smile at his father, which made Frank feel warm inside. He was so proud of Robert and what he'd accomplished. Mack had told his father about Robert's exploits in Vietnam. Frank also remembered what his brother Horace told him about Michael going to war against the gangsters and just felt good about his boys, even though he still believed they were suffering from Multiple Personality Disorder.

He was standing near the front door when he heard someone knocking.

"Now who could that be? I hope these boys did not invite any of their friends over. There's no space for any of those knuckleheads."

He opened the door and looked into his sons' face. Michael's face.

"Wow, how did he do that so quickly? Leave the room then switch into another outfit and make a new entrance in seconds."

He could not help but look back at the kitchen, half expecting to see Robert return, which he knew was impossible. He then looked back at Michael, whom he had grown to love. Then he heard Robert's voice behind him, so he looked back at the kitchen. Robert was returning from the kitchen and approaching his seat at the dinner table. He again looked back at Michael in the doorway, totally confused. He repeated the glancing back and forth several more times, then froze, unable to move. His mind began to count as he scanned the room.

"I see four of them right here. I can hear Ervin and Jack in the basement on the pool table. Horace is still eating at the kitchen table."

His eyes refocused on the man on the porch.

"I know I didn't have any kids outside this family. This must be one of my nephews, except he's too light, like my boys."

His mind finally returned to him, and he stammered, "Hello, young man. May I help you?"

The man said, "Hello, Mr. McCants. We've never met, but I've been waiting my whole life to meet you. I am your son, Michael. It's been a long time coming but I've finally returned."

The End

Epilogue

Frank's head was spinning. He had to sit down in the nearest chair. Mack saw what had just occurred with his father and slowly moved toward the open door. Martha, sitting next to Robert, noticed Frank's mood change, looked toward the front door, and fainted. Linda rushed to Martha's side, wondering what all the commotion was about.

Jack saw Robert with his back to the door and Michael standing at the front door.

"I knew it. I knew it. Two Michaels!"

He called Ervin and Horace out of the basement.

Richard walked out of the bathroom, wondering what all the commotion was about. He saw both Robert sitting in a chair and Michael standing in the doorway, dressed differently than he had been earlier. Then he realized that they were present at the same moment.

He began to mutter to himself, "I thought there was only one of them."

Louis mimicked Richard's reaction. Both of their wives, like Linda, wondered what all of the commotion was about. All of the children running around the house were mindless of the new visitor.

After a moment Martha regained consciousness, looked deep into Robert's eyes, and said, "What's going on? How are you standing in the doorway and sitting next to me?"

Tears welled up in her eyes and her lower lip began to quiver.

Frank was unable to stand.

The two German Shepherds, lying next to the couch, began to growl at the man at the door.

Robert had not turned around yet, since he was concerned about his mother. Her remark about the doorway, however, caused him to spin around. He looked at the man standing in the doorway, saw Michael, and wondered how the others could possibly see him as well. Then he looked internally, sensed his Dual, and realized something was off. He immediately thought about Dr. Patel and the shaman.

"What is going wrong?"

His CPU considered intervening, knowing Robert might have an adverse reaction to this intruder.

Robert alerted his Dual to the stranger in the doorway, then switched to Michael in front of the entire room. No one noticed. Michael saw the stranger in the doorway and almost lost it. He could still sense Robert, but, like everyone else, could also see him standing at the door. In different clothing. A man who looked exactly like him, yet someone he could not feel. A man who was not his Dual.

'Michael' cautiously entered the house, walked past a stunned Frank and, ignoring the barking dogs, approached a frightened Martha, extending his hand.

He said, "Mrs. McCants, I have been wanting to meet you since I learned my true identity. That you are my birth mother. You are as beautiful as I could have ever imagined. My name is Alexander. Michael Alexander. I am the son they told you had died at birth. In fact, I was stolen from the hospital the night of my birth. I've lived in Windsor all of my life, never knowing until very recently the truth about my past. The woman that raised me, my other mother, just died. I discovered the truth while going through her personal effects."

His voice was a blend of both Michael's and Robert's, yet his diction was Canadian.

Martha was unable to react to the suddenness of this news. That she had not lost her first-born twin child after all. She wanted to speak to her grandmother and her sister. Alexander understood her confusion and pulled back from her, lowering his hand.

He glanced back at Frank and became somewhat concerned that his abrupt entry may have been a mistake.

He turned to Michael and said, "You must be my twin brother. I am so glad to finally meet you."

He again extended his hand, but the Dual backed away.

Michael began communicating with Robert, but maintained his control of the engine, thanks to his training with the shaman. He did not want his CPU to intervene due to his confused state of mind.

Michael Alexander dropped his extended hand, looked at Frank and Mack, then said, "I'm sorry I'm causing so much confusion. I hope I'm not ruining your family dinner. Please forgive me but I just couldn't wait any longer. I thought it was time I came to meet my true family. I couldn't be happier."

Jack just smiled and thought, *Mom had triplets!*

.   .   .   .

Eight-hundred miles away a 97-year-old woman thought, "Oooowhey! So dats ware dat bois been all dem yars! Now da fun begins! Wishen I coulds be dar! Yessireebob!"

www.ingramcontent.com/pod-product-compliance
Lightning Source LLC
Chambersburg PA
CBHW051127300726
48981CB00024B/574/J